A Warlock's Secrets

by

Tena Stetler

Demon's Witch Series

This is a work of fiction. Names, characters, places, and incidents are either the product of the author's imagination or are used fictitiously, and any resemblance to actual persons living or dead, business establishments, events, or locales, is entirely coincidental.

A Warlock's Secrets

Cover Art by *Kristian Norris*

The Wild Rose Press, Inc.
PO Box 708
Adams Basin, NY 14410-0708
Visit us at www.thewildrosepress.com

Publishing History
First Black Rose Edition, 2017
Print ISBN 978-1-5092-1446-4
Digital ISBN 978-1-5092-1447-1

Demon's Witch Series
Published in the United States of America

Inside the house,

a shadow passed by the huge bay window. She held her breath. *Am I really going to go through with this?*

Walking up the steps to the house, she paused. Why would he leave such an expensive car sitting out when he had a four-car garage? She was stalling. Straightening her shoulders, she used the brass doorknocker. There was no answer. She knocked again.

The heavy oak door creaked open. Tristian stood shirtless, his abs rippled as he raised one muscular arm to lean on the doorframe. The skintight blue jeans hung low on his hips, and his hair tousled as if he'd not been awake long.

When he stared at her, with those huge blue-gray eyes, tingles careened up her spine. She covered her mouth in case drool pooled in the corners her mouth. He was one sexy male. She sucked in a breath and opened her mouth to speak, but nothing came out.

A brow arched, he peered questioningly at her then twisted to glance backward into the house. The sunlight streaming through the doorway accentuated several scars across his chest, rib area, and a healed slash across his back.

Who gets those kinds of battle scars and lives to tell the tale? Not going to ask. Maybe this wasn't such a good idea after all. She shifted prepared to run down the stairs if things got weird.

The corner of his mouth curved up in an inviting sexy-as-hell grin. "Good morning, Hannah. What a surprise."

Praise for Tena Stetler

Pre-review for *A WARLOCK'S SECRETS:*
"It is hard because now I have fallen for these characters too. I got wrapped up in the story so much that I forgot I was trying to take mental notes."

~Lisa H.

~*~

"I totally enjoyed [*A DEMON'S WITCH*]…fun paranormal romance, with enough sizzle and suspense to keep those pages turning, rooting for that Happily Ever After."

~Author Katie O'Sullivan

~*~

"Tena Stetler is a new author for me. What a nice surprise to discover a well written paranormal romance with a touch of fantasy. [*A WITCH'S JOURNEY* is] a story of witchcraft, dark secrets and second chances. This author nicely blended her two main characters with magic and romance to make it a fun read!"

~Books & Benches

~*~

A WITCH'S HOLIDAY WEDDING: "I had some doubts at first about the pairing of a witch and a werewolf, but author Tena Stetler makes it work! I had a lot of fun reading this unique paranormal story and seeing how they solve the problems that cropped up. This was a sweet and charming romance. I hadn't read the first book in the series (*A WITCH'S JOURNEY*). That said, I'm now eager to get my hands on the first book!"

~Reviewer Ashia - Reading Alley

Dedications

To my family and friends for all their support.
To my husband
who brainstorms and proofs my books with me.
My publishing house, The Wild Rose Press, Inc.
and my fantastic editor Lill. You're the best!
And my fellow authors at the Wild Rose,
who are always ready to lend a hand. What a team!
Last but not least, my wonderful readers—
I can't thank you enough!

Chapter One
Sometimes Life Sucks Bad

Summer Solstice, Twenty Years Ago

He lay in the dark, unable to move his arms or legs. When he opened his mouth, no sound came out. Sweat beaded on his forehead and trickled down his temple into his eyes, yet he couldn't wipe it away. A crash, then terrified screams assaulted his senses. His dad's voice drifted through Tristian's mind, but he couldn't make out the words.

A door slammed somewhere, and his eyes blinked open. A cylinder of filtered sunlight fell on the books spread open across his desk. He slowly raised an arm and relief flooded his consciousness. He bolted upright, staring into the rounded violet eyes of his little sister.

"Are you all right?" she asked her voice full of concern as she studied him.

He nodded slowly scanning the room. *A nightmare, that's what it was. It had to be.* He didn't have the talent of a seer like his mother. The precog abilities he'd inherited from his father were still developing but had never manifested in a dream.

His talents far exceeded the abilities of much of the Dragon Moon Coven, but he didn't take anything for granted. He was the first born to Rachael Shandie, a powerful witch, who served as High Priestess of the

Coven. His dad, Trent, equally talented, was considered High Priest, though he didn't officially accept that position. His vocation within the magic realm was in direct conflict with the requirements of the coven. Something no one talked about, though not from Tristian's lack of trying.

Raising a trembling hand, he brushed the blond hair from his eyes and grimaced. His pajamas wet with sweat stuck to his skin. The adrenalin subsiding from his body left him weak and shaky. He fell back against the pillows.

The argument last night with his father, regarding his vocation, must have manifested itself into the nightmare. *That's what it was, just a bad dream, nothing more.* Still he couldn't shake the foreboding feeling that knotted his stomach.

"Okay then. Aren't you ever going to get up?" she said impatiently, hands on her hips, her tiny foot tapping on the hardwood floor. Her gaze shifted to the huge suitcase sitting in his doorway.

He narrowed his eyes and glared at her. "Aren't you supposed to knock?"

"Yeah, I did…but you were…something was… wrong. I could feel…"

"It was only a nightmare. I'm fine. Now get out of here," he growled. The connection between him and his sister, Angelique, had always been strong, even though she was ten years younger.

"Can you help me get my suitcase to Willow's house?" She flipped her long wavy blonde hair over her shoulder. "I'm temporality banned from using magic after yesterday's fiasco."

"And how's that my problem? I'm not the one who

sent the brand new blender flying out the kitchen's bay window." He snickered, feeling a bit more like himself. "It dug a hell of a hole in Dad's garden. You're lucky there were no mortals around."

"There are never any mortals around up here." She shot back. "It was a minor miscalculation."

Tristian's eyebrow shot up. "Sure it was. Now get out of here. I'll bring the suitcase down in a minute."

Quickly, he showered and dressed in black jeans, a burgundy pullover with black vertical stripes and black boots he'd polished to a gleam last night. Still more than a little irked that his sister chose to accompany her best friend's family to Ireland for the summer solstice, rather than attend the coven's ceremony today.

Home from college for summer break, today he'd be inducted into the Dragon's Moon Coven as an adult member. Just a week after his twenty-second birthday, he looked forward to taking his place within in the coven with all benefits and responsibilities. A day that would be etched in his mind forever.

Footfalls pounded down the polished hardwood steps behind him and echoed through the family room with its vaulted ceilings. Angie, his twelve-year-old sister sprinted by him stopping only to yank open the door.

She tilted her head up to meet his gaze and smiled brightly. "Trist, they're ready to leave." Her face was flushed with excitement.

Tristian leaned his shoulder against the heavy wooden doorframe, ankles crossed, hands shoved in his jean pockets, and peered down at her. "Why would I help you, when you think so little of me that you won't even attend the coven's ceremony?"

"Aww, com'on Trist, you've been able to wield magic better than most the coven's members since you were my age. Not that I can't do the same," she said brightly.

"Gee, humble aren't you?" He sneered.

She shrugged. "Just the way it is, and you know it. But I've never been to Ireland. It's going to be so exciting with all the faeries, witches..." She twirled around on one foot, arms swinging out to her sides, paused to beam up at him. "Oh, just everyone there. You really aren't going to be mad at me, are you?" Her lilting voice wheedled, but her gaze was defiant, as usual.

Tristian blew out a breath and hugged his little sister. "Okay, Ang... This once I'll forgive you for abandoning me. But if I am granted special magical knowledge at the ceremony, I'm not sharing with you." A wave of foreboding washed over him, again. *Was something going to happen to Angie? Not possible, Mom would be aware. Besides, she hadn't appeared in his dream. Unless...the screams...were they hers?* He shook his head shoving the ominous feeling to the back of his consciousness, for the moment.

Angie sucked in a breath as her violet eyes flew open wide. "Is that possible. Is that what the ceremony is for?" She narrowed her eyes, gave him a hard stare. "You're just trying to get me to stay. Won't work." Angie sing-songed.

"I guess you'll have to carry your own luggage then." Tristian shrugged and crossed his arms over his chest.

"Fine." Angie surveyed the area quickly, raised her fingers toward the suitcase, and snapped. It disappeared. She giggled and raced out the front door, skidded to a stop, then ran back smacked a kiss on his cheek. "Don't tell, please," she pleaded.

Tristian grabbed his little sister by the collar and thrust a charmed, gold four-leaf clover in her hand. "For luck."

She closed her fingers around the charm and grinned up at him. "Thanks." She plucked a purple ribbon out of thin air and tied the charm around her neck. Grinning, she whirled around and barreled across the lawn to her best friend's house where her suitcase sat next to the front door.

He sighed. *She has no regard for the rules of magic, yet.* The knot tightened in his stomach. A harbinger of something yet to come?

"Ready?" His father, dressed in black slacks and a light copper shirt with black stripes, asked sprinting down the stairs.

"I am." His mom, Rachel's musical voice floated through the family room before she appeared in a light blue linen skirt and flowered top.

"You're driving." His father tossed the keys to Tristian then wrapped an arm around Rachael.

"Thanks." He reached one long arm up, snatched the keys out of the air, and strode out of the house to the sleek sedan. Equipped with a powerful engine, the vehicle was a dream to drive. When he fobbed the car door open, a taxi screeched to a halt next door and blared its horn. Willow's family along with Angie rushed from the house and climbed in the cab.

As the taxi pulled away, she rolled the car window down and waved wildly. "See you soon! Good Luck!"

Tristian waved back and slid into the car, started

the engine. His parents sauntered through the front door, closed and locked it. After they all settled into the car and left the city limits, Tristian glanced over at his father. "So Dad, about your job."

"Don't start." His father ground out, the lines around his eyes more pronounced, and he looked more tired than usual.

His mom glanced up from the paperwork in her lap. "Trent, it's probably time to…"

"No. End of discussion." His father's mouth set in a thin line, the jaw muscle twitched continuously.

Lips pursed, his mother returned her attention to the paperwork. Tristian wanted to scream. As he'd grown older, the worry in his mother's eyes, the midnight calls, his father missing in the morning all concerned him.

She'd confided in him that his father's profession was dangerous but absolutely necessary to keep the family and otherworldly creatures safe inside and out of the mortal world. His chest tightened, and his anxiety ratcheted up another notch. He was never prone to anxiety attacks, even during finals, always breezing through. Academics were never a problem. In fact, he was up for valedictorian of his class. After graduation, it was off to Harvard medical school.

His father's professional life never crossed paths with their family life. But Tristian couldn't help but wonder if one day the two might collide with disastrous consequences. Would the powerful protection spells his mom and dad cast over their home be enough to keep the family out of harm's way? *I gotta quit thinking like this.* He didn't understand why these thoughts kept bubbling to the surface; he slowed and coasted into a parking space.

"We're here," Rachel sang out, jerking Tristian out of his thoughts.

The family walked up the stone path to the huge log building, with a finely trimmed lawn, and well-kept gardens, his mother hung back and touched his shoulder. "Is something wrong?" she asked quietly, eying the group of elders quickly descending on them.

"I was going to ask you the same thing." Tristian held his mother's gaze.

She looked puzzled. "Why? Everything is fine." She smiled and turned her attention to the advisors.

He glanced from her to the group and shook his head, pasting a smile on his face. "Nope, just lost in thought."

"Your sister didn't mean to hurt your feelings."

He gestured dismissively with his hand. "Don't be ridiculous. It's a great opportunity for her. I understand. I'm certainly not a child anymore. But I couldn't let her off scott free. It's against the big brother creed."

"Oh, I know you're not a child. But this is your day to celebrate. Don't let whatever is on your mind spoil it." She paused as Trent turned and motioned them to hurry. "Let the celebrations begin."

He caught her sleeve. "Mom, I've got a bad feeling. Something weird happened this morning and…" He paused, something disconcerting flickered through her eyes, then it was gone. Or was it his imagination?

She studied him for a beat. "Oh, it's probably just nerves." Then she squeezed his arm. "Don't worry about it."

A group of Tristian's friends rushed up slapping

him on the back and urging him into the building. When he looked back, his mom and dad were embroiled in a heated conversation with the coven elders. *Gee, nothing new there.*

As he was whisked away with his friends, he tucked all serious thoughts out of his mind for now but couldn't shake the ominous feeling that something wasn't right.

He caught sight of Corra, a girl he'd been seeing recently and sauntered over to talk to her.

Her beautiful blue eyes brightened at his approach. "I have to run down to the basement to get plates, cups, and the ceremonial bowl." She batted her long black lashes at him, flipped her sleek raven hair over her shoulder, and raised a dark eyebrow with a mischievous grin. "Want to help?"

Glancing over his shoulder at his buddies, he winked and nodded toward Corra. "I'll catch up with you guys later. He slipped his hand around her waist. "Sure." Any opportunity to get her alone, he'd take.

At the bottom of the stairs, Tristian conjured a huge sparkling ball of light, tossed it into the air illuminating the entire basement area.

"You're showing off. We're not supposed to use magic frivolously." She fisted her hands on her hips. "Tristian Shandie."

He shrugged as she reached for the light switch on the wall and flipped it. Nothing happened.

"Guess we'll need my magic light after all." He smirked.

They walked to the wooden shelves on the far wall. The hair on the back of Tristian's neck stood up, a shiver shot up his spine as his mind's eye opened. His parents stood in the doorway to the kitchen upstairs. The scene played out in front of him as a loud explosion outside the lodge sent debris in every direction. A large piece of metal drove straight through the door and stuck there. Members of the coven visiting in small groups inside the lodge scattered and threw up protection spells. Tristian shielded Corra with his body, bringing her to the floor.

His heart thundered in his chest as he saw their actions came too late. The heavy wooden door flew off its hinges as a hulk of a creature strode through followed by several other creatures. He had to bend over to clear the doorway and took a stance just inside the door, feet planted shoulder width apart, his eyes narrowed, gaze moving from witch to witch. "Trent Shandie," he bellowed.

Peering from an adjoining room, his father was the first to recover and stared with disbelief at the unlikely group of werewolves, vampires, and demons. Trent leaned back toward his wife and whispered, "This is impossible. Dracon, the demon leading this group, was a member of a family hierarchy of demons I took down several years ago, on assignment."

Rachael stared at him in horror. "The ones that enslaved mortals, taking their land and forcing them to do their bidding?"

"The same, this is not going to end well. Where's Tristian?"

"I don't know. Last I saw, he was going into the basement with Corra to bring up stuff for the celebration," Rachel said quietly scanning the room.

Tristian opened his mouth to scream, but nothing came out. Willing his mind's eye closed failed, he was forced to watch in horror. It was like everything happened in slow motion.

His mother raised her arms quickly and murmured incantations, she swung her arms down forcefully. Metal spikes rose out of the floor surrounding the group of creatures, then the stakes bent over the top of the group, crisscrossing over each other until the outraged intruders were confined within the metal web. At once, the lodge filled with members of the coven casting spells of destruction, protection, and anything else that came to mind. But they were outnumbered as vampires, werewolves, and demons flooded inside.

Dracon bellowed again, and with a wave of his arm, the metal enclosure turned to ash floating to the floor. The group of creatures encircled and advanced on the witches. "Do you remember me demon slayer?" He growled, his fiery eyes finally locking on Trent standing in the doorway. "You killed my family. I'm here to return the favor."

Tristian tried to move but couldn't. His fingers tightened around Corra's arm. For a split second, he saw the horror on her face before his mind's eye resumed the scene taking place above them.

A ball of fire appeared in Dracon's hand, and he threw it at Trent. He forced the ball backward toward the demon, but as Rachel stood at his back, a vampire grabbed Rachel from behind, sinking his fangs into her neck. She flipped around on him, a wooden stake materializing in her hand; she forced it through his heart. The vampire fell to the floor dissolving into a pile of ash. Bile rose in Tristian's throat from the stench wafting down the stairs.

Trent's attention locked on Rachel's wound, just as

Dracon formed another fireball and sent it flying toward them. This one found its target, but not before Trent conjured crescent knives and sent them flying in Dracon's direction. Trent's aim was true, the knives severed Dracon's head, blood splatter covered the wall as his cranium hit the surface and slid to the floor, forming a pool of thick bloody goo.

Finally, Tristian broke free of whatever held him in place. He grabbed Corra's hand and rushed across the basement and up the stairs. Vampires, werewolves, and demons converged on them. Tristian was knocked to the floor and pinned there with a metal table leg driven through his leg, while a vampire grabbed Corra around the waist and disappeared with her.

Tristian sprawled on the floor, pain racking his body, the sickening stench of death all around made his stomach roil as he drifted in and out of consciousness. He saw his parents' scorched bodies lying lifeless on the floor among several dead or dying coven members. They'd waged a fierce battle, but in the end, it wasn't enough. Ash of vampires floated in the air, body parts from the demons and werewolves fighting alongside Dracon were scattered around the room. Once their leader was dead, the remaining creatures disappeared, leaving the surviving members of the coven in shock staring at the gory scene spread out in front of them.

Someone bent over Tristian, a sharp pain stabbed through him as metal was jerked from his leg and healing hands placed on his body before everything went black.

****

The throbbing in his head increased as he blinked in the dim light and tried to focus on the large black

11

blob wavering in front of him. His arms and legs were slow to respond to the commands his brain tried to give. Sounds of movement stilled him for a beat, he inhaled and coughed at the dank, dusty air. Propped in a chair, he squinted, now able to make out a hooded figure hovering over him.

A gravelly voice whispered, "Good, you're awake. I've woven a camouflage spell around you. We need to scatter, you know what to do, but make it quick. Once the spell wears off, you'll be discovered. You need to get out of here. It's not safe."

"Who are you? Where are my parents?" Tristian croaked as visions of the attack floated in and out of his mind.

The man pulled his hood farther over his face. "Dead. The creatures slaughtered most of the coven. It's best if you don't know who survived. Now, do as your father instructed in an emergency." He shoved a phone in Tristian's hand. "I've got to go; good luck." The man took a few steps then turned around. "Don't go home." He emphasized each word, then he was gone.

Tristian raked his fingers through his hair, then with a trembling hand pulled a folded piece of paper from his pocket. He dialed the number and waited, hoping he'd written the number down correctly at his father's insistence. Never in his wildest dreams did he think he'd ever have to use it. After the fourth ring, a female voice answered.

"Hello."

"Mrs. Coppervale?" Tristian asked in a shaking voice.

"Yes," Freesia Coppervale said pleasantly. "Who is

this?"

"It's Tristian…Tristian Shandie. Is Angie safe?"

"Yes, dear, she's outside with Willow." She paused. "Do you want…"

"No…need to talk to your husband, please," Tristian said trying to control his shaking voice.

"Of course." Freesia hollered for her husband. "He's coming. What's wrong?"

"Something terrible has happened. Don't let Angie know… I really need to talk to Mr. Coppervale, now."

Birch Coppervale picked up an extension. "Hi Tristian, what can I do for you?"

Relief flooded through him at the sound of Mr. Coppervale's voice. "The coven celebration…was attacked by creatures. My parents are dead…along with most of the coven. I don't know what to do, told the house may not be safe. You gotta help me."

"Son, where are you right now? No, don't answer that. Are you in a safe location?"

"I don't know. I couldn't get to them. I was in the basement helping Corra get… Oh, no. Where is she?" He pushed the thought out of his head. He had to get to a secure location, make sure Angie was safe. "Bodies are scattered all over. Don't know if anyone survived. I woke up under a camouflage spell woven by a stranger to avoid detection. He gave me a phone, and I called you."

"Who gave you a phone? Is someone there with you?"

"No. He left. Didn't leave a name. Told me to get out of here. Not safe."

"Okay, okay. Let me think—I want you to go straight to the airport using normal means. Call me when you arrive. Make sure you aren't followed. Are you able to maintain that camouflage spell?"

"Maybe, but the magic could be detected." Tristian got to his feet shakily, walked to the window. With a hand, he wiped a clean spot in the dirty windowpane, peered out recognizing his location." It'll take me about thirty minutes to get there from…"

"Don't tell me, get moving," Birch ordered. "Now."

Tristian disconnected the call, stepped into the fading twilight, and hailed a cab.

****

Birch Coppervale walked out into the room where his wife sat, hand covering her mouth, blinking back tears. Rachel and Trent were like family.

Freesia quickly wiped her hand over her face and put on a mask of normalcy. White as a sheet, she stared at Birch and then over to where Willow and Angie were playing outside. "What are we going to do?"

"We are going to get Tristian here as fast as possible. I need the members of the Faery Council to convene in Grandmother Lillie's house.

"I figured. I've already notified Lillie; she's alerted the council members. They should be there when you arrive."

"Good. The magic is strong there. Can you keep the kids occupied until we get a handle on this situation?"

"I can. You have a plan?" Freesia asked nervously.

"I believe so. We're going to need a lot of traveling faery magic. It's not safe for him to board a plane. If whoever did this is still around, we don't want Tristian bringing them here," Birch said, formulating a plan as he spoke. He looked at his watch, twenty minutes to go.

With a flick of his wrist, he joined the other council members convened in Lillie's house. Birch explained the situation as he knew it and asked for the council's help. Without all the facts, the council was reluctant to act.

An old faery sitting in her rocking chair in the far corner of the room listening to the debates said, "I can scry for the young man's location using my amethyst, but I need an object from him. If you can get me that and a map of Maine, I assume he is still there, we can get you on your way, Birch. You can intercept him before he reaches the airport then bring the both of you back here. Greatly lessening the chances of discovery."

"Good plan, Grams," Birch said eying the other council members.

The old woman smiled pensively and said, "Provided this council of scaredy cats, oh, excuse me, of faeries, can reach an agreement to provide the magic."

"I'm sure—" Birch began.

The old woman narrowed her eyes, continued as if Birch hadn't said a thing. "A young man's life is on the line while you dilly-dally around. Who of you wants his blood on your hands? Tristian isn't faery blood, but his sister is among us, and they are like family to the Coppervales. Birch and Freesia promised to look after the young ones in the event something happened to their parents. A faery's promise is their oath. The young man needs our help."

The debate among council members quickly died down after the old faery's words, all agreed to provide the magic necessary. Birch located a map. Freesia calmly asked to borrow Angie's charm. After a quizzical look, Angie freely took the gold charm from around her neck and handed it to her. She'd proudly shown off the charm after she'd climbed in the cab with Willow and her family. Within a few minutes, Tristian was located, and Birch was on his way.

Tristian stepped out of the third taxi he'd taken, a few blocks from the airport and checked for magic signatures or someone physically following him. Still feeling like it was all a nightmare. Detecting nothing, he stepped up on the sidewalk, just as Birch appeared beside him.

"Tristian, it's Birch, don't be alarmed." He touched Tristian's shoulders and said, "I'm taking you to safety."

Once on Irish soil, Tristian described what he had seen and heard. Inside the Coppervale's cottage in Ireland, with Birch and Freesia beside him, Tristian broke the news to Angie of their parents' death without relaying the gruesome details, naming a car crash the culprit.

Days later, Birch pulled Tristian aside. "I've received a couple of phone calls from your father's employer, Bruce. He said there are a few things he needs to discuss with you regarding your father's benefits and wishes in the event of his death. When you're ready, Bruce would like to talk to you. He is willing to meet you in Maine or to arrange for you to join him in D.C. My contacts in the U.S. indicate it is safe for us to return. Your home is intact, and all the protections cast by your parents are still in place."

"For how long? A day a week, or could they be waiting for our arrival?" Tristian shot back. "And why would my father's employer know how to contact you?"

Birch placed his hand on Tristian's shoulder. "Son, there is never a guarantee for the future. We take it as it comes and deal the best we can. I've booked a flight back to Maine for all of us under different names just as a precaution. As far as Bruce is concerned, apparently Freesia and I are listed as contacts in case of an emergency. Probably set up long ago before you were of legal age."

"What am I going to do? I don't know anything about raising a young girl. Mom and Dad are gone, how am I going to support both of us?" Tristian shook his head then put his face in his hands. "What about Corra and the other coven members? Is it safe to contact them?"

Birch's voice was calm and reassuring, "Let's take one thing at a time. You were told not to contact any of the coven members. Correct?"

"Yes. But…"

"Freesia and I will help with whatever you need. Eventually, things will get better, I promise." Birch pulled out a file from his briefcase, handed it to Tristian. "Your parents gave me this in case—of an emergency. It's instructions for you." He closed his eyes. "It won't be easy. There are a lot of things you need to understand. But we'll get through this together. I promise."

****

Tristian stepped out of the limo, walked across the sidewalk, and pulled open the door to The Wycked Hair Salon. His eyes wide like a deer caught in the headlights. All the magic signatures he sensed had him on guard, as a stocky silver haired man walked over to him, hand outstretched.

"You must be Tristian. I'm Owen, Bruce's right-hand man and salon manager. Welcome. We've been expecting you. How was your flight?" He smiled, in what Tristian assumed was an attempt to put him at ease. It didn't work.

He paused, stared at the older man in disbelief. *After all I've been through—how was my flight? Shit.* Unsure of his footing under the circumstances, he masked his emotions and attempted a blank expression. "Fine." He gave Owen's hand a strong shake. *Dad always said you could tell a lot about a man from his handshake.* The last thing Tristian wanted was these people to think he was weak or unable to handle himself. *Confidence, that's what I need to exude.* He straightened his shoulders and looked Owen squarely in the eye for a beat then turned his attention to the stairs.

A tall, muscular man silently descended the steps two at a time from the mezzanine to the main area. He strode across the floor right hand extended. "Tristian. I'm Bruce." He pursed his lips. "Nice to meet you. Wish it was under better circumstances."

Tristian nodded, surveying the Salon with incredulity. Witch's, demons, werewolves, the place was a melting pot of creatures, mixed with mortals. Then he turned his gaze to the mezzanine. The man standing in front him was a magical being, but the signature was masked so he couldn't get a read on him.

"Please join me in the office." Bruce motioned Tristian toward the stairs and led the way. Once in the office, Bruce closed the door, nodded to the navy-blue leather chairs arranged in front of his large glass-top desk. He eased down in one of the leather chairs as Tristian sat in the other one. "I am so sorry for your loss. Your father was a great man and will be missed terribly." He ran his fingers through his shoulder-length hair, paused for a moment as if assessing the young man sitting before him. "How are you doing?"

Tristian snapped, "How do you think I'm doing?" Suddenly, his shoulders slumped, his brave façade faded. "Sorry…it's too much." He blew out a breath and wished Bruce would quit staring at him as if he was a bug under a microscope. "I'm okay, considering."

"Life's dealt you some terrible blows. I'm afraid I'm not going to make it much better."

The sheer raw power that suddenly rolled off Bruce shook Tristian to his very core. Realization dawned as Bruce dropped the disguise of his magic signature. Tristian's gaze hardened and locked on the demon sitting beside him. "I understand there are things I need to handle regarding my father?"

"Handle. Not exactly…" Bruce paused for a couple beats. "However, it's imperative to your continued existence that you understand exactly what happened to your parents, and why. Your father was my enforcer. I am the Demon Overlord of the Western Hemisphere. Together we made sure everyone played by the rules."

Tristian sucked in a breath and swallowed hard.

There was a light tap on the glass door to Bruce's office. "Owen said I was to join you?" A tall older man with salt and pepper hair strode into the office glancing from Bruce to Tristian.

"Yes. Paul this is Tristian, Trent's son."

Paul's eyes widened. "I didn't know he had a family. Guessed he had a wife hidden away somewhere as he seemed more settled in recent years." He blew out a breath and turned his attention to Tristian. "You look like your father, a bit taller and muscular, but…" Shaking his head, he looked from Bruce to Tristian. "I'm really sorry for your loss. Your dad was the best partner I've ever had."

"Yes, he was," Bruce said. "Now we have to protect Tristian, while he learns to protect himself. The creatures that killed Trent, saw Tristian, made the connection, according to the coven. They'll come looking for him to exact revenge." Bruce leaned back in his chair, pinched the bridge of his nose with his thumb and index finger.

"So how do you intend to do that?" Paul asked his jaw muscle twitching.

"If he is willing, you'll mentor him, as Trent did you." There was no negation in Bruce's voice.

"I have to go back home. Our neighbors won't know what happened to me. They were part of Father's plan," Tristian protested.

"I've already explained the situation to the Coppervales. They will look after the house and its contents until such time it's deemed safe for you to return. Birch agrees with our assessment."

"May I consider the offer? I have to return to college to finish my…" He scanned the stony faces of Bruce and Paul. "My life as I know it is over. Isn't it?"

"Unfortunately, if you want to stay alive, I'm afraid so." Something caught Bruce's attention. He glanced toward the door.

Tristian scrubbed his hand over his face. "Could I have a few minutes?" He drew in a breath, and it hissed out between his teeth. "Am I able to…"

The office door flew open. Birch marched in and stood beside Tristian. "I figured you'd be resistant." He nodded in Bruce's direction. "Excuse us for a few minutes—please."

"A few minutes. If the young man leaves this building, you know he is dead," Bruce said over his shoulder as he and Paul stepped outside the room.

Birch glanced warily at the closed door. "Since I am sure everyone in this building is under surveillance, I'll keep it quick. There is a price on your head." He nodded in the direction of the men outside the door. "And they know it. You don't want to endanger anyone in Misty Harbor." He raised an eyebrow and gave Tristian a knowing look.

"What about An—"

Birch shook his head vehemently. "I will take care of the house and its contents. Everything will be waiting for your return."

Tristian nodded in understanding. *Bruce didn't know about Angie. The Coppervales will take care of her until I can return and do it myself. Don't want anything to happen to her.* He blinked back the tears burning behind his eyelids. He'd wanted to know what his dad did, well, he'd find out first hand.

"For the time being, let Bruce protect you until the culprits are found, which according to my intel, won't be long. Then we'll discuss settling the estate and all belongings, which will be returned to your care. Understand?" Birch locked gazes with Tristian.

"I do. You knew, didn't you?"

"Yes. We'd had long talks with your dad and mom. But after so many trouble-free years, we figured your dad had a foolproof system." He put his arm around

Tristian. "Know we are keeping tabs on everything, though you don't see or hear from us."

Chapter Two
Time to Rearrange the PlayBook

Present Day

Recent years with Angie had been difficult to say the least. She declared her independence by quitting the career path Tristian arranged for her and fleeing the family home while he was on assignment. When he returned, his sources located her. He pulled in favors for her protection until he could cast the spells himself.

In damage control mode, rather than confront her, he'd waited for an invitation that never came. Finally, he made an unannounced visit to her shop, only to discover she was out of town with friends. *What a goddamn mess.*

He'd sucked it up and waited for her return. Willow seemed accommodating but mum on where Angie had gone. Eventually, Angie returned and consented to dinner with him. However, she insisted on extremely tough ground rules for future visits. He agreed to her terms, and their parting was more amicable than he'd hoped.

Tristian slid into the seat of his sleek, powerful, sports car, started the engine, and flipped on the windshield wipers, glad this frigging day was nearly over. When he glanced in the rear-view mirror, tired gray/blue eyes stared back at him before he slid designer sunglasses on. The sun was peeking through the cloud cover. It appeared the rain wouldn't last much longer. He left the airport terminal parking lot and turned toward the highway that would take him to Misty Harbor, where the family home, his home was located. A weight lifted from his shoulders having made amends with Angie. But she'd made it abundantly clear, she'd made a life for herself in D.C.

All the way home, he tried to come to terms with her decision. She wasn't coming back, and he didn't want to return to an empty house—not right now. Tires squealed as he jerked the steering wheel. The car skidded sideways into the parking lot of the little diner where he occasionally got a bite to eat. He straightened the car out, coasted into a space, and turned the engine off.

Sitting behind the wheel, he combed fingers through his damp, dark-blond hair in an attempt to look presentable. *Aww to hell with it.* He shoved the car door open, unfolded his six-foot-four inch frame from the vehicle, slammed the door, and set the alarm.

Cheerful red checkered curtains hung in the windows, funny he'd never noticed that before. Probably because it was usually in the dead of night when he stopped to grab a bite. The late afternoon sunlight bounced off the glass door to the diner as he yanked it open. The aroma of fresh French fries, hamburgers, and homemade cherry pie wafted out into the cool spring air. He strode through the diner, slipped into a red vinyl booth in the far corner, and stared out the window for several minutes. The sounds of food being prepared, dishes clinking together, and the ding of a bell when the cook called "order up" somehow took the edge off.

The door opened again, and a woman stomped inside. She had shoulder-length wavy, red hair, a sprinkling of freckles over her nose, and the brightest blue eyes he'd ever seen. She was curvy in the right places, not like the skin and bones women prevalent these days. He shook his head. *How did men find those types attractive?*

The wooden chair scraped across the tile floor as the woman jerked it out from under a table not far from Tristian's booth. She plopped down on the red padded vinyl seat and shoved her wet hair out of her eyes, blew out a breath, and leaned back in the chair. The woman stared into space for a beat, then closed her eyes, shook her head slightly.

A waitress with a nametag that said Nan stopped by his table. "What'll you have?"

"A cup of coffee."

"Got fresh baked cherry pie that goes really good with a scoop of ice cream." She tapped a pencil on the order pad she held in her hand.

"A cup of coffee."

"Okaaay, but you don't know what you're missing." She turned and flounced over to the table a red-haired woman occupied and laid her hand on the woman's arm. "Didn't go as well as you'd hoped?"

"You could say that. The big announcement was that the company is relocating to be part of a National Cyber Intelligence Center being established in Colorado Springs. Shadow Hawk Cyber was one of the first companies tapped to be a part of it." She slapped the menu down on the table.

Nan tilted her head slightly and peered at the

woman questioningly. "You don't want to move? I've heard Colorado is beautiful. Great skiing, hiking, biking, you name it; Colorado's got it." She paused for a couple beats, tapping her pencil to her lips. "Except the ocean. It's land locked. Suppose it has mountain lakes."

The red-headed woman huffed out a breath. "Relocation isn't the problem. I'm an Irish citizen and getting a top-secret security clearance is impossible. Without it, I can't work for the company. Well, that's not exactly true. The owner of the company said I needed to apply for a Limited Access Authorization. Supposedly, I would have no trouble getting that since my expertise is needed."

"So...why not apply?"

"I looked into it. Seems it's harder to get than my boss thinks. LAAs are granted in rare circumstances where the non-U.S. citizen possesses a unique or unusual skill or expertise that is urgently needed. Can't get higher than Secret clearance. I'm the only one in the company that has a—certain skill set. But since other companies are also clamoring to be part of the NCIC, you can bet they'll have people with my skill set that are U.S. citizens."

"Gee...that's too bad. But you're not just going to give up, are you?"

"Tonight—I don't know. On a positive note, the move won't be complete for eighteen to twenty-four months. Boss says I can fly under the radar until that time."

"What about becoming a citizen? You plan to stay in the states. Right?"

"I hope so. But I don't want to give up my Irish

citizenship, either." She sighed.

Tristian clinked the empty coffee cup against the saucer and stared at the waitress.

Nan patted the woman's arm and frowned, then jerked her head in Tristian's direction. "I'll be right back." She rushed behind the lunch counter, whisked the coffee pot from the warmer so quickly the scalding coffee nearly sloshed over the rim.

Tristian hid a grin behind his hand at her response. *Mortals were so predictable.*

Nan paused, let the liquid settle, and walked to Tristian's table, filled his cup. "Sorry about that."

He nodded and gave her an obligatory smile.

Several customers entered the diner talking loudly and laughing. They settled into seats on the opposite side of the room. Tristian was glad they didn't invade his area, as he contemplated doing something he'd never done before. He slid out of the booth and ambled over to the red-headed woman's table. "Rough day, huh?"

She glanced up at him warily. "You could say that."

"I understand. Had one of those myself." He pulled out a chair and glanced over at her. "Mind if I join you?"

She shrugged, "Suit yourself." and motioned absently to the chair he leaned on.

He offered his hand. "I'm Tristian."

She hesitated for a beat, then clasped his hand lightly. "Hannah."

"Nice to meet you, Hannah." He eased into the chair. "Overheard you're from Ireland. Been here long?"

Pausing, as if deciding how much to tell him. Since he'd already overheard enough, she said, "I attended college in the states. Right after graduation Shadow Hawk Cyber recruited me. I've been there ever since. My friends are there." She paused. "What about you?"

"Family problems. Didn't feel like going home."

"Wife?"

Tristian snorted and gave a half laugh. "No way. Not married."

She raised a well-shaped red eyebrow questioningly and pursed her lips. "Uh huh."

"Really. I just came back from a visit with my little sister. I raised her after our parents died." *Why the hell am I spilling my guts to this woman?*

Her eyes softened. "Oh, I'm sorry for your loss."

Waving his hand in a gesture of dismissal he said, "It was a long time ago. Now she's on her own. Started a business with her childhood best friend. Looks like she's gone for good." He shifted in his seat and grimaced. "We didn't part on the best of terms when she moved out. Hell, she didn't even tell me she was leaving." He blew out a breath. "So, I had business where she moved. I stopped by to see her—we went out to dinner and things are better now."

"Well, that's a good thing."

"Mostly... Don't like the ground rules she insisted I adhere to, but she's a grown woman." He shrugged, stood, and walked to his booth to retrieve his cup of coffee. Took a sip.

"Lonely, huh?" Hannah said softly.

"No... Yeah," he admitted, settling back into the chair.

Nan stopped by their table. "Can I get you two

anything?"

Tristian shook his head then changed his mind. "A burger and fries." He glanced at Hannah. "Want something?"

She scraped her bottom lip through her teeth. "Yes, I'll take the same. Separate tickets." She said quickly.

He raised a brow but said nothing. *I've learned my lesson about crossing strong willed women.*

As Nan turned to leave, Hannah added to the order. "Oh, could I have raspberry tea?"

"Iced or hot?"

"Hot."

"Sure thing. I'll be right back with the tea." Nan flitted off to toward the other tables.

"Could be a while before you get your tea." Tristian watched the waitress change her demeanor as she approached the table full of young men laughing and talking.

"Yeah, a table of hunks. Good thing I'm in no hurry."

"So, do you live around here?" Tristian turned his attention back to her.

"Yeah. One of the reasons I accepted the job was the area. Small town, close to the ocean, and I found the cutest cottage on the bluffs overlooking the sea. Most mornings I eat breakfast watching the waves crash to the shore, the seabirds swoop and dive for their meals while screaming to defend their territory." A laugh bubbled up from her throat. "Sometimes the birds make quite a ruckus."

Nan was back with the tea and more coffee. "Your orders will be right up," she said cheerfully.

"Oh, I know. I've observed the same some

evenings."

"Do you live near the bluffs?"

"Sort of. But I live on the outskirts of town," he said trying to be vague. *Probably said too much already.* "You know a person can hold dual citizenship. Especially, in the industry you work in. It's not uncommon."

"Really? To be honest, never thought about it. But I did apply for citizenship in the U.S., told me it would be six months to a year. The company helped cut through the red tape." A slight smile curved her lips. "Maybe, things aren't so bleak."

"Of course not," Nan said as she set the steaming plates in front of Hannah first and then Tristian. "If you need anything else, just holler." She flounced off to the other tables.

Taking a big bite of his burger, he discovered he was starved. "Sleep on it," he said around the bite of burger. "Things always seem better in the morning." He swallowed then chuckled.

She poured ketchup on her plate and dipped French fries in the puddle of red. "Yeah." She sat quietly for a couple of beats chewing. Her gaze flicked up to him. "You're not that..." She swiveled around in her chair to look out the window at the parking lot. Sucked in a breath. "That midnight blue low slung sports car isn't yours, is it?"

"Maybe." *I knew I'd said too much. She's too damn easy to talk to. Time to go.* He quickly finished his meal.

"You're not that recluse—" Her hand flew to her mouth as red patches bloomed on her cheeks. "I mean..." she stammered. "You don't live on that huge piece of land with the castle-like house overlooking the ocean?"

Tristian was silent as he contemplated a response. Took a gulp of coffee. He intentionally didn't mingle with the townspeople anymore, and this was why.

"I'm sorry, I didn't mean to—I've driven by that house so many times, wondering...well, it's none of my business." She took another bite of her burger, washed it down with tea.

He blew out a breath. "Guilty as charged. My business often keeps me out of town. When my sister went away to college, I didn't have any reason to rush home. So..."

"I understand."

"Do you?" He raised a brow and pushed away from the table. "It's about time I head toward home, got a lot of work to do." Tristian stood abruptly. "It was nice to meet you." On his way out the door, he stopped and handed Nan a fifty-dollar bill. "That's for both meals and your tip. You did a great job." He yanked open the door, shoved his sunglasses in his pocket, and strode into the dusky evening. *How long was I in there?* He glanced at his watch, nearly seven o'clock.

On the drive home, Tristian replayed the interaction in his head. The only thing he regretted was that she knew where he lived. In his business, anonymity is necessary. He had enjoyed the interaction. If circumstances were different, he'd consider asking her out. One night stands were getting tedious and unsatisfying. Lanterns atop tall lampposts came on automatically, shedding soft glow in a wide swath as he steered the car up the winding driveway.

Climbing out of the vehicle, Tristian walked up the

path, disarmed the security system, and unlocked the door. A familiar scent of lavender wafted through the room as he took off his coat, hung it in the hall coat closet. He glanced at the air freshener plugged into the outlet, noting it was nearly time to change it.

Slowly descending the stairs to his wine cellar, he checked the labels on several bottles before choosing one and trudging back upstairs. After pouring a glass of wine, he glanced at the secure message system. No calls. He sighed and settled in his chair in the great room, swirled the burgundy liquid in the glass, glanced over at the cold hearth.

Flicking his wrist, fingers extended toward the huge stone fireplace, red-orange flames tipped in blue shot up the logs, crackled and hissed like a newly awakened dragon. Though he used it more than most, using magic frivolously wasn't a good idea, but tonight…he just didn't give a damn. Angie would have lectured him, but she wasn't there. Leaning back in the recliner, he took several sips of wine then set his glass on the table and closed his eyes.

The next time he opened them, sunlight was streaming through the gap in the curtains. He stretched and kicked the recliner into a sitting position and padded upstairs. In the shower, the warm water cascading down his body eased the muscles stiff from spending the night in the recliner. He grabbed the soap, lathered his skin, and rinsed. Toweling off, he decided to prep his vegetable garden today.

Before he'd left for D.C., the rose bush canes were turning green, and a few leaves had started to bud. In the flower gardens, green sprouts poked through the earth, promising spring was on the way. Sean, the gardener, wasn't due to return for another month.

Dressed in tatty jeans, well-worn running shoes, a sweatshirt, and work jacket, he collected a shovel then tossed four bags of garden soil into the cart and wheeled them out of the shed. After a couple hours, sweat trickled down his forehead, and his damp shirt clung to the contours of his back and chest. Shrugging out of the jacket, he tossed it on the still brown grass. One foot on the shovel and one firmly planted on the ground, a shadow fell across the garden. He glanced up and grinned. "Hi, Birch. How you been?"

"Oh, can't complain. Yourself?" Birch Coppervale said conversationally leaning on the handle of a hoe.

"I'm doing good. Got a head start on prepping the garden."

"So I see. Sean is going to have your head if you used up all his supplies before he gets back." Birch knelt and scooped up a handful of dirt. "Looks like you have a good mix in here, should produce well this year." He stood brushing off his pants and eyed Tristian. "Well—how'd it go?"

"Not bad, actually. When I first arrived and stopped by the shop, Willow said Angie had gone on holiday with friends. So, I reviewed the paperwork with Bruce and checked in with Willow before I left. She still hadn't heard from Angie. But she invited me to dinner with her and a boyfriend, Caleb. We had a good visit.

The Krystal Unicorn, that's what they named their new age store, is doing very well. It's nice. They stock a lot of herbs, crystals, books on a wide variety of topics and stuff." He scrunched up his face, then scrubbed a hand over it.

"Willow told us she had met someone, but we've not been to visit yet. Figured we'd let her get settled and wait for an invitation." He held Tristian's gaze.

"Well, I couldn't wait," Tristian growled.

"Still too controlling, too overbearing. You're going to have to let Angie go her own way, or you're going to lose her," Birch said.

Tristian huffed out a breath. "I know. I know. But she did return before I left. She showed me around the place, and we had a nice dinner. We agreed on ground rules that she expects me to abide by if I want to remain in her life. And I do, so I'll do my best. But it's hard. Given what happened to our parents."

"That's another thing I wanted to discuss with you. It's time you tell her what really happened."

Tristian shook his head vehemently. "No."

"It could go a long way toward making her understand why you've been so tough on her. Let's face it; yours is not a typical brother-sister relationship. And if you don't come clean with her, I'm going to tell her. You're risking that she'll find out someday from someone other than us. Then there'll be hell to pay for everyone who lied to her. I'm not willing to take that chance. She is as much a daughter to me as my Willow." His knuckles turned white as he gripped the handle of the hoe, stared up at Tristian.

"I'll give it consideration."

"You better give it a hell of a lot more than that."

"Are you threatening me?" Tristian asked.

"No, son, it's a promise," Birch said sharply.

"What are you two fussing about now?" A melodic voice floated on the breeze. Birch's wife wandered over to stand beside her husband, her long black hair blowing in the breeze. She was barefooted as usual wearing worn jeans and a t-shirt, a pastel sweater tied around her shoulders.

"Good morning Freesia." Tristian wrapped an arm around her and squeezed. "Nothing." The sweater looked a lot like ones Angie favored.

"Nothing, my ass. Angie again?"

"Yes," her husband confirmed.

Tristian glared at Birch. "He wants me to tell Angie what really happened to our parents. I'm not ready."

"Well—she's a grown woman, doesn't need protection from the truth anymore. The question is not whether or not you're ready. There's a lot of things you should have told her. She is out in the world, on her own. What happens if she meets other creatures? What if they find out…? Never mind. I can see by the defiance in your eyes, nothing we say…" Anger flashed through Freesia's eyes then softened.

"You're right. I'll figure out a way to tell her."

"See that you do. The burden is wearing on you. We see it. You spend way too much time alone. Angie's moved on with her life, and so should you. Find a woman that matters. Enjoy life."

So someone can wipe out everyone that matters to me. Like they did to my parents? Hell no. His temper vibrated at the end of its tether. Out of respect, Tristian held his tongue. Those thoughts were better left unsaid.

Birch interrupted as if he knew what Tristian was thinking. "Come enjoy dinner with us tonight. You can tell us all about Willow's Caleb. Did you like him?"

Tristian blew out a breath, his temper under control again. "You know, from the little I saw, he was a nice person. He treats Willow like she's a princess." Tristian paused for a few beats, considering. "I liked him okay, for being a man that's dating a woman I consider my sister. He was okay. And the way she looks at him—" Tristian let out a low whistle.

"Well, that's something," Birch said a wide smile curving his lips. He clapped Tristian on the shoulder. "See you at dinner." He took his wife's hand, and they ambled back across the grass, where the occasional green blade appeared, promising spring was right around the corner.

Tristian spent the rest of the day in the gardens. Sean be damned. Working with the earth, watching things sprout and grow, always took the edge off. He put the garden tools away, showered, dressed in black jeans, black and red pull-over, polished his boots, and joined the Coppervales for dinner.

Chapter Three
Should She or Shouldn't She—Probably Not the Best Idea in the World, But It Had to be Done

Hannah drove past his house every day, trying to convince herself to turn up the steep driveway to where his home perched high on the cliffs. It resembled a stone castle, less the moat. Sitting on a large piece of land overlooking the ocean to the front and bordering a lush forest to the back. Even in the early spring, you could tell the manicured lawns and garden had been well cared for during the growing season.

From rumors she'd heard around town, he was gone a lot and had a staff of employees to take care of things while he was away. The man was more a myth than reality. Reclusive—but he'd not seemed like that when she'd met him. Lonely is how she would describe him. But there was something else off about him, besides the lack of social skills. Her talents warned he wasn't as he appeared—his true self was cloaked.

Why she cared what he thought, she would never know. But she did. Infatuation…that's it. Plain and simple. Her parents would have an absolute fit. He wasn't like them. And she could face serious consequences if… *Oh, that was plain ridiculous. I've met him once, and it didn't end well. All I want to do is apologize for the things said before he abruptly left. That's all.*

She stopped the car at the turn-off, flipped on the blinker, hesitated only a beat before turning the steering wheel and hitting the gas. *No turning back now.* Parked in front of his house was the same sports car he'd driven that night. Maybe he was getting ready to leave.

The fact she couldn't read him worried her; she didn't want to get involved with a—serial. Hannah shook off the thought. Inside the house, a shadow passed by the huge bay window. She held her breath. *Am I really going to go through with this?*

Walking up the steps to the house, she paused. Why would he leave such an expensive car sitting out when he had a four-car garage? She was stalling. Straightening her shoulders, she used the brass doorknocker. There was no answer. She knocked again.

The heavy oak door creaked open. Tristian stood shirtless, his abs rippled as he raised one muscular arm to lean on the doorframe. The skintight blue jeans hung low on his hips, and his hair tousled as if he'd not been awake long.

When he stared at her, with those huge blue-gray eyes, tingles careened up her spine. She covered her mouth in case drool pooled in the corners her mouth. He was one sexy male. She sucked in a breath and opened her mouth to speak but nothing came out.

A brow arched, he peered questioningly at her then twisted to glance backward into the house. The sunlight streaming through the doorway accentuated several scars across his chest, rib area, and a healed slash across his back.

Who gets those kinds of battle scars and lives to tell the tale? Not going to ask. Maybe this wasn't such a good idea after all. She shifted prepared to run down the stairs if things got weird.

The corner of his mouth curved up in an inviting sexy-as-hell grin. "Good morning, Hannah. What a surprise." He paused for a couple beats staring down at her. "If you are done ogling me, is there something I can do for you?" His resounding voice flowed smooth and deep. "Or...

Panic set in, her brain wouldn't engage, and her mouth took off on its own. "I...I didn't mean to wake you. Only wanted to apologize for whatever I said the other night that pissed you off," she stammered. *God— Can I embarrass myself anymore?* Her cheeks felt like they were on fire as she whirled away from him in an attempt to compose herself. When she turned around, he'd leaned one shoulder against the doorframe, crossed his arms over his sculptured chest, but his smoldering gaze over her body should have incinerated the clothes she was wearing.

Resting her hand on her hip she tilted her chin up, her gaze met his. "Like what you see?" *Oh my god, where did that come from?* Her hand flew to her mouth again. "Anyway, I'm sorry." She turned and sprinted down the steps. By the time she reached her car, he was leaning nonchalantly against her driver's side door. "How did you do that?"

"Practice." He blinked at her. "Why don't you come in and have a cup of coffee? Obviously, you are having caffeine withdrawals. I warmed up a couple of cinnamon rolls and apple fritters. Would you like one?" Not waiting for an answer, he sauntered up the steps.

Her knees went weak; she licked her lips.

"Coming?"

"No...I have to go," she stammered. "I was on my

way home after a run. But thanks for the invitation."

"Suit yourself." He strolled through the doorway and paused turned back to peer at her. "Sure?"

Her stomach growled loudly. *Traitorous organ.* "Maybe just a bite and a big cup of coffee." She plodded up the stairs and followed him into the kitchen filled with the aroma of warm cinnamon and apples.

"I'll be right back." He sprinted up the stairs and returned dressed in a shirt unbuttoned halfway down his chest. "Sorry about that. Don't want to be rude running around half naked." Tristian whisked a pan of delicious looking treats from the oven and placed them on the counter.

Hannah eyed him. *Still nearly half naked, but I like what I see and he's proficient in the kitchen. Huh.*

Reaching into the cupboard, he pulled out a large mug, poured it full of steaming coffee, and set it on the table in front of her. He jerked his chin toward a carved wooden chair, "Have a seat."

She eased onto the chair as he deftly took the rolls from pan to plates, carried them to the table. The sunlight streamed through his kitchen window, as he crossed to the table.

"Anything else I can get for you?"

"No," she said quietly, her mouthwatering. "Um— Where'd you get those? Never mind, none of my business."

With his long fingers, he picked up a cinnamon roll and took a big bite, washed it down with a swig of coffee. "Now tell me again why you are on my doorstep at this time in the morning?"

"You left so abruptly the other night. I must have said something to upset you. Sometimes I say things before my brain processes the comment."

"Nope. I had work to do and needed to get back to it. I enjoyed our conversation that evening."

"Would you like to have dinner sometime?" she blurted.

"I'm tempted, but no. I'm not good at relationships. Married to my job. On call twenty-four-seven." He took another drink of his coffee. "Most women don't tolerate that type of schedule well, and I hate confrontations away from the job."

"Oh. What do you do for a living?"

Tristian paused for a couple of beats. Took another bite of the roll and chewed. "Private security." His tone of voice warned no further questions.

"Okay, well—thanks for the apple fritter. I'd better be on my way. If you change your mind, my cell phone number is on the card." She flicked a business card toward him. It whirled and fluttered landing on the table beside him.

He picked it up, turned it over a couple times in his large hand. As he was about to return the card to her, she bolted across the kitchen, through the living room, and out the door.

How stupid could I be? He's not interested. Just as well, he's not one of us. However, when she glanced in her rearview mirror, he was standing in the doorway a smirk curving his full lips. There's something about him.

****

A split second after he ambled toward the door, her vehicle wheels spun and left dust trails down his driveway as she drove away. Shrugging, he returned to the kitchen tossed the card in the trash can and finished eating. All the while, his gaze returning to that trash can. *What the hell is my problem? Getting involved with a woman is not an option. Look how it ended with my dad.* He shoved up from the table as his phone rang.

"What's up boss?"

"Glad I caught you. We have a problem down south. Seems a rogue demon, werewolf, and vampire have joined forces. They're intimidating political candidates in an attempt to rig the election outcome. The front runner is missing."

"So why not send a mediation team?" Phone to his ear, Tristian walked over to the trash can and fished Hannah's card out. Tucked it in a drawer by the sink.

"It's beyond that point, according to Bobby and his team. He's down there now."

"Okay…On my way. What about the vamp? Want me to handle him too?" Gulping down the rest of his coffee, he washed the mug and set it in the dish drainer.

"No. I've already contacted the Vampire Council. Lady Rose is sending someone to clean up that mess." A tap, tap, tap came over the phone.

Tristian chuckled to himself at hearing Bruce tap his pen against the glass top desk in his office. An indicator he didn't like the situation at hand. "Got ya. I hate cleaning up ash all over everything."

"Let me know how it goes." Bruce gave him directions to the location.

"Of course. You'll have my report immediately after the situation is neutralized."

Tristian hung up and punched in Bobby's number. It rang only once before he picked up.

"Figured I'd be hearing from you. On your way?"

"Yeah. Fill me in."

"That frontrunner's body was found a few minutes ago. Drained dry. The candidates are in hiding. A vamp seems to be running the show, but demons, changelings, and the werewolf have had words recently. It's a powder keg."

As Tristian talked on the phone, he sat at the computer and made airline reservations. "I'll be there by nightfall. Made your team's return reservations. Sending them to you via email. Should give us enough time for you to fill me in, and we go our separate ways."

It was silent on the other end for a minute or two. "Got the email confirmation. See ya soon."

Tristian swiped his finger across the screen and stuffed the phone in his pocket.

Chapter Four
Change is Difficult. But When Life Blindsides You
Upside the Head, Maybe You Should Listen

Exhausted, Tristian finished the report and emailed it over his secure server to Bruce. Leaning back in his high-back black leather office chair, he rubbed his eyes and stretched his arms above his head.

Hannah had danced around the fringes of his mind on the plane ride back home. If that wasn't enough, Birch's words drifted through his dreams. Distractions were deadly in his business. When he closed his eyes, damn if she wasn't there again.

This time, he heard Birch's words whispered through his consciousness. *Shit, Was it a faery spell? Naw, Birch wouldn't do that to me. Or would he?* After several minutes Tristian strode to the big bay window in his office, stood there with his hands tucked in the front pockets of his jeans. The man who was like a second father to him was working in the yard next door.

When Tristian picked up the phone off the desk and punched #1, he was still undecided.

Bruce answered on the first ring. "Tristian, good to hear from you. Just got the email, looks like things went off without a hitch."

"Yeah, by the time I got there, the assassin from the Vampire Council, Stefan, had lit up the vamps involved. Bobby and his team had set a trap for the others, I came in, shot the werewolf with a poison dart, lobbed fireballs on the demons left as they scattered." Tristian scrubbed his hand over his face. "Comparing my body count to Bobby's, a couple underlings may have escaped, which could mean trouble down the line. But for now, the town is secure, the election…well…the creatures left their mark on it since the frontrunner is dead."

"Not good."

"No, but Bobby vetted the remaining candidates. None of them has ties to the magical community. We covered our tracks before leaving."

"Having Bobby plant that story about possible terrorists was brilliant," Bruce said.

"It's the nature of the times, a convenient scapegoat for the mortals." Tristian raked his fingers through his hair and rubbed the back of his neck. "Anything else going on?"

"Nope, checking on the rumblings you reported of a high-ranking demon looking for revenge, so far nothing. Sent emails out to other Overlords and Lady Rose, for good measure."

"Yeah, it's unnerving, my sources are afraid to talk. I've hit a brick wall. And that almost never happens." He blew out a breath, wisps of blond hair feathered over his forehead as he shifted slightly.

"Tristian, what's on your mind?"

"I'd like time off. Personal issues need to be resolved, without worrying about an assignment looming."

"No problem—I'll put other teams on alert. How much time do you want?"

"Couple of weeks, maybe three at the most. It's

been a long time…"

"You've got months of time built up, don't worry about it. Are you all right? Anything you want to talk about?"

"I'm fine. It's time to make a few changes."

"Okay. With the demon situation simmering, I still want to follow protocol. Check in every couple of days. Will that work?"

"Sure. And I know if I forget you'll send the cavalry out to check on me assuming the worst."

"Wasn't going to state the obvious. You're the one who set the procedures in place. Enjoy your time off."

"Thanks." Tristian ended the call and yawned. He pushed up from the chair, ambled upstairs, showered, and fell into bed.

****

For the first time in years, Tristian woke up without an agenda. He tugged on a pair of worn jeans and sprinted downstairs to the kitchen where the first slice of sunlight beamed across the floor. The inviting aroma of freshly brewed coffee filled his nostrils, he sighed, thankful for the automatic timer on the coffee maker.

Rummaging through the drawers, his gaze settled on the quarry. He snatched Hannah's business card, flipped it over in his hand, and examined the handwritten phone number on the back. A cell number. He turned on his computer, using a special computer program, he traced the number to a local address. Was that her home address? Must be, the address indicated a location on the bluffs. Shadow Hawk Cyber's building was located in the opposite direction on the northeast edge of town.

Saturday morning, he glanced at his watch, six-thirty, maybe a good time to catch her for breakfast. He shrugged into a shirt and slipped his feet into running shoes. *It's been a while since I've worn these.* He grabbed his keys, set the security alarm, and closed the front door behind him.

The sports car coasted to a stop in front of a cream-colored house with blue shutters and a nicely landscaped yard. The curtains were closed, no signs of life in the cottage. He rang the doorbell and smiled at the Irish jig it played. No one answered the door. This time, he knocked. Dropping his hand to his side, he felt her presence coming up the street, he turned a broad smile spreading across his face.

Dressed in tight-fitting jogging attire, she skidded to a stop several yards from her porch and stared at him wide-eyed.

Leaning his hip on the porch railing, he winked at her. "Guess it's my turn to apologize for my rude behavior the other day." He jerked a thumb toward his chest. "Not a morning person. I was hoping we could start over while I took you to breakfast. You haven't eaten, have you?"

"No—but you already made it quite clear... And how did you find where I lived."

On a laugh, he said, "Security specialist. Remember? Anyway, I've changed my mind, but if you'd rather not..." Tristian stopped himself right there. First instinct was to hurl a flip response and leave. In truth, he liked her spunk and wanted to get to know her better, despite his fear of getting too close. "Come on; give a guy a break."

Hesitantly she approached him. "You're not some

kind of cage fighter, are you?"

For a couple beats he blinked at her incredulously, then with a bark of laughter, he scrubbed his hand over his face. "No. Where on earth did you get such an idea?"

"The scars on your torso."

He nodded in understanding. "Security comes with risks."

"Yes, but...I think we'll just leave things as they are. But thanks for the offer."

"Have it your way." Temper flared; he turned and strode back to his car, yanked open the car door, then he glanced back. She was still standing on the porch. "You don't know what you're missing." He sent her his best devastatingly smile, slid into the car, and waited.

She stepped off the porch and walked toward the vehicle, then stopped.

Encouraged, he rolled down the window. "Second thoughts?"

She chewed on the side of her cheek. "Only if you quit being so secretive."

"It's the nature of my business. If I told you what I do, I'd have to kill you, and that would defeat my purpose and intentions. You'll just have to trust me on this."

Looking doubtful, she sucked in a long breath and blew it out slowly. "Okay. I've got to shower and change, so I'll meet you at the diner in twenty minutes."

He considered offering to help her but thought better of it. "Fair enough." He did a small fist pump inside the car out of sight. "I'll see you in a few." *This dating shit is tougher than it looked. One night stands are so much easier, no entanglements.*

****

Taking his time, he drove the long way through town on the way to the diner. It had been a while since he cruised his hometown, Misty Harbor, for the heck of it. A new scattering of homes filled what used to be empty fields, several new storefronts had popped up, and the high school had two new additions and appeared to be in the middle of building another. On the bluffs appeared to be a new upscale restaurant. *A good place to take Hannah for an early dinner and a walk on the nearby beach.*

By the time he pulled into the diner's parking lot, his stomach was in knots. This was all foreign to him, as he never had a reason to impress anyone. Before he had a chance to process the feeling, Hannah pulled into the lot and parked beside him.

Nonchalantly, he pushed his door open and walked around to her car, waited for the lock click, then tugged on the handle, holding the door open for her.

"And they say chivalry is dead." She smiled up at him.

The knot in his stomach loosened as he held the diner door open for her and breathed in her lilac and orange blossom scent. Air whooshed behind him as the cracked glass door slowly closed. Nodding to a waitress, he ambled over to a corner booth farthest from the entrance and waited for Hannah to settle into the seat. He slid in beside her.

Nan rushed over with a pot of coffee, flipped the cups over on the table, and poured rich dark liquid. "Nice to see you guys again. What can I get for you?"

"Give us a couple minutes." His nostrils flared at the delicious coffee aroma. "Hey, something happen to your door?"

Nan glanced over her shoulder and frowned. "Yeah, the other night after closing, a couple thugs tried to rob the place as we were leaving. Cook used a baseball bat to convince them it was a bad idea."

"Good thing there were two of you," Hannah said.

"Oh, we never close without at least two of us, sometimes three. Safety in numbers you know. I'll be back." Nan flitted off to another table.

Tristian opened the menu. "Do you eat breakfast here often? What's good?"

"Yes, quite a bit, lunch mostly. But I hear the ham and cheese omelet with mushrooms is good. If you like mushrooms."

"I do. You don't?"

"Not really. I'll have the hash brown casserole with two eggs, bacon, and orange juice."

He raised his arm up signaled to Nan they were ready. She held up a finger and nodded.

A few minutes later, she took their order and promised it wouldn't be long. An uncomfortable silence passed between Tristian and Hannah.

"So—do you return to Ireland often?"

"I try to make it across the pond at least once a year. I spent last Christmas with Ma and Da, but my sister couldn't make it. A bad storm in Montana snowed her in for days. But we try to talk at least once a week." Hannah paused as Nan brought their order and set plates of steaming food in front of them. "How about you? Just your sister?"

He picked up a fork and cut into the omelet. "Yeah. Tell me about your work. Do you hack the hackers and ride off into the sunset as heroes?"

Nearly choking on a bite of hash browns, she took a sip of water and stared over the glass rim at him. "Something like that. Like you most of my work is secret. Writing code to prevent hackers from getting access to sensitive materials in the private sector and now the government. They finally realize the private sector is so far ahead of them, that their outdated security practices are actually a threat to national security."

Taking a piece of toast, he wiped up the remnants of his omelet and said, "Even though you can't get the clearances required, you are still able to work on…" He popped the food in his mouth.

"Oh, I'm still assigned to the private accounts. I've applied for citizenship, so we'll see how that goes. If the guys working on government contracts run into a problem." She motioned air quotes. "I unofficially help 'em out."

"I see." More relaxed now, he noticed a faint magic signature. Glancing around the room, he excused himself and walked to the restroom. The farther away he got from her, the weaker the feeling. It was her. *How'd I miss that? She isn't the usual classification of otherworldly creatures.* Intrigued, he ambled out of the men's room, as three tough-looking teens sauntered in, perched on stools at the lunch counter talking loud, and demanding service.

Cheerfully, Nan said, "I'll be with you guys in a minute." She had a tray full of food as she passed by them. One teen grabbed her elbow causing her to nearly drop the tray. She jerked loose, glared at them, then her eyes widened. The tray precarious balanced on her shoulder and palm, she made another attempt to deliver the order to the awaiting table. Another of the teens stood up in front of her, blocking her way.

Tristian stepped out of the alcove between the teens and Nan. He should have moved on, minded his own business, not meddle in minor disputes. But—he turned to face all three, noting that one had a huge bruise on his forearm. The kid pulled his jacket on, covering the bruise. The others sneered.

"When you bump into someone you say excuse me," Tristian said calmly.

The teen with the bruise said, "Maybe YOU do." His friends snickered. The cook came out of the back as Nan tried in vain to step around the teen.

The muscle in Tristian's jaw pulsed, then he grabbed all three and escorted them out the door. Once outside, he tossed them to the ground with little effort. "Now, you have a choice, scramble up and disappear, which will only delay your arrests."

The young men squirmed on the pavement but appeared to be unable to right themselves.

"Or you can wait for the cops to arrive. Coming back to the scene of the crime was your first mistake. You've been identified. Your second was causing a commotion."

Wailing sirens, red and blue flashing lights engulfed the little diner. A police officer rushed to the teens on the ground, handcuffed them, and yanked boys to their feet.

The officer's gaze flicked to Tristian. "What happened here?"

Tristian shrugged. "You'll have to ask the waitress. I escorted the boys outside after they harassed the woman. They tripped and fell to the ground when I released them."

"Oh, that's bullshit," one teen said. "He shoved us then held us down."

"Yeah," the two others chimed in. "We couldn't get up?"

Tristian shrugged again. "Apparently, they have trouble telling the truth also. You've several witnesses inside." He turned, started back into the diner.

"Stick around. We may need to talk to you again." The officer said as another officer helped load the young men in the patrol car.

"Of course," Tristian said, then shook his head and strode into the diner. *This is exactly why I stay home.* Hannah stood in the middle of the diner. He touched the small of her back guiding her to the booth.

"You all right?" she asked.

"Yeah, fine. But I'm ready to get out of here. How about you?"

"Didn't the police officer ask you to stay?"

"Yes, but with all the witnesses, he doesn't need me and will soon forget the role I played in this whole frigging situation." He lightly snagged Nan by the arm as she scooted by. "Check please. We are going to be on our way. You know how to contact us if necessary."

Nan glanced around, then nodded. She fished in her apron pocket, pulled out a slip of paper. "Breakfast is on the house orders of the owner. Thanks for nabbing the robbers."

Tristian shifted uncomfortably from foot to foot anxious to be out of there. "No problem." He offered his hand to Hannah as she stood, wrapped an arm around her waist, and guided her out of the diner. "How about a ride up the coast?"

"Sure, as soon as you explain how you held those teens down without touching them." She smiled up at him knowingly. "And don't give me that crap about telling me or killing me."

A slight grin curved the corners of his mouth. "How about on an as needed basis, and you don't need to know?"

A soft laugh bubbled up from her throat. "If I had to guess, I'd say you're a warlock with well-honed powers." She tilted her head up toward his. "Would I be right?"

His grin faded and was replaced with a stormy expression. "Where would you get that absurd idea? They merely tripped and had trouble getting up. I suggested they stay put until the police showed up. Simple as that."

"Right. Well on that note, I'll see myself home." She turned to her car and opened the door.

For a moment, he considered letting her go. *Women are more trouble than they're worth anyway.* That's when the meddling voice of Birch wafted through Tristian's mind. *She's moved on, so should you. Damn faeries anyway. I'm sure he's using some kind of magic to do this to me.*

"Okay, you win. But only if you tell me why you are disguising your magic signature." He leaned against the car a smirk on his face.

Her eyes rounded and she stared at him, mouth slightly agape. "I'm sure I don't know what you're talking about."

He loved when she got flustered and her light Irish lilt became quite pronounced. It was a kind of turn on, he had to admit. "How about we take a ride and work out all this secretive stuff." Tristian opened the passenger door and motioned for her to enter. A fine mist began to fall, it sparkled on her long red eyelashes—he hoped the moisture would encourage her to make a quick decision.

Hannah straightened her shoulders, her chin jutting out. Her gaze holding his without blinking. Slowly she closed her car door, leaned against it. "Okay, but the way this is going to go is, I ask a question, you answer. You ask a question, I'll answer, and we have to be truthful. No skirting the issue or the question asked. Fair enough?" She adjusted the purse strap on her shoulder.

Waiting a couple beats, he pursed his lips and nodded. "Sounds fair, but personal only, no work-related inquiries."

"Agreed." She tossed her jacket into the car and slipped into the buttery leather seat.

Giving one more glance at the activities inside the diner, he strolled around the car and eased into the driver's seat. When he turned the key in the ignition, the engine rumbled to life. The dashboard lit up like the cockpit of an aircraft with a variety of lights and gages. It's what he enjoyed most about the car, well, the zero to eighty acceleration in seconds wasn't bad either.

"Nice ride." She commented her fingers tracing the contours of the buff colored seat. "Don't drive her much."

Grasping the shift knob, he thrust it into gear. "What makes you think that?" He raised a sleek dark butterscotch brow, glanced over at her.

"The tires are close to new, the leather still has the new smell to it, and there are few fingerprints on the dash, though it's trimmed in chrome. So, either it spends a lot of time in the garage, or you use magic to keep it pristine." She snapped her fingers. "Which brings me to my first question. Warlock or not?" She settled back in her seat and turned to observe his expression.

Features schooled into a blank expression, he said, "Warlock. What type of magical creature crawls under your human appearance?"

A heavy sigh left her lips. "If I tell you—oh well— you won't stick around long anyway."

His eyebrow winged up, again. "Why would you say that? We're just getting to know each other. So far, I like what I see." Then under his breath added, "Which is rare."

"Why rare?"

"Nope, answer the question," he insisted, covering the fact he'd been surprised she'd heard his afterthought.

"I'm—a shifter—of sorts. My family are all— shifters."

Tristian rubbed his forehead. "I find that intriguing. You shift at will? Into what?"

"Yes, at will…the rest is on a need to know basis, and you don't need to know." She gave a half laugh and licked her lips nervously, which left a moist sheen to her full lips.

Enjoying that he made her nervous, he leveled his gaze at her. "I thought we agreed, none of that crap."

"Take it or leave it, that's all I am going to say at this point." She paused. "So, do you use magic in only your personal life?"

When he punched the gas, the car's tires spun

tossing gravel in its wake as he turned out of the parking lot onto the street. "Not often. Don't need to."

The diner disappeared in the rear window. The street was wet from the mist now turned to drizzle. Tristian turned on the wipers and relaxed into his seat. The clouds thinned on the horizon, the squall would be short lived which fit into his plans nicely. "Are you dangerous in shifter form?"

"Can be. Honestly, I don't change that often, only a handful of times since leaving Ireland."

"Interesting."

"Your family is magical then? It's just you and your sister."

"Yes. How about you? Only a sister?" he asked.

"No…I have a younger brother also. He is still in Ireland. Gavin helps Ma and Da at the pub. He'll take it over once they retire. I guess only my sister and I inherited the wanderlust from Ma." Hannah laughed. "She wants to someday retire and travel, but Da is going to be a hard sell on that, but she'll win. He'd do anything for her."

"Your parents own the pub?"

"Yes, it's been in the family for generations. My da took to the pub business. His brothers are in the commercial fishing trade."

"So why come to the states?" Tristian slowed the car and turned onto a road leading to the cliffs, the trails to the beach wound down from there.

She rolled the window down and inhaled deeply, the breeze blew strands of her red hair across her face. "I love the fresh clean scent after a rain." She glanced over at Tristian.

The sun peeked out through the dissipating clouds

as he stopped the car next to a trail and waited expectantly for her answer. Reaching across the seat, he smiled and brushed the wisps of hair from her face with his fingertips lightly touching a smattering of freckles across her cheeks. He lingered for a couple beats before trailing a finger along her jaw. Her creamy white skin was so soft, her hair silky. He liked the feel and leaned in wondering if her lips were…

"Education and opportunity," she quickly replied leaning away. "We had family that helped me get into a prestigious college known for computer sciences. Then my sister followed."

His hand dropped to the console. "She's a computer geek too?"

She laughed. "No…Brandy was more interested in ecology and wildlife. She's a park ranger in Glacier National Park."

He glanced out the window. "Rain appears to be over for now. Want to go for a walk? We can follow the trails to the beach."

She hesitated for a moment, then slipped her arms into her jacket as he opened her car door.

Chapter Five
A Perfect Gentleman—Too Good to be True?

And her body was never found... She shook her head to dislodge the voice from her mind and followed him to the trail. He took hold of her hand and intertwined their fingers as they walked the rocky coastline until the trail wound through the brush and trees down to the beach. Waves crashed against the shoreline, and wind gusts brought the ocean spray raining down on them. The sun hung low in the sky as she pulled her jacket tight around her.

The man was a puzzle. One minute he's gruff and unresponsive, the next patient, attentive, and talkative. It's like he's at war with himself. *Damn he's intriguing and—sexy as hell.* She liked the air of mystery surrounding him. If she was honest with herself, the hint of danger that lurked around him was a turn on too. *Ma and Da would not approve.* She snickered.

"What's so funny?" Tristian stopped in mid-stride and stared at her.

"Oh, nothing. Just that my attraction to bad boys is alive and well. My parents…"

He quirked an eyebrow. "Boys? I don't think so. Your parents?"

"Wouldn't approve of you." She snickered again. "And I used the term boys loosely, meaning males." Her gaze slithered over him from top to bottom.

"Believe me, I'm well aware you're not a boy."

"I'm certainly glad you noticed." He paused for a couple beats. "Your parents—does it matter?" he asked sliding a seductive glance in her direction.

"It should, but it doesn't. Where are we going?" The ocean breeze stirred, bringing with it the scent of brine and a chill. She shivered.

"Are you cold?" He wrapped an arm around her waist, drawing her close. "We should head back anyway. Felt good to get away from prying eyes for a bit."

"It did. I wasn't sure at first, but… It was a nice ride and walk. Thank you."

"Since you survived being alone with me, this time. How about dinner at the new restaurant on the cliffs?"

She looked into his large smoldering blue-gray eyes, mesmerized for a moment. It was bewitching how his eyes changed from blue to green tinged with gray depending on the light. "I'd like that."

The spell he seemed to weave over her was one of her own making. She was sure of it. But she couldn't remember ever being so attracted to a man so quickly. They'd only met a few days ago, yet, she was so drawn to him it was scary. Who knew what else would follow, if she didn't get a grip on herself and rein in her traitorous body.

Her kind wasn't allowed such luxury. Intimacy had major consequences in her culture. She was positive he was nowhere near ready to take those steps now, if ever. A fun romp in the sack wasn't in their future. There were no exceptions.

"Here we are. I'll get the car started it shouldn't

take long to warm up." He reached around her for the door handle but paused leaning into her, effectively pinning her between him and the car. Even after everything she'd just told herself, somehow it didn't matter. His warm body pressed against her made her heart race, her arms crept around his neck, she arched against him, and breathed in his alluring spicy scent.

His fingers caressed her cheeks, then he buried his hands in her hair as he covered her mouth with his demanding a response. She gave freely to the passion of his kiss, desire spun through her as he deepened the kiss, his tongue stroked and danced with hers. Too soon, he raised his mouth from hers and gazed into her eyes for several seconds. Then he rested his cheek against the top of her head for a beat, breathed a kiss on her hair inhaling deeply before straightening. One corner of his mouth curved up in a half smile as he bent once more brushing his lips over hers, then opened the car door.

"Better get you home." Tilting his head, he eyed the sky. "Looks like there's a storm brewing."

Easing into the seat, she blew out a breath as he closed the door and sauntered to the driver's side. Tugging on her shirt, she tried to center herself after that searing kiss. He was as good as he looked. She ran the tip of her tongue around her lips still moist from the kiss and sighed.

By the time they picked up her car at the diner and arrived at her house, the rain was coming down in sheets, lightning crashed all around. She shoved open the door, dashed up the path, Tristian sprinting behind her, and took refuge under the covered porch.

"Are you sure you don't want to come in for a

while, at least until the storm subsides?" she asked.

He eyed the darkening sky. "Looks like we're in for an all-nighter. Thanks for the offer, but if I came in, I wouldn't want to leave." He leaned in and kissed her. "I don't think we want to go there—yet. Thanks for a lovely afternoon."

She stood on tiptoe and returned the kiss, lingering and savoring every moment she was in his arms.

"I'll pick you up Saturday night around seven for dinner?"

She nodded and touched her fingers to her lips. "You haven't put me under a spell, have you?"

Tristian laughed aloud. "Not yet, but am seriously considering it." He caressed her arm before turning to sprint down the path to his car, he stopped and waved before ducking into the vehicle.

Fishing the keys out of her purse, she unlocked the door, pushed it open, and stepped inside. When she flipped on the light switch, her cottage was bathed in a warm golden glow. She tossed her keys on the light oak coffee table in front of the brown leather couch with buff accents and plopped down momentarily.

The fireplace she'd stacked with wood and crumpled newspaper before leaving called to her. A warm crackling fire would chase the chill of the early spring weather. She pushed up from the couch, took matches from the mantel, struck one against the rock fireplace, bent over, and lit the edges of the paper, then tossed the match among the logs. She flopped back on the couch, pulled out her phone, and tapped in her sister's number.

Brandy answered on the first ring. "I had a feeling it was you. What's wrong?"

"Nothing—everything." Hannah launched into the situation at work, her application for citizenship, the possibility of relocating in the next couple years to Colorado.

"So…what's really bothering you?"

"I just told you," Hannah insisted.

"Nooo—you told me things that will shape your future down the road. What's going on?"

She huffed out a breath. *Sis always knows.* "I met a man. He's unlike anyone I've ever known. Tall, dark blond hair and beautiful blue-gray eyes, square jaw and his kisses…" She sighed. "He makes me feel—I can't explain it. Darkness and danger roll off him in waves, but he's also charming, caring, and so damn sexy. It's like he's at odds with himself."

"Sounds hot and yummy…but disastrous for you. He's not one of us," Brandy said flatly.

"No. He's a warlock." Hannah picked at the seam on the couch between the brown and buff.

"Oh, Hannah, you don't want to mess around with a warlock that wields black magic."

"That's not it. His magic is powerful, but it's not dark magic. It's something inside him, a sadness that engulfs him. His parents died when he was young, and he raised his little sister. He's had a rough life, but I can't get a sense of him. It's like he's immune to my talents. He works some kind of security but won't tell me much about it."

"Your soft heart is overpowering your brain. You need to walk away while you still can."

"I can't—Don't want to. I'm drawn to him and he to me…I think."

"I'm coming out there. Then we'll see what's

what."

"No. That would only make things worse. If I can get him to trust me enough to... Well, he's already told me about his parents and his sister. I got a sense that it's not something he tells anyone. The info kinda slipped out when we first met. Both of us were having a really bad day."

"Information like that doesn't just slip out. He's playing you, like a fine fiddle."

"No, he's not. I can tell that for sure. Trust me, sis. If I'd wanted a lecture, I'd call Ma. I needed someone to talk to, to listen to me, so I could maybe figure this all out."

"Did it work?" Brandy snorted. "By the way, trust is a two-way street."

Ignoring her sister's jab, she said, "Not exactly, but...talking with you has helped me sort a few things out. How about you, hear from that skirt-chasing slime you left in Ireland?"

"Nope. Maybe he's finally taken the hint. I mean what more can I do? Told him I didn't love him, wouldn't marry him if he was the last male on earth." Brandy huffed out.

Hannah giggled. "That's cold. Put a dent in his huge ego I bet."

"Couldn't be helped. I tried letting him down easy, and he offered to come live over here. Couldn't have that, now could I?"

"Nooooo. Absolutely not. Sis, I gotta go, five in the morning comes awfully early."

"Don't I know it. Are you going to be seeing tall, dark, and dangerous again?"

She hesitated a couple seconds. *If I tell her the*

truth, she'll be on a plane out here. That's the last thing I need. Wish I hadn't called her. "Probably not," she lied.

"Coming to your senses, are you then?"

"Only time will tell. Talk to you next week. Love you."

"Right back at ya."

Hannah ended the call feeling worse than before. *Now on top of everything else, I worry about when Brandy will show up on my doorstep. I just made things a whole lot worse.* She yawned and put the kettle on for a cup of soothing herbal tea before bed.

Chapter Six
How Can the Right Decision be so Difficult for One Man?

Standing under the cold spray of the shower, he shivered. But at least the heat in his crotch subsided. This was the third cold shower he'd taken since leaving her cottage the night before last. He replayed their last conversation in his head and wondered if she wasn't the one bewitching him. Every time he thought of her, lust zinged to his groin. Turning the shower off, he toweled dry as the doorbell rang. *Who the hell is that?* Yanking jeans off the back of a chair, he pulled them on and sprinted to the door.

"Birch, what are you doing here?"

Birch grinned. "Now is that any way to greet a friend?"

"It is if you show up unannounced at this time of night." Tristian's voice held a sharp edge, but he grinned, held the door open wide, and motioned Birch inside.

"I can't stay. Freesia wanted to see if you've eaten yet? We're having a late dinner and thought you might like to join us."

He thought for a moment, then his stomach growled loudly. He'd worked in the gardens all day, trying to keep his mind off her, which didn't work, attest the cold shower. "Let me put on shoes and a shirt, and I'll be right over."

"Good. That's want I wanted to hear." Birch turned with a wave and walked toward home.

****

Dinner was lobster tail, biscuits, fine wine, and friendly conversation until Tristian's tongue got a little too loose.

"Noticed you've been around more than usual, taken some time off?" Birch asked casually.

"Yeah, thought about what you said. Told Bruce, I needed some time off to take care of personal matters. Wasn't a problem."

"I would hope not. First time in what—ten years?"

"Something like that." He shrugged, took a sip of wine.

Been spending a lot of time in town," Freesia said, clearing the table, then setting out plates of strawberry shortcake.

"Some." *Ahh...now the reason of for the invitation rears its ugly head.* Tristian took another drink of wine, leaned back in his chair, and narrowed his eyes at Freesia. "Out with it."

Freesia put her hand to her chest in a gesture of feigned surprise. "Nothing. Nothing at all. Glad to see you out and about, not moping around."

"First of all, I don't mope. Second, what I do is my own business," he said sharper than he meant to. A small town talked, which is why he kept a low profile. He'd bet his life that someone told Freesia about him and Hannah. He wasn't going to offer any information, on the off chance, he was wrong about their motive. "So how is your garden doing? Any sprouts?"

Freesia's gaze flitted between her husband's and

his. "Nan said they caught the hoodlums that broke into the diner, and…"

There it was, the bait for their fishing expedition. He finished her sentence for her. "I was instrumental in their capture, then left the diner with a red headed woman. Is that what you're trying to ascertain?"

"I'm sure I don't know what you are talking about," Freesia said indignantly red creeping into her cheeks.

"The jig is up, hon." Birch met Tristian's gaze. "Yes, Frees, heard you were seeing a young woman, then she appeared at your door the other morning. Son, if you're trying to keep her a secret, don't have her coming to your door in broad daylight when Freesia is stalking you." Birch barely got the last words out before he roared with laughter. He wiped his eyes. "To top it off, a couple hours later she came rushing out of the house, jumped in her car, and sped off, while you stood in the doorway with only jeans on. It's a good thing we're the only two houses on this bluff, or…"

"Enough," Tristian growled. "Yes, I've been spending time with Hannah, that's her name. We're friends and I enjoy her company. End of story."

"Well…Not exactly. Ernie's teenage daughter was walking up the path from the beach with her boyfriend the other afternoon."

"That's it. I'm headed home. Thanks for the delicious meal." Tristian grabbed his jacket and bolted out the door.

Birch right behind him, grabbed hold of his sleeve. "We only wanted to make you aware of the rumors. Making yourself scarce while Angie was in college, only strengthened the lore of the recluse in the big house on the ridge. Now you're out and about, people are going to talk."

"I was going to cut her loose anyway." He jerked away from Birch.

"Don't be an ass. Obviously, you have feelings for this woman. It's been twenty years. You're safe. No one here knows who you really are, nor what you do for a living. Get a life before it's too late, and you die a bitter, lonely old man." He grasped Tristian by both arms and gave him a shake. "There are no guarantees in life. Take a chance and live rather than exist." Birch shoved him away and stalked toward the house.

Unable to let it go, Tristian said, "If I'm alone, no one gets hurt."

"But you." Birch shot back shaking his head and closed the door.

God, he hated it when Birch was right—and knew it. Tristian changed into sweats and running shoes, took off across the land toward the forested area of his property. After several laps around his and the Coppervale property, he slowed to a walk. The full moon washed everything in silvery shadows as he stood on the edge of the ridge and watched the tide ebb and flow. This was not the way he'd planned his and Angie's life. Therein lies the problem. Angie, headstrong and independent, wasn't going to let anyone plan her life. He should have known better, but she didn't know—because he'd never told her what could happen, or about their parents, or the magic world. Birch was right about that too. She had to know, and he would tell her, but the timing wasn't right—yet. He'd provided her a protective existence growing up. Was he wrong?

Tomorrow night he'd see Hannah, have a nice dinner and—*Aww to hell with it, things will look better in the morning.* On his way up the porch steps, he glanced at the Coppervale's house where lights still blazed in the windows. He'd always thought the faeries kept strange hours. They were usually up no matter what time he arrived home.

Inside his house, he kicked off his shoes and shed his clothes as he climbed the stairs to the bedroom. A warm shower eased his tired muscles. After flipping the spray to massage, he stood under the stream a few minutes longer. Steam covered the mirrors and bellowed out from the shower when he opened the glass door to step onto the vibrant blue, plush bath mat. He toweled off and crawled into his lodge-style log king sized bed where the first thing to dance through his weary mind was Hannah. His dreams drifted through different scenarios, but they all had one thing in common—her. The last sequence had him cursing his imagination and wishing she was still under him as he opened his eyes and squinted at the sun already high overhead. He rolled to his side and grabbed the phone off the nightstand. This was the latest check-in he'd done since taking leave. Leaning up on one elbow, he scrolled to the number and pressed the green icon.

"Well, well…you did remember us. Seconds to spare in the check in time frame. Seriously…too close for comfort."

"I know. Sorry. Late night."

"I hope you were getting laid." A low male chuckle came through the receiver.

"Hate to disappoint. Had to run off adrenalin before I could sleep. Didn't get to bed until the wee hours of the morning…why am I telling you?"

"Don't know boss."

"Check-in complete. Talk to you tomorrow." Tristian disconnected the call and flopped over on his back, threw his arm over his eyes as if he could make the world disappear. Finally, he got up, yanked on worn jeans, a dark blue T-shirt, and boots. After wolfing down a couple toasted asiago cheese bagels and a large mug of steaming coffee, he strapped on the gauntlets that held wrist blades and slipped into his black duster. He checked the inside pockets for the proper weapons and strode to the practice range hidden in the trees behind his house. After three hours of practice with magic weaponry, a variety of guns, his favorite crossbow, and wrist blades, he was satisfied and returned to the house to clean up for his date.

A knot in the pit of his stomach grew as he pulled on black suit pants, light gray shirt with thin black stripes, a black European cut jacket, and polished black boots. The front door closed and locked, he sprinted across the porch and down the stairs. A low whistle caught his attention as he opened the car door. Scanning the area, he spotted Birch and Freesia walking along the path to their house.

"Since you are still on leave, are we to assume you are all dressed up for pleasure rather than assignment?" Birch chuckled as he and his wife passed by the entrance to Tristian's driveway.

"I don't know how you do it. Always—never mind. Pleasure is the plan. Don't wait up." Tristian snickered as he slid into the sports car and sped off. Stopping only once to pick up a bouquet of a dozen long-stemmed lavender roses in a mother-of-pearl colored vase. A dark violet ribbon was tied in a bow at the top. After carefully examining the flowers, he nodded and handed the florist two hundred-dollar bills. "No change needed."

Chapter Seven
A Romantic Dinner, Drive on a Moon Lit Night,
Satisfaction Guaranteed—Not

Tristian pulled up in front of Hannah's cottage and cut the engine. For a few moments, he sat there fingering the dark violet ribbon, then drew in a deep breath and let it out slowly. *I can make this work. Honesty is the key. But how much can I tell her— safely?* He unfolded his tall frame from the vehicle, grabbed the roses, then strode toward the door. When he knocked, a vision in light blue opened the door. He sucked in a breath. "Wow! You are absolutely stunning."

Dressed in a shimmering, one-shoulder dress that hugged her curves, she smiled shyly. "You're early."

A quick glance at his watch, he brought his gaze back to her. "Couldn't wait to see you." He handed her the flowers.

Eyes rounded, she sniffed the bouquet. "They're beautiful. Thank you so much." She padded to the coffee table and gently set them down. Beside the door, she slipped her feet into pale blue heels, picked up a frosty white leather coat from the couch, and returned to the door. "I'm ready."

"Great." He helped her into the coat. Unable to stop himself, he turned her toward him, took her face in his hands, gazed into her eyes, brushing his lips over hers. Trailing kisses along her jawline, he breathed a kiss in the pulsing hollow at the base of her throat, lingering only a moment. When she wrapped her arms around his neck and curved into him, he went hard, hoping there'd be no cold shower tonight. "I think we better get going, before..." he whispered against her ear.

She turned, nuzzled his neck, placing a soft kiss there. "I suppose so." With a sigh, she turned to set the alarm, waited for him to exit, and locked the door. "Have you been to this place before?"

He opened the passenger door and waited for her to settle in the seat. Leaning over, he fastened her seat belt, caressed her cheek with his finger before straightening. "No. Noticed it was open for business the other day when I was cruising through town. Thought of you."

"How sweet." She looked out the window as they approached the restaurant. "Appears they have valet parking too. Wow, this town has never had a place like this."

"I hope you don't mind, but I'd like to skip the valet parking. Don't want anyone touching my car without me being present." He shrugged.

"No problem. You'd be surprised at what people will do to cars...trackers—"

He lifted a brow. "No, I have a pretty good idea." Scanning the lot, he steered the car into a space flooded with light from the parking lot lamps.

Hannah giggled. "I guess you would, being in security." Reaching for the door handle, she pushed the door open, only to find Tristian already there offering his hand.

The building had a rock exterior, double glass doors with an etching of a lighthouse on one side, a rocky pier on the other. As they passed through the entrance way, a man dressed in formal attire greeted them.

"Do you have reservations?" he asked quietly.

"Yes, for two at seven under Shandie." Tristian glanced beside the man at the ice sculpture of a lighthouse lit from beneath with soft blue LED's. "Nice." He touched the small of her back and drew her to him.

"It's beautiful."

"This way, please. The maitre d' led the way to an intimate corner table. In the center, the candle's flame wavered slightly with their approach. "Is this to your liking, sir?"

Tristian surveyed the large room. The white starched linen table clothes covered wooden tables, crystal water goblets and stemware sat on each table beside cloth napkins neatly folded. "Yes, it will do nicely. Thank you." Tristian held the wooden captain's chair with an upholstered seat for Hannah, then moved a chair closer to her but still with his back to the wall.

"This is really a nice place." She took the menu from the waiter, dressed in a black suit with a white shirt, who had joined them.

"May I get you something to drink while you look over the menus?" he asked.

"Yes, a bottle of your finest Chardonnay."

"Of course. 2006?"

"That would be fine." Tristian leaned back in his chair and watched Hannah unfold her napkin, delicately place it in her lap, arrange the silverware, then turned her deep blue eyes up to meet his.

"What? Did I do something wrong?" Hannah kept her hands in her lap and held Tristian's gaze. "It's been a long time since I've been to a place like this. Surprised they built one in our little town."

"No. You do everything exactly right." He glanced at the waiting line that formed out the door, then at the dining rooms where there wasn't an empty table. "Looks like it's pretty popular."

The waiter returned and presented Tristian the bottle of wine, label up. "Is this what you had in mind, sir?"

"It's exactly the one. Thank you."

The waiter popped the cork and poured the sparkling golden liquid into the wine glasses. He paused and glanced at Tristian.

"You can leave the bottle on the table."

Any more news on the work front?" Tristian placed his napkin in his lap, then swirled the wine in his glass, sniffed, and took a sip. "This is excellent."

Hannah picked up her glass and took a sip. "Yes, the vanilla note is delightful with a hint of fruit and oak."

She knows her wine. He didn't know why, but it pleased him.

The waiter brought a basket of rolls then asked, "Are you ready to order?" He looked first to Tristian, who nodded to Hannah.

Hannah sat her wine glass down and smiled up at the waiter. "Yes, I'd like the lobster ravioli."

"And I'd liked the poached lobster." Tristian handed the menus to the waiter.

"I'll be back with your salads shortly." He turned

on his heel and strode across the room.

Hannah took another sip of wine. "Work is good. My boss turned the clearance situation to the higher ups who claim to be able to expedite things. My citizenship test is a couple months away. There's a lot to study for, so the timing is good."

"Will you be relocating with the company sooner?" The knot in his belly tightened.

"No. The big wigs are going first to finalize the location, and the building arrangements then purchase the latest and greatest equipment. I'll be one of the last to go, because when it was initially thought I couldn't get a top-secret clearance, the company shifted all civilian clients to me."

"Doesn't that make your workload heavy?"

"Job security." She laughed. "Besides, I've worked with most of these clients for a couple of years. It's comfortable knowing we've met their expectations. In a crisis, they trust we can handle any situation, quickly and confidentially. That makes my job easier in a breach."

"What you are saying is that the government is a pain in the ass."

"No—it's an unknown factor. The private sector we handle has the latest encryption software, secure networks, and top of the line hardware. Whereas, the government has always lagged behind. Now they realize it, and updating their systems is going to be a monumental task. Think about it. Cyber security, government style is going to include, offices, aircraft, ground vehicles, telecommunications, and the list goes on."

"To job security." He chuckled, tapped his glass to

Hannah's, and took the last sip as the waiter brought their entrees.

After the waiter left, Tristian poured more wine.

Hannah cut into the ravioli, forked up a piece, and slid it into her mouth. She closed her eyes. "Mmmm, this is excellent! Never tasted better."

Tristian chewed a piece of poached lobster, swallowed. He pointed to the dish with his fork. "It's delicious."

After the meal, he ordered dessert and coffee. Placing his large hand over her small delicate one, he brought his gaze to hers and was lost in the depths of her deep blue eyes. *How could I drag her into my world of treachery and expect her—their relationship to survive—even thrive?* He struggled to shake the haze from his mind. Her gaze locked on his and held for a moment. He leaned over, brushed his lips lightly over hers, not caring who was watching.

She ran the tip of her tongue around her moist lips and smiled. "What are you thinking?"

"Hannah, I'm not good at—" He cleared his throat, tried again. "These last few days have been the best I've had in a long time. I enjoy your company and would like to make our relationship mutually exclusive." He blew out a breath. "What do you think?"

She gave a soft laugh. "As far as I'm concerned, it always was." Hannah entwined her fingers with his. "You're a tough man to figure out. So many layers. But I'm willing to give it a try."

The waiter paused at the table, coffee cups on saucers and plates of cheesecake topped with strawberries sat on a tray he carried. "Coffee and dessert, sir."

Tristian nodded. The waiter put the items on the table and strode away.

Still holding on to Hannah's hand, he brought it to his lips, brushed them over the back of her hand, and released it. "Guess we should enjoy the cheesecake." He glanced out the window at the sliver of moon and bright stars. *Great night for a ride.* "Let's finish our dessert and see if they will give us the coffee to go."

"You want to go cups in a place like this? What do you have in mind?" She took a bite of cheesecake, closed her eyes, savoring the flavor. "Exquisite."

Seeing her expression, he forked up a piece of the cheesecake with several slices of strawberries on top. Popped it in his mouth, savored, then swallowed. "Why not? It's a beautiful night, I'd like to take you for a ride before we call it a night."

"How about we finish dessert and stop by the specialty coffee shop and get lattes?"

"Much better idea."

After a relaxing drive, he pulled up in front of her cottage, cut the engine and leaned over, took her mouth with his, then deepened the kiss. Her flavor spun into him, as his tongue twined with hers in a sinuous dance. She moaned; he'd aroused her passion as his grew stronger. Heart pounded as his fingers feathered along the side of her breast. Trailing kisses down her neck, he flicked his tongue lower to the cleavage between her breasts then kissed his way back to her lips. Raising his mouth from hers, he stared into her eyes. His breathing increased as his fingers continued to explore.

Her pulse quickened, matching his heartbeat, she hesitated then whispered, "Would you like to come in?"

"We both know I shouldn't, but…" Getting out of

the car, he walked to the passenger door and opened it. He leaned in to unfasten her seatbelt, brushed aside her soft hair with his fingers and breathed a kiss at the base of her neck, lingering a beat. Finally, he straightened and offered his hand to assist her out of the car.

She took his hand, swallowed hard, and stepped onto the curb, the heel of her shoe caught in a crack, she pitched forward into his arms. He smiled seductively as he swept her into his arms, carried her to the door.

"Saved by my gallant knight in a sleek sports car." She giggled and unwound her arms from around his neck as he lowered her to the ground.

"I'm afraid I'm no one's knight, but save you I did from a nasty fall."

Hannah pulled the keys from her purse, unlocked the front door, and deactivated the alarm. "Come on in." Her voice wavered. She toed off her heels and kicked them against the wall. "Don't believe I'll be wearing those anytime soon." Padding barefoot across the floor, she stopped at the doorway to the kitchen. "What can I get for you?"

Shrugging out of his coat, Tristian's eyes raked boldly over her as he closed the distance between them. She sucked in a breath when he took her in his arms, holding her against his growing excitement. "Are you sure this is what you want?" he said breathlessly, his lips hovering over hers, then he took her mouth hungrily. His one hand caressed the side of her breast, along her ribs, waist and curved around her butt cheek pressing her against him. "We have too many clothes on."

"Wait. Before we go any further, there's something we need to discuss." She pressed her hand against his chest. He pushed at her elbow and her arm encircled his neck. "The consequences of making love to me are…"

He lowered his lips to the swells of her breasts, reached for the zipper in the back of her dress, and tugged it down to her hips; the dress slipped off the one shoulder, pooled on the floor. He went hard at the sight of her beautiful, nearly naked body. "Step out of the dress."

Unbuttoning his shirt with shaky fingers, she ran her fingertips over the contour of his naked chest and licked kisses across his jawline, nibbled on his ear lobe then whispered, "Our lives could change forever. You need to—"

"Later." He growled and swept her up in his arms, unceremoniously deposited her on the couch. She squealed, struggling to keep him from crawling between her legs.

"We can't." Squirming beneath him, she finally stilled enjoying his ministrations.

"We can seek pleasure without compromising you." The sexual haze engulfing them thickened. He kissed her belly, sucked her nipples until they were hard, trailed kisses up her neck. Finally, he pressed his lips to her mouth, teasing her lips apart with his tongue, thrusting inside to stroke her sweet mouth, her flavor mixed with the evening's wine spun through him. He caressed her throat, slipping his hand between her breasts, and lower. She arched against him as he slid her panties aside and his fingers coaxed, teased, danced and dipped between her spread thighs until she cried out in pleasure. He smiled against her warm moist lips.

"My turn," she murmured. Slipping from beneath him, she tugged his zipper down pushing his trousers and briefs to his knees. She kissed her way along his sculptured chest, feathered her fingers over his taut abs and lower, he groaned, arched up as she reached her destination.

Chapter Eight
Tristian's World Spins Out of Control and Takes Hannah With It.

Tristian strode to the mailbox, gathered his mail, and continued into the house. He tossed the mail onto the dining table, picked up a large manila envelope, and slid his finger under the flap. When he drew out the photograph, his eyes narrowed; he snarled and flipped the picture over. In neat script, the words read "Your sister has a secret." He stared at the photo of his demon boss and Angie strolling along the street, fingers entwined, she smiling up at him. The streetlights cast a golden glow across the couple.

All the threads fit together in a web of deceit. Recalling that both his boss and sister were missing the weekend he arrived in D.C. Angie on holiday with friends, supposedly. Bruce away at his estate. Willow seemed nervous at first when he appeared at the shop. *She was in on it.* The flames of fury engulfed him. Out of the closet, he grabbed his black duster, shoved his arms into the sleeves, and checked his magic arsenal, poison darts, and arrows. He added poisoned arrows conjured for demons and his silver dagger. He grabbed his crossbow from the shelf, raised his arms, and disappeared.

He materialized on the fringes of the parking lot behind The Krystal Unicorn. Bent over at the waist, hands resting on his knees, Tristian was exhausted due to lack of sleep from the night before and the use of magic to port from Maine to D.C. Somewhere in the back of his mind a voice screamed, *What the fuck are you doing? You know better than to go into a fight fueled by emotion clouding your focus and judgment.* He mentally slapped the voice away. Bruce's midnight blue SUV pulled up to the back door of The Krystal Unicorn. Bruce leaned over toward Angie when Tristian caught his attention standing several yards in front of the vehicle, stalking forward.

Tristian bellowed, stopped, aimed his crossbow for the middle of the windshield, an inch or so more to the driver's side and released the silver-tipped arrow. That little voice was back. *Don't do it.*

The arrow penetrated the windshield, split the rearview mirror, and lodged in the headrest an inch from Bruce's neck. Blue liquid oozed from the tip of the arrowhead, and a stream of red mist escaped from the other end of the arrow. Surprisingly unaffected, Bruce leaned over and kissed Angie as the mist began to disappear. Tristian roared in anger and rushed toward the SUV. In a blur of movement, Bruce and Angie exited the car. Willow opened the back door and yanked Angie inside.

When Bruce turned, Tristian buried a dagger between Bruce's neck and shoulder. Blood spurted from the wound, soaking his shirt in seconds. Tristian swaggered forward as his boss staggered and fell against the wall of the structure and slid toward the ground. Tristian watched in horror as Bruce raised his hand, a white-hot electric bolt surged out of his upturned palm and struck Tristian in the center of his chest, he stumbled backward. Before he could recover, Bruce dislodged the dagger and lunged toward Tristian, dagger held out in front of him. Bruce drove the dagger into the small of Tristian's back and jerked upward. He screamed in pain and crumpled to the ground, rolled to his side, took aim, and released another silver tipped arrow from his wrist gauntlet. He eased his head to the ground, his vision dimmed, the arrow hit the inside of Bruce's thigh, the target being the femoral artery before everything went black.

****

When Tristian regained consciousness, he was sprawled on an unfamiliar bed. Tobi's face swam in and out of focus as he blinked his eyes. "Where am I?"

Tobi, the wife of Bruce's right-hand man, stood hands on hips, her wild auburn hair with green streaks fanned about her face as she stared down at him. "The question is not where, but what the hell were you thinking. You stupid bastard. You tried to assassinate your boss, the Overlord of the Western Hemisphere." She shook her head. "You'd be dead if it wasn't for your sister. Owen took pity on you and brought you to our home to recover. Willow and Angie worked tirelessly to save your sorry ass." Tobi rolled him over gently and changed the magic herb patch on his back.

"He… Angie." He tried to raise up, the pounding in his head and shooting pain in his back was excruciating, his stomach roiled. "Hannah. Where's Hannah?" he mumbled, then succumbed to sleep again.

Tristian drifted in and out of consciousness, but didn't know for how long. When he finally could stay awake long enough to put a sentence together, Tobi and Owen stood at his bedside. "How long have I been out of it?" Shifting in the bed was less painful than it had been previously, he peered up at Owen.

"About seventy-two hours. We need to get you up and dressed. Bruce wants a meeting," Owen said.

"No way." Tristian shook his head vehemently, then put his hands to his head in an attempt to stop the pounding.

Owen waited a couple of beats. "That wasn't a request. You tried to murder your Overlord and his mate. Lucky you're not dead or imprisoned." He put an arm under Tristian's arms and lifted. "Now, I'll help you get vertical. The injuries are healing nicely, but you have a way to go. The meeting is in twenty minutes."

As Owen angled Tristian up, his stomach roiled, and he tried to stop the onslaught of stomach contents unsuccessfully.

Tobi rushed over with a trash can.

Pain shot through his back as his diaphragm spasmed. At last he was able to take a deep breath and pushed the rest of the way up to a sitting position. Tobi wiped his face with a warm wash cloth.

"Owen, the son-of-a-bitch was seeing my little sister without talking to me. I don't want her involved with a demon. Especially, if he's my boss." He spat out between halting breaths.

"That's not your choice, and you might as well know, it's more that dating. And you better get used to it. Angie was a willing participant, as you know she must be. The rest... Well, you have fifteen minutes now."

Tristian tried to jerk away from Owen and fell back against the bed. The injuries to his spine and internal organs were severe. He hissed out a breath. Slowly,

Owen assisted him to his feet, again, where he wobbled then straightened taking a few steps on his own.

"Are you strong enough to conjure clothes? Yours were destroyed in the battle and aftermath of trying to save your life. Angie nearly lost her life trying to save both you and Bruce."

"Of course." He drew his arm along his side and was instantly clad in jeans, navy sweater, and black boots. Sweat trickled down his face at the effort.

****

Arriving at The Wycked Hair Salon after hours, Tristian leaned on Owen as they climbed the stairs to the mezzanine. He paused breathing hard, his hand braced against the wall for a couple beats outside Bruce's office.

"These are for your own good." Owen snapped his fingers to effectively restrain Tristian with magic.

Tristian jerked, his jaws clenched in anger, he narrowed his eyes at Owen in rage.

"Trust me, it's safer this way." Owen knocked on the metal frame of the open glass door. Bruce's head turned, and he motioned them in. Angie stood behind his chair, Tobi made herself at home on the white leather couch. Owen escorted Tristian to one of the leather chairs in front of Bruce's desk.

Hatred sparked in Tristian as his gaze met Bruce's, then swept over Angie. He'd never seen or felt his sister so filled with rage. Sorrow knotted his stomach nearly causing him to retch.

"There's no need for the magic shackles. We've done enough damage to each other. Don't you think?" Bruce rose and met Tristian's gaze. "Tobi, Owen, and Angie, give us a minute alone. Close the door behind you," he commanded.

"Boss, I don't think that's advisable," Owen said.

"Don't question my decisions." Bruce pointed to the doorway.

Angie stood and moved behind Bruce, her hands on his shoulders. "I'm not going anywhere."

Tristian's rage boiled over as Bruce tilted his head and grinned up at Angie. "Okay, you can stay only because I love looking at you."

Tristian stood, poised to leap over the desk. In a split second, he collided midair with Bruce, as he knocked him to the floor, breath whooshed out of him. Bruce held him to the floor, hands on his shoulders and slight pressure to his injured back. Tristian let out a low moan, his body jerking. He heard the door open and saw Angie's feet start toward him then she disappeared out of his view.

Tristian's body slumped to the floor as Bruce informed him that Angie had consented to be his mate and at Bruce's estate they had consummated that union over the weekend, before the attack.

Bruce helped Tristian into a lounge chair, then paced the office floor to the window. "We have bigger problems. Demon Lord Rezar is back and out for revenge. It seems he didn't appreciate our efforts to kill him nor banish him to the underworld."

"We should have killed the son-of-a-bitch, when we had the chance," Tristian said vehemently. "If it hadn't been for Paul—we would have."

Bruce nodded.

Angie walked over to the lounger, sat on the arm, reached behind her brother's neck rubbing at the stress knots. "Tristian, you and Bruce have trusted each other for decades. We've done nothing wrong. I wanted what Bruce offered more than anything in my entire life. I love him. I have no regrets, only that I've hurt and angered you. Can you honestly say that if we'd come to you sooner, you would've acted any differently?"

He hung his head. "No. I can't." *I should tell her what happened to our parents. Then she'd understand—Or would it drive a bigger wedge between us? I couldn't bear it.* He remained silent, even though Birch's words reverberated in his mind. "You know Rezar is going to come after Angie, once he discovers you've taken a mate."

Angie returned to Bruce's side. "You guys know I'm right here."

Bruce smiled at her. "All the more reason for you to accept Angie's decisions and for us to rebuild the trust we've enjoyed throughout our working relationship. You've twenty-four hours to decide before I take Angie to a safe house until this is over." He switched his gaze from Tristian to the door. "Owen, Tobi, please come in here."

Quietly, Owen and Tobi slipped inside, closed the door, and took a seat on the couch.

"Nowhere will be safe," Tristian argued, his fingers digging in on the arms of his chair.

"That's where you are wrong. She will be in the safest place on earth."

"What makes you so sure?"

Bruce rested his head against the chair. "You're free to go. But you may want to consider your woman? She could be in grave danger as well. Although, it's a far stretch that he would suspect such a relationship."

"You mean I'm free to go home?" Tristian smirked

and raised an eyebrow incredulously.

"I never intended to hold you against your will, only to make sure you healed. Your attack on Angie and I will be dealt with later."

Tristian leaned back against his chair, closed his eyes. His back throbbed. *Hannah was innocent in all this. I shouldn't have tried to… Doesn't matter now. All that matters is that she's safe.* He sat up and stared at Bruce. "I'll accept your offer for Hannah. But I need to talk to her. Explain."

"Not a good idea. She doesn't have a secure phone. I'll send security to go get her. You're welcome to write her a note explaining the situation when she is picked up. Where can we find her?"

"She won't come with—Hell she doesn't know what I do. She won't understand."

"You can address all that when she arrives."

Angie padded to Tristian's side, pushed him gently forward to check his back. "It's healing nicely, but you are nowhere near battle ready. Staying with Owen and Tobi for a few more days until Hannah arrives is a great idea."

"Yeah, we'll put up with him. But where are we going to put Hannah up?"

Bruce sighed and reached into his desk drawer pulling out an iridescent disk. Tossed it to Owen. "My apartment has substantial security in place, no one knows about it with the exception of you." He glanced at Owen. "And Angie."

"Thank you." Tristian scrubbed his hand over his face, rubbing the back of his neck.

"Of course. I didn't want you to find out the way you did, but…" Bruce waved his hand in a dismissive gesture.

"How the hell did Rezar escape the underworld? Is he still wearing the collar?"

"Called in favors. He still wears the collar, so he has no power, and is weak, but has others to do his bidding until he is recovered. At least that's what my sources tell me. Last known location was the far east."

"They're reliable?" Tristian shifted in his chair, locked gazes with Bruce. He didn't like his sister aligned with a demon, but Bruce was one of the good guys. *If I'd been honest with her about our parents' death, this wouldn't have happened. I'll tell her as soon as I get Hannah—Shit, she's going to hate me. Women.* He huffed out a breath.

"I'd trust them with my life." Bruce nodded.

Tristian's jaw clinched, the vein in his temple pulsed. "Good enough for me. I'm in 'til the end, as I've always been."

"I've your oath that you'll have my back, as I'll have yours, should it be necessary?"

"Of course, she's my sister. I don't like what she's done, but I'll learn to live with it. As far as between us, business as usual."

After discussing the possibilities of Rezar's escape and plans to neutralize him permanently, Bruce called an end to the meeting. Tristian left with Owen and Tobi.

Chapter Nine
Telling the Tale—Better Late Than Never

Tristian turned the door handle and hobbled into the apartment. Hannah rushed to him, throwing her arms around him. He pulled her to him and buried his face in her soft red hair. Her body wrapped around him had never felt so good. Yet, trying to have a life outside his professional life…was going to be tough.

She backed away and leveled her gaze at him. "What the hell is going on? You need to tell me now."

He paced away from her. Stopped in front of the big picture window, looking out over the city. In an apartment owned by his…what exactly was Bruce? His boss definitely…his sister's demon mate, brother-in-law to be? Oh yeah. Tristian ran his fingers through his hair rubbing at the base of his neck, where the nerves were bunched and aching. "It's not that easy."

"Not that easy. Are you out of your mind? Let's recap the last few days."

Spinning around to face her, eyes flashing with anger. "I never should have tried to have a life with you. It just can't be done."

Hannah's mouth fell open, she collapsed onto the couch. "What… After all this…" She jumped up and slapped him hard across the face, leaving a large red hand print. "First, I get a phone call from a woman I've never heard of, Tobi, she says there's been an accident.

Then she tells me to pack a bag and hangs up."

Tristian backed away, touching his hand to his cheek. *It stung like a bitch.* "It couldn't be helped."

Hands fisted on hips she continues, "But wait it gets better. A few hours later, a security team shows up at my door and informs me that I'm going with them. My life is in serious danger and you are—They've been sent to take me to you—refusal is not an option. At this point, I am scared out of my mind."

"I couldn't leave you alone, unprotected under the circumstances," Tristian said hands clenching and unclenching at his sides.

"Let's talk about those circumstances. No one will tell me anything. Why? Because it's your tale to tell." She threw her arms over her head and let them drop to her side.

"There wasn't time. The altercation, threats, things were happening too fast." *She doesn't need to know I attacked Bruce, yet. Later—I'll...*

"Wow, that's the most information I've gotten out of anyone to date," she said caustically.

"That's enough," Tristian roared. *The medicinal herbs for pain are wearing off. Every time, I move, pain shoots up my back.*

"Oh, no—not even. I'm not allowed to leave this apartment—condo—whatever it is."

"This whole thing was a bad idea. I'm truly sorry. But for you—at this time—there is no way out. You voluntarily tied yourself to me, even after I told you..."

"Told me what? You would be gone a lot, sometimes for days, weeks. I figured you were special forces... Never in my wildest dreams did I figure it would be for the Demon Overlord of the Western

Hemisphere. Who now I discover is involved with your little sister."

"I told you before the less you know the better."

"Well—the days of keeping me in the dark are over. Spill it, or I'm leaving on the next plane out of here."

"No…you're not." He yanked his coat off the back of the chair, clenching his teeth at the pain. He gave her a cold stare and strode out the door.

She followed him. "That's it, run away." She paused, tears streaming down her face. "I'll be gone when you get back."

He turned on his heel and barked out orders to the two men standing guard outside the door. "She is not to leave the premises."

The men blocked her going any farther even though she tried to push her way through. She met with a wall of muscle that not so gently guided her back into the apartment and closed the door.

Outside the building, Tristian stopped, pounded a fist against the brick wall, whirled at the sound of footsteps. He glanced around and saw one of his men standing at a discreet distance. His head pounded, body ached, he leaned his back against the cool wall. *What am I doing? I brought her into this world—I can't just walk out. Send her back…to what. I don't want to, I need her. Oh…my God. Am I in love with her?* He shook his head in disbelief.

****

Hannah cried, screamed, and finally flopped down on the bed. Nowhere to turn, she called the only person she knew here—Tobi, the woman who'd greeted her at the apartment upon her arrival, who also worked for

Bruce. She explained a little of what had happened, what to expect and cautioned her, contact with her sister was forbidden. Before Tobi could answer, Hannah hung up the phone.

She didn't care who saw her transform, she had to get out. Quietly, she walked into the living room where French doors led out to a balcony and carefully tried the handle on one door. It turned. When she pushed it open a crack, the hinge creaked. She paused, turned to see if anyone would come in to check on her. Nothing. Pushing it open farther, she slipped outside and closed the door carefully.

If she shifted out here, her clothes would be shredded and scattered all over, and when she returned to human form, she'd be nude. *Bad idea.* Could she throw her clothes down to the ground, behind a bush and retrieve them later? She stared down the three stories. There were a few bushes beside the building.

Thankful for the darkness, she slipped out of her clothes, tied them in a bundle, made sure no one was watching, and tossed them to the ground. Luck was with her, and the bundle landed behind the tree nearest the corner of the building. With a deep breath, Hannah transformed and took flight, soaring over the structure high into the sky. Her multicolored wings shimmered in the moonlight as she banked and faded into the inky darkness.

Anger and feelings of helplessness subsided as she drifted through the night sky. Free. *Not one of the smartest things I've ever done. I don't know where…* She circled high and spotted a wooded area, she was completely out of the city. Landing on her rear paws, she drew her wings against her body and padded deep into the trees. Her semi-neutral colors blended nicely in the dark. But she couldn't stay here without being discovered. Somehow she had to retrieve the bundle of clothes. By now, Tristian would have discovered she was missing, no way she could get close enough to get her clothes. *Unless...*

A light mist began to fall; she was so tired. Hannah in gryphon form settled behind a large tree, her eyes drifted closed for what felt like only a few minutes. When she heard the rustle of leaves, felt movement not far, her eyes fluttered open, then her head jerked up. Tristian dressed in jeans, sweater, boots, and a black leather duster sat, legs stretched out in front of him, arms crossed over his muscular chest, head resting against the tree opposite her. A slow smile curved one side of his full lips. His eyes sharp, shifting from hazel to green with blue flecks, and assessing her. Next to him, was her bundle of clothing. She should be afraid, but she wasn't. He'd never given her any reason to fear him, though from the snippets of conversation she'd overheard, it seemed he was a dangerous warlock.

He shifted and sat up straighter. The other side of his mouth curved up in a sexy as the devil smile. "I have to admit in all my travels, assignments, and battles, I've never seen a gryphon. Believed they were myths of Irish folklore. But here you sit in front of me, an exquisite specimen proving me wrong." He shook his head, blond hair falling over his face. Brushing it aside with his long fingers, his gaze held hers, then swept over her body slowly. "Found the apartment a bit confining, did you?"

She blinked her large eyes and nodded.

****

Tristian had never seen such a beautiful combination of colors and textures on a creature. *I'd love to run my fingers along her enchanting body. But better not right now. Best if we could reach some common ground in this situation.* Head, shoulders, and front talons of an eagle, the rest of her body and hind quarters that of a lion, covered in a combination of coppery colored fur and sleek feathers, a sharp, tawny beak and huge cornflower blue eyes. Her wings were folded against her body, but wisps of bright-multicolored feathers peeked out.

"We have a lot to discuss, and it would be easier if you were in human form. Though I find your current form absolutely beautiful." He waited a couple beats, and when she didn't move, he pressed on. "Have it your way, I'll go first."

She held his gaze and waited.

"I find myself it this situation because I acted without thinking. I received a picture clearly indicating my little sister and my Demon Overload boss were having an affair of the heart. Didn't like it." He raked his fingers through his hair, leaving little rows. *My sister mated to a demon. I've failed on so many fronts.* He cleared his throat. "Renegade demons, werewolves, and vampires attacked our coven and killed our parents during what was supposed to be a celebration. Angie was in Ireland with Willow's family. But I never told her what really happened. My bad."

She shifted, shook out her wings, then tightened them against her body.

Drawing his knees up, he braced his feet against the ground. "I'll get around to it, soon. I wanted to keep her away from the magic world, but instead she was drawn to it and now is mated to a demon. My parents would hate this situation." He threw his hands up in the air. "Not just any demon, the Demon Overlord of the Western Hemisphere and my boss, Bruce. In an uncontrollable rage, I ported to D.C. and tried to kill him, also endangering my sister."

She blinked her eyes slowly, leaned forward as if intent on every word.

He hung his head. "Normally, I keep a cool head—never meant for any of this to happen." He paused not wanting to expound on the situation but ultimately told her every disgusting detail of the battle, the meeting, and the reason her life could be in danger. Because of him. *I don't understand why I feel it necessary to confide in this woman.*

She made a keening sound that was almost sympathetic, he thought. But her blazing gaze said differently.

"I'm Bruce's enforcer. My team and I neutralize those that will not conform or break the laws of magical creatures endangering the delicate balance between us and mortals. Usually, my team tries to mediate the situation, however, if they fail, I move in and extinguish the perpetrators."

Pausing a beat, he dared to glance into her eyes, expecting to see shock or disgust. Yet, none of those emotions appeared in her eyes. *Could it be understanding?* He must be mistaken. She shifted, tilting her head to one side as if to encourage him to continue. At least that's what he assumed.

"One such demon lord, Rezar, was left alive due to circumstance beyond our control, but we managed to banish him to the underworld, collared him so he couldn't wield magic. Now, he's escaped and sworn revenge on Bruce, myself, and anyone we care about." Tristian pushed up from the ground, brushed his hands together and paced. "That's about it in a nutshell."

She blinked, shook herself, and cocked her head sideways in question, then glanced at the bundle of clothes.

He held up the bundle. "Couldn't have you wandering around naked, though I wasn't sure what to look for at first. A sleek coppery feather and bits of fur left on the balcony gave me a hint. I track creatures for a living but wasn't sure how far you'd gone. Figured you'd head somewhere that provided cover until you came up with a plan. I wanted to get to you before you did."

She unfolded her body, which was a good eighteen inches above his six feet six inches, yanked the bundle up in her beak, and pranced out of sight. The sun was cresting the eastern horizon as he heard rustling from where she'd disappeared.

"I'm sure I caused you to flee, but you didn't have much of a plan. Did you?" He blew out a breath and hoped to hell she'd join him soon. The one-sided conversation was getting tedious. On the positive note, without any incendiary comments from her, he was able to tell his tale without losing his temper. *Where do we go from here?* Surveying the area, he figured they were somewhere in rural Maryland, he hadn't paid attention on his way here. Since meeting Hannah, his methodical, calculating, and meticulous attention to detail brain seemed to have flown out the window. *What is happening to me? If I don't get back on my game, the consequences could be deadly.*

She sauntered into his line of vision a hand fisted on her hip. "If I understand the situation correctly, I can't safely return to Maine and my job. I took a quick leave of absence without explanation because I'm caught up in a web of—" She shook her head. "Some asshole is looking for you and your compadres because you didn't finish him off. Did I miss anything?"

"That's about the gist of it."

"Unless you plan to support me, I need to contact my employer ASAP with an explanation. I can't afford to lose my job. What about my citizenship test in six weeks? I left my book at the cottage, I'd made several notes in… Oh, well…"

Tristian scrubbed his hand over his face. "I don't have all the answers." He rubbed the back of his neck. "There is a secure line in Bruce's office." Suddenly, he snapped his fingers. "Bet the phone line in the apartment is also secure. You can use that to contact your employer."

"I'll tell them family emergency and when can I return?"

He let out a harsh breath. "A month or two at the most. Depending only how long it takes to locate Rezar and eliminate him. Then you're free to go."

"Is that what you want?" she asked staring him down.

"Yes." He paused and drew his top lip through is bottom teeth. "No. If I didn't care for you, I would have left you in Maine to fend for yourself. But I've fucked everything up so bad, with you, my sister, my—boss. I understand if you want to leave." Tristian slammed his fist into the tree trunk. Pain radiated from his hand up his arm, shoulder, and spine. He groaned.

"Do you think for one minute that I would have come with the men you dispatched after me if I didn't..." She hesitated and peered at the floor, then tried again. "Didn't care for you. I could have easily escaped and flew off. But I didn't. I was scared shitless that something terrible had happened to you. Something you may not recover from. What I expect from you is honesty, from here on out. Clear?"

He could only nod. Unable to believe she was going to or at least it sounded like she was going to give him another chance. "So, you'll stay with me at the apartment until we track down Rezar?"

"Yes, provided you keep me in the loop. If you have to leave to find him, tell me, don't yank me around. It's imperative I take the citizenship test." She emphasized the last two words. "I need my book." She yanked her arm back, her hand balled into a fist as if she was about to hit something, but at the last minute drew back.

Tristian bit back a grin as his phone buzzed. Reaching into his pocket, he jerked it free, checked the screen. "We gotta go." He glanced at Hannah as he put the phone to his ear. "Yeah, Ruben, I found her. We'll be back shortly. I understand, probably for the best."

Disconnecting the call, he tapped the screen again, scrolled to Birch's secure line and put the phone to his ear.

"What in the hell happened?" Birch greeted him after several rings. "Where have you been?" Birch's voice dropped. "What did you do?"

"We'll discuss it later. Right now, you and Freesia need to disappear for a while. You remember Rezar?"

Birch remained silent for several seconds. "Yeah,

the one that got away a while back. Responsible for Paul's death."

"He's back and out for blood. No one associated with either Bruce or me is safe."

"Understood. We closed your house up when Willow called and brought us up to speed. We'll be gone within the hour. Take care of yourself and Hannah. You realize it's a different game now."

"I do." He reached out and grasped Hannah's hand, pulled her into him, wrapped his arms around her, and they disappeared.

Chapter Ten
More Trouble, a Location, and a Plan

"What in bloody hell are you doing?" Were the first words out of Hannah's mouth when he released her inside the apartment. "Creatures could trace your magic trail here."

"What would you have me do? Grab a cab to D.C. from somewhere in Maryland? I don't have wings, which by the way could have put you in the enemies' cross-hairs along with me as I tracked you. No more acting before thinking." He paused a moment. "For either of us." His full lips kicked up in that damn sexy as hell grin again.

She tried to squelch the heat rising in her body. The effect he had on her was disconcerting, and she didn't like it one bit. *Tied to one woman for eternity—he probably had a different female in his bed every night.* She snorted, then covered it with a cough. "Agreed. What do we do next?" Walking over to the couch, she plopped down, glanced around, somehow the room seemed brighter than she remembered.

Tristian narrowed his eyes at her. "We aren't..." Before he could get his point across, a loud knock sounded on the door, then it flew open. Owen stood in the doorway.

"Tristian, what the hell are you doing? Up and disappear for hours, your men tried to cover for you, but out tracking a woman?" Owen's hands clenched and unclenched as he paced across the room, stopped and stared out the window before turning on his heel to face Tristian. "I know you're new to the relationship shit, but—" He lifted a gray bushy brow. "Bruce and Angie left for the safe house hours ago. They've arrived safely…wanted you to know."

"Good," Tristian said a bit harsher than intended. "While I was off tracking Hannah, I was working on a plan. No doubt Rezar's spies have figured out something is amiss here. My team has been in town for several days, which in itself is unusual. Bruce has the same woman by his side for more than a day or two, so they know she's something special. And lastly, I've spent a lot more time here than normal. How about we use that to our benefit?"

Owen glanced suspiciously at him. "What do you suggest?"

"Use Hannah and me as bait to flush out whoever is watching us. Hopefully, the magic I spun around the apartment building will keep our enemies guessing for a while. However, if we play tourist…"

"Absolutely not. You got a death wish?"

"No," Tristian said calmly. "We make it appear as if Bruce is on holiday. I'm covering with your help and have brought my lady. Act as if we suspect nothing. Scatter the team leaders, then covertly have a few return through untraceable means, with the new faces we have in the ranks as security for Hannah and me."

Owen rubbed his chin with thumb and forefinger. "Could work…if we're careful. With Hannah as part of the equation…it's too risky. She's untrained."

"Let me worry about Hannah. She brings her own

skills to the table."

"That's what I am afraid of." Owen glanced at Hannah. "With all that has transpired, it's too risky."

"So, you suggest we wait, like sitting ducks?" Tristian sneered. "You got a better idea?"

"No. But I want to talk it over with Bruce. Not going to have it over my head." He walked into the room used as an office in the apartment and closed the door.

"I'm not sure I want to be used as bait," Hannah said carefully.

"I don't see any alternative. They might get sloppy if we appear to have no idea we're being watched. From the information Bruce obtained, Rezar himself is still out of country. His men are not going to make a move without him being here. It's personal for him. If we can flush out one of them, question them about the plan, we'll be in a good place."

"What makes you think they'll talk to you?" Hannah asked.

"I have my ways," Tristian said, a wicked smile spreading across his lips. He stood in front of the window, hands behind his back watching the activity on the street. When he whirled around, he flicked his fingers and flames shot up from the fireplace. "Bit chilly in here. Don't you think?" He ambled over to the sofa and eased down beside her. "I won't let anything happen to you. I want time to see how things play out between us. Kinda of a rough start. It's going to get better." Leaning over, he gently brushed his lips over hers, something he'd wanted to do since he'd found her safe. But she could be so prickly.

The door to the other room creaked open, and

Owen strode into the living area. He shot Tristian a look and nodded toward the outside door. "A word."

Tristian leaned backward, stretched his arms across the back of the couch, then stretched his legs out, in no hurry to get up again. As he was preparing to push up, Hannah patted his arm.

She stood. "I need to make that call we discussed, Tristian. May I use the phone in the office? It's a secure line?"

"It is," Owen said as she started toward the other room.

"Fine. I'll be a few minutes." Her gaze slid from Tristian to Owen, then she walked through the door, closed it behind her, and picked up the phone. Before she dialed her boss, she listened to the voices on the other side of the door.

****

In the other room, Tristian smirked. *Nice move Hannah.* He turned his attention back to Owen.

"Bruce is uncomfortable with your plan and with your woman. But agrees sitting around waiting for something to happen is not advisable. So, he is leaving it to your discretion as usual." Owen gave him a hard stare. "He's putting a lot of trust in you after your actions. I wouldn't screw it up if I were you," Owen warned.

"Have no intention of doing so," Tristian said smugly. Anger still simmered inside him, but he had to let it go for the benefit of them all. *Angie made her choice, I'll have to live with it.* He gestured for Owen to sit beside him and pulled out of his pocket a tourist map he'd picked up earlier and unfolded the map, smoothing it out on the coffee table. The two men discussed

Tristian's plan, the number of men needed and the time frame in D.C. They also discussed the leaders and teams assigned to move out when Rezar and his group came stateside. Tristian wanted to be prepared to move on a moment's notice. He sensed no matter what scenario he envisioned, they could be caught by surprise.

****

Hannah finished her conversation and sauntered out the door. "All set. But I have to check in with them routinely. If one of my systems encounters a problem, I'll have to access a secure network and computer. Will that be a problem?"

"Shouldn't be," Tristian said getting to his feet stiffly. "We are going to be playing tourist. Have you ever been to D.C?"

"No."

He folded up the dog-eared map and tossed it to her. "What would you like to see first?"

She caught it and peered up at Tristian as he pulled a book out of thin air. "What's that?"

A mysterious smile crossed his lips and sparkled in his eyes when he turned the book over. "It appears to belong to you." He waved the book in front of her, but when she reached for it, he jerked it higher. "It'll cost you."

"Then I don't need it that bad." She continued to eye the book. "That's mine. It's my study guide for the test." Narrowing her eyes, she sighed. "What do you want for it?"

"A kiss," he said without hesitation, a seductive smile played at the corner of his lips.

She loved it when he flirted with her. He was so

serious much of the time. "Fair enough, but you have to tell me how you got it. I left it on the nightstand at home."

He pointed to his lips with an index finger.

On tiptoe, she brushed her lips over his lightly, then grabbed for the book, knocking it out of his hand. "Debt paid." She snickered and took a couple steps back from Tristian, the book safely tucked behind her.

Owen chuckled. "She's got your number Trist. I gotta get back to the Salon. I'd appreciate you keeping me in the loop, and no more disappearing," he said firmly. "Either of you." With a wave, he opened the door and was gone.

"So how'd you get this?" Hannah held the book, fanning through the pages.

"It was out wandering in the universe, and I snatched it." His lips twitched, unable to hold a straight face—he snickered.

She leaned forward and raised a hand as if to slap at him. But he slipped neatly out of reach. Out of the book's pages, a piece of paper fluttered to the floor.

"Birch and faery magic. I don't know how he does it, but the book appeared in hand when you saw it." Tristian stooped and picked up the slip of paper and read it. "Figured your lady might want this. We're gone. Be careful, you're being watched. But he's out of country. B."

"Well, that's cryptic. Who's out of the country? The bad guy?"

"Sounds like it. Now, where do you want to go tomorrow?" He glanced at his watch. "We still have time to join a tour of the White House."

"Getting a tour of the White House is difficult.

Don't you have to get with a senator or representative, congressman, or something?" Hannah asked.

Tristian snorted. "Usually, but… I have connections. As many suspect, those types are not all that they seem. Would you like to see the White House?"

"Yes. I'd like that."

"Done." He pulled out his phone and touched the screen. After a quick conversation, he hung up and smiled at her. "Tomorrow at 7:30 a.m."

"Wonderful." She sat down on the couch and spread the map out on her lap. "The Spy Museum sounds interesting. Maybe you could pick up a thing or two." She giggled and turned her attention back to the map. "I've always wanted to stand next to the Lincoln Memorial, have my picture taken, and see the Reflecting Pool. It's the largest of the many reflecting pools in D.C. Then if no baddies come out of the woodwork, the Library of Congress. I could spend a whole day there with exhibits, lectures, and gallery talks that breathe life into the collections housed inside. Not to mention the reading rooms."

"Wow. I've created a monster." He chuckled. "This is serious, you know. The baddies to which you refer are dangerous."

"I know, but it's the only way I can deal with the not knowing when or if. Don't like being bait."

"Understood. We'll keep you safe. Now back to the fun… I'd like to see the United States Botanic Garden, how about you?"

"Sounds good. You're a gardener, aren't you?"

"On occasion, when Sean is off." He shrugged sitting down beside her. "Otherwise, he doesn't want me messing with his precious dirt and plants. Okay, our schedule for the next few days is set." Tristian touched his screen again, this time calling Owen. "We'll be spending tomorrow morning at the White House. Ruben and a couple new faces will join us."

"Great. A good place to be, impossible to lurk, especially on such short notice." He paused, cleared his throat. "Or should be. Other plans?"

"Yeah." He set out the plans as discussed with Hannah. "I'd like to keep Ruben with us and rotate the newer men daily. Do you want to be included in the planning session for taking down our enemy?"

"Nope. Keep me informed. If anything changes on this end, you'll be the first to know."

Tristian ended the call and turned to her. "Ready to call it a night, or do you need a midnight snack?"

****

Up before dawn, Tristian and Hannah wolfed down a couple of bagels with egg and cheese, orange juice, tea, and coffee. The salon limo took them to catch the Metrorail at Federal Triangle. The driver said, "I've other pickups but should be back long before you are ready to return. You have my cell, in any event."

Tristian nodded, grabbed Hannah's free hand, and hurried through the rain. Dressed in black pants, boots, and a deep maroon sweater, he stood at the visitors' entrance to the White House, his arm lightly wrapped around Hannah's waist. She shook out the brightly colored umbrella, then folded it up. Her pink and blue striped sweater remained dry, but the black ankle boots and light blue slacks were damp from the rain. Three other couples waited behind them when two men dressed in dark suits greeted the group.

"Good morning and welcome. My name is Rob." He pointed to the other gentleman. "And this is Adam. We'll be your guides for today."

Tristian took his driver's license from his pocket and nodded to Hannah as she held on to her passport tightly. She handed it to one of the men, who looked at her then back at her passport.

"Irish citizen, huh?" He glanced at the passport again and flipped through the pages then turned it over in his hands.

"Yes, sir. But I work…"

"We are taking in the sights before returning to work in Maine," Tristian said smoothly surveying the room, then smiled at a tall, red-haired man hurrying toward them.

"Sorry, I'm late. These two are special guests and have been vetted already." The man motioned toward Tristian and Hannah while reaching for their ID's from the guide.

Adam hesitated a couple of beats, narrowed his eyes then shrugged, handing the ID's to the man. "No one told us about special guests," he murmured to Rob who made a sound of agreement.

Tristian nodded to the red-haired man. "Hannah, this is Stan, he works in the Chief of Staff's office." Tristian turned his attention to Stan. "Any problems with the luncheon arrangements?"

Stan smiled. "None at all. Should have sunshine by the time the tour is complete. You can go ahead with the group. I'll meet up with you in the Rose Garden after your tour. Enjoy." He turned on his heel and strode down the hallway.

They joined the group and toured the first floor.

The guide turned to glance at them and continued with her speech. "The first floor of the White House Residence is known as the "State Floor," because this is where formal receptions of state are held."

Tristian found it interesting that this floor was at the same level as the second floor of the West Wing and the East Wing. The Residence seemed to sit on higher ground. He studied the bust of Abraham Lincoln, while Hannah stared out the huge windows.

"How do they maintain security with all this glass?" she whispered to him.

He shrugged. "Bullet-proof glass?"

She glared at him. "Be serious."

"I am." He grinned. "Okay, maybe there's a bit more going on here than simple mortal security."

"That would explain a lot." Hannah snickered.

Next stop, the library decorated in red and gold, she found the room fascinating. But in another room on the first floor, she smiled at the dishes displayed for each administration. "That's a lot of dishes to keep clean." She pointed to the glass cases displaying the tableware, then slipped her hand into Tristian's.

He trailed behind her when the view from the yellow oval room's balcony held Hannah's attention. The tour guide frowned. "Keep up. The second and third floors contain the first family's private quarters as well as guest entertainment areas."

Waiting until Tristian and Hannah passed by, the tour guide pointed down the hall. "Now for the West Wing, which has expanded and undergone several renovations since 1908, the year it was built." The guide droned on. "During that time, Teddy Roosevelt moved his office from the second floor to the oval office where it has remained the official workplace of the President."

At this point, Tristian and Hannah left the rest of the group to meet Stan in the Rose Garden. A table for two was prepared with lunch waiting for them. Tristian held Hannah's chair for her and smiled at her awe-struck look. "The food will get cold if you continue to stare at your surroundings."

"This is where they hold state dinners. How did you? How?" She glanced at Stan as he stood talking with the wait staff. "Are you trying to impress me?" She drew in a breath and coyly looked up at him from under her long red lashes.

"Is it working?" he asked, as her wide smile reached to her beautiful cornflower blue eyes.

"Yes." She took her cloth napkin and delicately placed it in her lap. The rain clouds from earlier gave way to a few fluffy white clouds and a pleasant light breeze tousled her hair.

Tristian picked up his chair, which sat across from Hannah, and set it beside her. His hand gently brushed down her arm while he eased into the chair and spread a napkin in his lap. Stabbing a fork into a bite of salad, he surveyed the area for threats. Their conversation was light as they finished their meal. Dessert was a delicious piece of cherry pie with a large scoop of ice cream. Looking at it made his mouth water.

Before Hannah spooned up a bite of pie and ice cream she giggled. "Does this have anything to do with the fact that George Washington was purported to have chopped down a cherry tree?"

Tristian chuckled. "And couldn't tell a lie? But that's all hearsay you know." He said playfully, surprised that his usually serious demeanor gave way to relaxed and playful nature when he was with Hannah. He couldn't remember feeling like this since…in a very long time. "If you're finished with lunch, I'll call the limo, and we'll head over to the International Spy Museum."

"Now that sounds like fun." She touched the napkin to her mouth, put it on the table, and stood. "I'd like to walk around the garden a bit before we leave."

"Sounds like a plan. Stan is on his way. We'll stretch our legs in the garden before hoofing it over to the Metrorail to meet the limo."

Before long Tristian and Hannah were whisked away in the limo on their way to the Spy Museum. Inside they discovered a museum dedicated to how espionage and spies shaped the course of history from Roman and Greek Empires through the Cold War to present day.

Hannah looked over the interactive spy experience offered by the museum. "I'd like to try being an undercover agent and work with a team, solving puzzles, and completing tasks in an effort to intercept a secret arms deal. Maybe prevent nuclear war?" She giggled softly behind her hand.

With a butterscotch brow raised, Tristian snorted. "Really? Not enough real life intrigue?" he whispered, his lips skimming the soft shell of her ear. She shivered against him as her cheeks heated. "Like my undivided attention?" he said, lips brushing against her throat.

She pulled way and narrowed her eyes at him. "Not here… This will be fun."

"For who? I don't think my men would agree. But…if you insist. Stay alert."

"Always."

After the sixty minutes of playing secret agent were up, Hannah not only intercepted the secret arms deal but prevented nuclear weapons from getting into the wrong hands."

"You are a natural. Let's head back and get ready for the Kennedy Center musical extravaganza this evening. We have dinner reservations at seven."

"We have plenty of time." She laughed. "I want to do the Spy in the City experience."

"No. Too hard for the men to keep track of us."

"Please…" Hannah wheedled. "I haven't had this much fun in ages."

Tristian paced the floor and talked into his earpiece. His thunderous expression smoothed into a thoughtful one as he turned to her and whispered, "Okay, Ruben thinks he can hack into the specialized GPS device used to guide us to hidden clues in the area surrounding the museum. If he can, then we'll do it. If not, too risky."

"Super. We can do the one-hour operation."

"Then I have your word, no more spy games."

"Yes, sir." Hannah snickered and rushed over to sign up for the next one-hour circuit of operation. Once she had the GPS in hand, she glanced at Tristian.

Listening intently, he nodded. "He's in."

"Gee double espionage," she said quietly.

"Shhh…off we go."

An hour later they had the password for a secret weapon, and the game was over. A man at the counter said, "Well played. Been here before?"

"Nope, spy—"

"Just lucky. We had a great time." He took Hannah

by the elbow and led her out of the building into the waiting limo.

"I was only going to say spying was fun." She huffed.

"Couldn't risk you would say something else. Loose lips and all." He pushed the button on the side of the door, a partition between them and the driver went up, then he muted his earpiece.

She bristled. "I would never compromise..." Hannah glanced at the smirk on his lips and reached out to slap at him.

"Too slow." He grasped her wrist and pulled her to him, brought his lips down on hers in a feather light touch with tantalizing persuasion. She moaned softly against his lips and quivered as his fingers danced along the side of her breast, ribs, and hip. He reveled in her softness and reactions to his ministrations. *I want her. I've got to get to the bottom of why she won't share my bed.*

She wrapped an arm around his neck caressing the tendons in the back of his neck, fingers running through his hair. He trailed kisses across her jawline and inside the neckline of her low-cut sweater where his tongue dipped between her soft mounds, she arched up to him, giving him more access. His fingers slipped under the waistband of her pants and traced a sensuous path to ecstasy.

Chapter Eleven
An Unexpected Twist with Deadly Consequences

Hannah stepped out of the limo and sucked in a breath as she stared at D.C.'s foremost performing arts center. She'd read somewhere that it was divided into three main theaters and five smaller venues. But she was not prepared for the enormous location. While attending college, her roommates had insisted they watch the lighting of the Christmas tree at Kennedy Center, but…she blew out a breath.

"Our show is in the Concert Hall. It's this way." Tristian gently slid his arm around her waist, hand at the small of her back, and guided her forward. Once seated in the premier seating, he glanced around to locate his men.

"Everything all right?" Hannah asked, following his gaze to behind their box seats.

"Yes, verifying our security. No threats. We can enjoy the show."

At the end of the evening, Hannah stood to follow the crowd out.

"This way, doll. We have a couple of hours. I'd like to take you to the rooftop terrace. From up there under the full moon, we can see the Lincoln Memorial, George Washington University, Watergate Complex, and the outstanding city skyline. But you have to promise me not to fly off."

She elbowed him in the ribs. "Oh my—It's gorgeous. Everything looks so different lit up in the night. And look at the hauntingly beautiful full moon."

"Full moons are for lovers."

"Which we are not."

"Oh, I wouldn't say that. We need to talk about your—our problem," he whispered against her neck as his warm lips breathed a kiss against her skin.

A shiver of hot desire zinged up her body and down to her very core. *I don't know how much longer I can resist. I want him as badly as he desires me. But the consequences...*

"Let's go check out the restaurant before it closes." His lips curved up into a teasing and sensuous smile. One that fanned the flames of her desire as she leaned into him, felt his arousal against her.

Her pulse raced even as he pulled away, took her hand and guided her in front of him to the restaurant.

****

The next morning, they toured the Lincoln Memorial, paused for pictures, then spent the rest of the day at the Library of Congress. Tristian patiently waited as Hannah poured over the books available. By the third day, Tristian and his men had yet to see any suspicious activity. Perhaps Rezar's men were still with him, out of the country, but it didn't make sense not to post guards. Hannah gave the situation a fleeting thought, as she got ready for the United States Botanic Garden tour. Tristian looked forward to this tour the most. She could feel it. His love of gardening and plants seemed at odds with the persona of a tough guy he presented. She knew better. The man was caring, gentle but protective which was at war with the assassin he was. The tangle of personalities was what he didn't want anyone to see. But deep inside, she felt his turmoil and was determined to support and love him, regardless of the requirements of her kind. *I guess I've made my decision. Ma and Da I'm sorry. Forgive me.* She looked up and blew out a breath.

Tristian turned and peered down at the concern etched on her face. "Is something wrong?"

"No, no, not at all. The sound of the fountains splashing inside and the lighted ones outside are magnificent. The fragrant flowers are all so beautiful. I'd love to have a glass greenhouse like this." She spun around in a full circle, arms out, as air whooshed out of her.

"I suppose you want the two courtyard gardens with streams and fountains as well?"

She nodded. "It's not much for a powerful…"

He put his index finger to her lips. "I'm afraid I'd have to draw the line at the ten garden rooms under the glass." Tristian smiled, intertwining his fingers in hers and continued down the winding pathway.

By midafternoon Tristian stopped and pulled out his phone to check the time. "Let's find somewhere to get a bite to eat." As he was about to slide his phone back into his pocket, it rang. He looked at the caller ID and touched the screen. "Hi—what—I'll be right there. Call in all teams, I want to pick those accompanying me. Wheels up in less than an hour." His jaw set in a firm line, color draining out of his face, he stared at Hannah. "We have to go. Now." At a fast walk, he tugged her through the crowd and out the first door he came to. They sprinted toward the waiting limo. In between gasps for air, Tristian filled her in. "Angie's been snatched from the dream world. The Vampire Council's assassin has located her inside an isolated cabin in Cherryfield, Maine. He has eyes on her as we speak. Lady Rose has commanded him to wait for our arrival." He yanked opened the limo door and shoved Hannah inside, slid in beside her, and slammed the door. The driver hit the gas.

"Why don't you port to the Salon?" She pulled her jacket around her and shifted to look at him. "Wouldn't it be faster?"

"Because we don't know who is watching and could be intercepted in between while we port. We'd be extremely vulnerable until we reached The Wycked Hair Salon. Not willing to risk you."

"What? I don't understand. I can take care of myself." She bristled, squared her shoulders.

He snorted. "You don't have to." He took a deep breath, his voice calmed. "I need you to stay at the Salon with Tobi and Owen. They'll take you back to the apartment when it's deemed safe. I'll meet you there when this is all over."

For the second time in Hannah's life, she had no idea what was going on and no control. She shivered as fear closed in. "How long will you be gone? You're not completely healed from your last altercation. How do you snatch someone from his or her dreams? That is what you mean?" Hannah asked. She'd never felt so helpless, so…

"Indeed, it is. Angie is a seer in addition to her other talents. Rezar must have invaded her dreams, separating her spirit from her body. A dangerous situation." The limo slowed to a stop in front of The Wycked Hair Salon. Owen yanked open the door.

Tristian bounded out of the vehicle. After two steps he turned, hurriedly leaned in, grasping Hannah's hand, and gave a tug that sent her flying out of the limo and into his arms. "Sorry. Need to get inside."

****

Once in the Salon, Tristian took command, calmly issuing orders and setting in motion the plans he'd established, tweaking it as necessary. In the middle of the well-ordered departure, his phone rang. "Bruce. We're on our way out. Anything new." Tristian nodded. "I'll get back to you when I know more. You're going to wait there to help her return to her body once I free her."

"Yes," Bruce said tersely, filling Tristian in with the circumstances as he understood them concerning the Vampire Council and its assassin, Stefan.

"Good. I'll be in touch." Tristian ended the call, turned quickly to locate Hannah. Strode to her and grasped her by the shoulders. "Do as Tobi and Owen tell you; I'll be back soon." He pulled her to him hard and brought his mouth down on hers; the kiss was urgent. "I—I—" He cursed. "I'll be back." He couldn't get the words out he wanted to say. They'd have to wait until he returned.

On the plane, he went over the plans in his head. Once airborne, he paced, playing out alternate scenarios. Bringing someone back from the dream world wasn't something he'd done often, actually never. Fury raged inside him, he tamped it down. Emotions had no place in his profession. Anger had nearly gotten him killed a short time ago. A lesson he'd not soon forget. After what seemed like hours, the seatbelt warning sign lit up. Tristian plopped down in a seat and fastened his belt. The plane taxied to a stop and the group hustled out the door and into the waiting vehicles. The sun dropped down behind the horizon. It would be dark soon, better cover for the rescue.

"Ruben," Tristian called. "You and your team surround the property and wait for my orders. Maps are on your phone. Should be no surprises. Everyone's com's working?"

"Yes, sir."

The cars will drop us a quarter mile from the site, we'll go in from there. "I'll meet up with the vamp in front of the house, and we'll handle it. No one goes in or out of the line once you set it up. Got it?" Tristian turned on his heel then stopped. "Don't engage the creatures unless I tell you."

"Yes, sir."

He narrowed his eyes meeting the gaze of each man. "It's my sister in there."

"And Overlord's…" Rubin stopped mid-sentence, swallowed hard at Tristian's scorching gaze. "Your sister. Right. Understood."

"We have to get her out before we engage the enemy."

Rubin nodded and rushed off to join his team.

Tristian slid into the driver's seat, glanced at his phone's screen while waiting for the others to settle, then drove into the night. Stopping the vehicle a quarter mile from the property, he waved Ruben's team on and motioned his team to spread out behind him. As they made their way through the underbrush, the noises of the night filled his ears, the bass of the frog's croaks, shrill chirp of the crickets, and the buzz of mosquito's swarming around his head. They timed their steps with the natural rhythms of the night, hoping to avoid detection until he spotted Stefan.

A twig snapped, and there was movement up ahead. A quick flash of light then darkness. A signal the vamp was ready. Tristian motioned his men to follow, a few yards from where the light had flashed, Tristian signaled his team to hold their position and silently touched in the phone number Bruce had given him.

At the first ring, a low voice rumbled, "Tristian."

"Stefan we're set." Tristian turned the phone off and crept closer, giving a night owl's call. The vamp silently joined him. Motioning to the window in the back corner of the house, where an eerie blue phosphorescent glow reflected in the glass.

In a hushed tone, Stefan said, "I'll wait for you to get to the window. Then I'll charge the front door at the same time you enter the window, draw their attention outside. The men will flee once I enter and grab the Council's Harbinger, a double-sided ax. I can wield it, as I am of true blood and will terminate Rezar then the rest of them. You escape with the innocent."

"If we encounter a problem, my men will move in."

"Won't be a problem. Now go," Stefan said impatiently.

At the sound of the front door shattering as Stefan kicked it in, Tristian materialized inside the room where Angie floated in a blue bubble. *So, that was how Rezar was keeping her alive.* Tristian raised a hand to the warlock guarding his sister.

Angie's voice pleaded inside her brother's mind. *Don't hurt him. If not for him, I would not be alive.*

Palm still facing the guard, Tristian muttered words

under his breath, and the guard slumped to the floor. He touched the bubble, easily slid his fingertip through it, a blue haze seeped out around his finger. Tristian pulled it back, sucked in a breath, and began the incantation as he crept around the bubble; a smoke-filled layer surrounded the bubble. Standing as close to Angie's body as possible, without rupturing the enclosure. His mind reached out and touched hers. *You realize I've never done anything like this before.*

She nodded her violet eyes wide open assessing his every movement. *You can do it. You've always taken care of me. I love you. Now get on with it. Stefan can't hold 'em off forever.*

Tristian cursed, held his palms flat as he murmured words in cadence, pushed his hands through the first smoky barrier and through the bubble taking hold of Angie's essence with both hands around her waist and shoved. The bubble collapsed in around her. As she faded, a gnarled hand caught hold of the blue phosphorescence tail attached to her filmy dress. Before Tristian could reach the body attached to the hand, they were gone.

"Noooo, Bruce watch out." Tristian roared then fell against the wall. Stefan crashed through the door and stared at Tristian. "What's wrong? Are you injured?"

"No. The bastard got hold of Angie's essence and was pulled through to the other side where Bruce is waiting."

Stefan leaned on the jewel encrusted handle of the bloodied double ax. "From what I've heard, the Overlord will enjoy finishing the demon off." The vampire swung the ax up on his shoulder. "I've called for the clean-up crew. Your men took out a few creatures that escaped while I was otherwise engaged." He motioned Tristian through the door, and they walked out on the porch where demon and vampire ash still swirled in the breeze. The two negotiated their way down the steps and over several body parts strewn over the front yard of the cabin.

"One renegade demon is unaccounted for and may have escaped." His jaw clenched as he rubbed his chin with thumb and index finger. "Council will put a bounty out on his head. Won't be long before he is terminated."

Shit. I'd hoped to get 'em all. "Keep us in the loop. I'll put one of my teams on it as well. We don't want another incident." Tristian raked his fingers through his hair, then shook the demon and vampire ash from his hand before extending it to Stefan. "Good job. Thanks."

The vamp shrugged and clasped Tristian's hand. "Just doing my job." He strode off into the night as Tristian stood a moment more, his black duster flapping in the wind.

Chapter Twelve
Celebratory Home Coming, Elegant Dinner Plans,
and Unexpected Events Stir the Pot.

Once Tristian and his men boarded the plane, he attempted to contact Bruce via phone. The call went to voice mail. He fidgeted, shifted in his seat. *Waiting was a bitch.* Finally, half-way through the flight, his phone rang.

"Bruce. It's about damn time."

"I was a little busy. Angie is safe and sound. She's here with me. Rezar is dead. The rotten bastard stabbed me in the thigh with a dagger. It was his last act. I used his own dagger, with a little magic to gut him. But now, I really I gotta go. Fill you in on the details when you get back." Bruce disconnected the call, and Tristian stared at the screen. *Damn demon.*

The sun was high in the sky as the company jet touched down on the runway. Tristian and his men clambered down the stairs.

At the base of the steps, he paused. "Take a couple of days off. The Vampire Council has assigned a task force to search for the missing demon. When we regroup, I'll touch base with Stefan and see what progress has been made in the capture. If necessary, Rubin, your team will assist the vampires."

"Got it." Ruben turned to the others and motioned a release.

The ride to his apartment was uneventful. He waved to the driver while exiting the vehicle. Exhausted, Tristian trudged down the apartment hallway, opened the door with a thought. Hannah rushed to him, nearly knocking him over, and flung her arms around his neck. "I was so worried. Glad you are back. You okay?" She leaned back and surveyed his body."

"I'm fine. Happy to be back. Angie's safe, and Rezar is dead."

"I heard. Tobi called, but she didn't have any more details." She rested her head on his chest with a sigh of relief.

He picked her up and whirled around once before setting her feet on the floor. Burying his face in her wavy hair, he breathed her in. Never had the mixture of honeysuckle and lilac smelled so good, replacing that terrible stench of the cabin from his nostrils. Raised up on tiptoe, she turned her face up toward his, her lips softly brushing his jawline. He reveled in that delicious sensation and relaxed against her, covering her mouth hungrily.

****

She gave herself freely to the passion of his kiss. The sensation sent the pit of her stomach into a wild swirl. Raising his mouth from hers, he gazed into her eyes. The depth of his emotions swept over her, affection, desire, trust, and weariness reflected in his eyes. Additionally, never had she felt such turmoil in an individual. She guided him over to the couch and eased down with him. His embrace tightened.

"So glad to see you," he murmured.

His warm breath tickled against her cheek. "Tris, if

you'll loosen your arms, I'll get the herbal tea I prepared. It'll relax your muscles and ease the pain in your back."

"No." He nuzzled deeper into her neck, his tongue teasing a path to her earlobe, and along her jawline. He rested his head wearily on her shoulder.

Hannah leaned into him, gently caressing his shoulders and chest until he finally released her.

"I had no idea how good it would feel to have someone waiting at home for me. Now I know why my parents risked it all for family." He sighed and relaxed against the back of the couch. "I'll take that tea now."

She padded into the kitchen, took a couple mugs from the cupboard, and picked up the kettle that simmered on the stove. Pouring the steaming liquid into the mugs, she spooned in a bit of sugar and added milk to hers. When she set a mug in front of Tristian, a bottle of Jameson's whiskey appeared out of thin air and poured a generous amount into the mug, then disappeared with a pop. "Needed something stronger, huh?"

"Oh yeah."

"Tell me what happened. Since you're back, I assume Angie is too?"

"Yes. The bastard clung to her essence as she passed from the bubble to her body. Upon his arrival, his last act was to drive a dagger into Bruce's thigh."

Hannah sucked in a breath. "Oh God... Is he okay?"

"Of course. Bruce finished him off with his own dagger and demon magic, a potent combination." Tristian couldn't help but grin.

She detected a note of pride in Tristian's voice.

"So, things are better between you two on a personal level?"

Tristian glared at her for a beat. "I'm working on it. But our professional bond is strong."

She nodded, glanced into the mug, took a sip, and leveled her gaze over the rim at him. "You do know that if you'd been completely honest with your sister, things might have turned out differently. And on that note—"

He narrowed his eyes. "I don't want to talk about it." Tristian shifted slightly away from her in his seat.

She gently cupped his chin and turned his face to meet hers. "I'm sorry—but this has gone on long enough. It's time she knows exactly what happened to your parents. It will help her to understand your rage and actions. Clear the air. A fresh start for everyone."

"It's not that easy," he said stubbornly. Gulping down the tea, he hissed as the hot liquid burned his throat.

She hid a smirk behind her hand. "Tristian, I know what you are, know what you do, and I'm still here. We can't move forward until you release that terrible burden you've carried for twenty years. She's not a child anymore. Angie is a grown woman with a right to know. Besides, according to Tobi, Angie is aware that you're still keeping something from her. Bruce has kept your secret since he figured it out, waiting for you—"

He sat up straight and glared at her again. "What did you tell Tobi."

"Oh, get off your high horse. Nothing. I would never betray your confidence. Tobi gave me a lot of insight while you were gone."

He groaned. "I never should have—"

"No, probably not. But it can't be undone and you"—she paused and locked eyes with him—"had no choice. Want some more tea?" She pushed to her feet.

"No." The bottle of whiskey appeared again and poured into his mug.

"Well, I do." She sauntered into the kitchen, poured a mug, and sniffed the steam. "Mmmm. Smells good." She sliced a couple of bagels and popped them in the toaster. "You really should eat something."

He mumbled something unintelligible.

"I'm fixing bagels, I have blueberry cream cheese." *I know that's your favorite.* "You look like you could use a nap after the bagels. Then maybe later go out to dinner?"

"Mmmm sounds good." He stifled a jaw-popping yawn behind his hand. "You'll join me in a nap?"

"Of course, but no hanky-panky." She smiled. *He'll be asleep before his head hits the pillow.* When the slices popped up, she spread the cream cheese on the warm toasted bagels, set them on plates, added napkins on the tray, and carried everything into the living room. Tristian had sprawled across the couch and was softly snoring.

She brought a fresh mug of herbal tea and touched his hand. He jumped, his hand drew back in a fist. Hannah jerked two steps backward.

"Don't ever sneak up on me." Reaching for a bagel, he took a huge bite and washed it down with the tea. "Fresh mug, huh?" He caught her hand and pulled her down beside him, waggling his eyebrows. "How about we take a shower before that nap?"

"As long as you don't fall asleep in the shower and drown." She giggled.

"Oh, you'll keep me awake." Tristian's voice purred as he set his mug on the table. Then took Hannah's from her hand and set it down. He feathered his fingers along the soft sides of her back, her waist and hips. "Don't you think it's about time you tell me why you won't let me make love to you?"

She drew in a long breath, desire heated all the right places and butterflies danced in her stomach. "Probably." Even as she tried to tamp down the yearning, her pulse raced and her traitorous body arched against him.

Tristian pulled her into his lap and whispered, "I would never hurt you. If that's what you're afraid of." Gently he slipped his arm under her knees and around her back, cradled her to his chest and stood, walking toward the bedroom. "Let's see about that shower."

****

A cool breeze blew tousled Tristian's hair as he held the apartment building door open for Hannah. The last rays of sun faded into red, purple, pink streaks across the blue sky. A limo waited at the curb to whisk them to Fiola's Restaurant for the best Italian food available in D.C. Tristian made reservations and insisted on a secluded corner table. Upon arrival, the waiter showed them to a table in the corner, wine chilling and the flame swayed on the candle in the middle of the table. Hannah's eyes rounded as she sucked in a breath at the large bouquet of dark red roses in a clear crystal vase sitting beside her place setting.

The waiter glanced at Tristian with a slight smile. "Is everything to your satisfaction, sir?"

"Yes, thank you." He discreetly put money in the man's hand and pulled out Hannah's chair. After she was settled, he pulled out the other chair and placed it beside her, eased down into it.

"Wow, you've been back how long?" Hannah said in hushed tones.

Taking the wine out of the ice, he poured the amber liquid into the glasses. "Long enough to know what a lucky man I am." He reached for her hand. "I wanted to let you know just how much I appreciate you. My life is not an easy one, but coming home to you—makes—" He swallowed hard. "I love it. I'd like to give this relationship thing a try, if you're still willing."

"Well, I have to say I am going into this with my eyes wide open. Especially after spending a few hours with Tobi."

He huffed out a breath. "I'm going to have a talk with her."

"You'll do no such thing," Hannah said louder that intended, then lowering her voice. "I wanted everything out in the open, and you couldn't seem to understand that concept."

He shook his head. "Still, she had no right."

"I know. They're your tales to tell. But your secrets are spilling out all over. You talk in your sleep or I guess actually, it was when you were unconscious? Which is how Tobi learned about me. That's why we compared notes. You said some things about the death of your parents and Angie tying herself to a demon. Tobi put two and two together and wanted to know if she was right. I neither confirmed or denied the scenario she set out. Which, by the way, was pretty damn close to the truth."

Resting his head in his hands, he stilled for several beats. "And she didn't say anything to Angie?"

"Nope. Figured it was up to you. But…if you keep procrastinating—" She shrugged. "Anything is possible."

"This is not what I had planned for this evening. I wanted to talk about us."

"Okay, let's do that." She lowered her voice to a whisper. "You know what I am. Along with that is a…" Hannah paused for a beat, lowered her long, red lashes and stared at her hands. "My kind mate for life, which means once the relationship is consummated, there can be no other mate for me. It's forever. We believe in marriage and life-long commitment. I wasn't… I'm not sure that is something you can live with." When she slowly peered at him from under her thick lashes, there was a heart-rending tenderness in his gaze. It surprised her.

"Commitment was never in my plans. But neither was having a relationship with someone like you. I want to see where this thing between us goes, if we consummate it, I won't leave you."

"Oh, that's great. Just what a woman wants to hear." She yanked her napkin out of her lap and pushed up from the table. "I've heard enough. I want to go home." She blinked back tears.

Tristian stood and grasped her hand. "You are taking this the wrong way."

"It's crystal clear."

"Then your crystal is cracked. What I meant is that if we decide to consummate our relationship, I'll be ready to face commitment and we'll wed."

"Face commitment? Really. Commitment to another for an eternity is something you do willingly. Not something you have to face." She shook loose of his hand and turned away.

He raked fingers through his hair and reached for her again as people in the restaurant stared. His face flushed. "I'm mucking this up, and I can't seem to help myself." He rubbed the back of his neck. "I've never had a problem talking to women, but with you—things are different. Maybe—because it matters. Never did before. Give me five minutes...Please."

He was ready to throttle her, she felt his anger building, but she couldn't tell if it was at her or himself. *Interesting.* "Ok, you've got five minutes." She gave the people staring at them a "mind your own business" glare, then glanced at her watch, eased back into the seat.

Settling in the seat, he put his hand over hers and held tight, as if she would try to flee. "Commitment is not something I ever considered after seeing what can happen. No one ever mattered enough for me to think about it. Then you come waltzing into my life and nothing...will ever be the same. The idea is growing on me. It's not that I'm saying never... With everything that had happened recently, I am trying to get my head around all of it and deal with it. As you so eloquently put it, I should have told Angie."

"I didn't mean to put blame on you. It's possible if you believe in fate, she was meant for him, and nothing was going to change that."

He sighed. "I've never opened up to anyone like I have to you. So, if you believe in fate..." His gaze held hers.

"We belong together. It's just going to take you a while to get there." She leaned back against her chair. "I'm ready to order."

"Exactly." He blew out a relieved breath and picked up the menu.

She raised an eyebrow as she felt his emotions settle into a calm but decided to say nothing. Soon she would have to explain her many talents to him. But for now, knowing his emotions and having the ability to soothe them would remain her secret.

The waiter arrived at their table. She ordered Maine lobster ravioli. He requested beef rib eye and handed the menus to the waiter. Over the three-course meal, the conversation was light.

"Bruce has offered the company jet to take us home tomorrow whenever we're ready." He took the final bite of steak, chewed for a beat or two, and sipped on his glass of wine. "I'd like to introduce you to my sister, Bruce, Willow, and the group at The Wycked Hair Salon before we leave. I figured leaving around early afternoon would give us a chance to sleep in and get everything together for the trip."

"Sounds good. I'll notify my boss when we arrive. I imagine work is piling up." She leaned back to allow the waiter to remove her plate along with Tristian's. Another server brought two pieces of tiramisu. Hannah forked up a small bite, slid it into her mouth, and closed her eyes. "Mmmm. This is fantastic."

"Best in D.C., they advertise. I've never eaten at other Italian restaurants in the area, so we'll have to take their word for it." He forked up a bite, popped it in his mouth savoring the flavor. "Yep. Delicious."

After scraping the last crumbs of tiramisu from her plate, she peered up at Tristian, who was staring off into to space. "Penny for your thoughts."

He blinked a couple of times and met her gaze.

"Thinking about how much things have changed. You ready to go?"

She pushed up from her chair. "Yes. It's been a long day—or series of days."

Tristian turned his head trying to hide a yawn. "I agree. Have you ever been to Niagara Falls?"

Her eyes flew open at the change of subject and she paused for a beat. "No. When I started my job, I had a list of places I wanted to see in the U.S. But then work took over and I only got to a couple, close to home."

His eyes sparkled with mischief as he tucked her hand through his bent elbow then walked into the brisk night air. He led her around the corner of the building and pulled her in tight, his lips slowly descended to meet hers. His lips were warm and sweet on hers and suddenly the crashing sound of waterfalls surrounded them and a cold mist settled on her skin.

A warm poncho wrapped around her as her eyes rounded, she sucked in a breath. "What the hell?"

Gales of laughter floated on the air as she looked at Tristian.

"I believe this is one of the most romantic places on earth. At least in my mind." He shrugged. "Don't you? We have the star-strewn night sky, waning moon, and the spectacular lighting effects on the falls." He kissed her cold cheeks, nibbled down her neck, and breathed a kiss at the base of her throat. Turning her to face the falls, he wrapped his arms around her again and held her close to his chest as they stared at one of nature's exhibitions of raw power and beauty. "During the day, its view and mist off the water is breath-taking, but at night…that's where the real magic is."

She cuddled against him, her womanly curves pressed against his strong chest. Desire surged through her. He wrapped a blanket around both of them. *Never a dull moment with this warlock, a man I'm quickly falling in love with.* Giddy with excitement, she giggled taking in the unbelievable expansion of beauty before her.

****

He'd taken a big chance using magic to bring her to Niagara Falls. Some women didn't like porting from one place to another on a whim without warning. But Hannah was different in so many ways, he'd risked it because using words to express his feelings had failed miserably. He hoped she'd understood what he was trying to convey. *I'm in love with her.* The thought hit him like a punch to the gut. *Where in the hell did that come from?* "How about we book a room and port back in the wee hours of the morning?" He peered up at the building across the way. "Bet one of those dark rooms facing the falls is available. We could watch the falls from the warmth of a suite." *And see where it leads.* A seductive rumble rose from his chest.

She tipped her head back to look at him. "Oh, I'd love that, but won't people worry if we don't return to the apartment?"

"That's what cell phones are for." He pulled the phone out of his pocket and wiggled it between thumb and index finger.

Chapter Thirteen
Overdue Introductions, Surprise Announcements &
an Unexpected Trip Keep Things Interesting

All the magic expended last night caught up with Tristian this morning, he was dragging ass helping load the luggage in the limo. The rules of magic use for personal gain were tough. But given his recent triumphs over evil, he figured the balance was tipped toward him at the moment and well worth the cost. Hannah bounced out of the sliding glass doors of the hotel, gave him a smacking kiss on the lips, before sliding into the limo seat to check her phone. Closing the trunk, he slipped in beside her.

"Ma and Da have called several times during your absence when Tobi wouldn't let me use my phone. My sister, Brandy, has called twice as many times. If I don't answer their calls soon, they will be at my cottage looking for me. When I'm not there, Brandy will scour the town until she finds out what happened. She's a park ranger in Glacier National Park and has resources."

"It should be safe to call them when we head to the airport." Tristian conceded gathering her against him. "Good enough?"

"Okay."

He smothered her mouth with demanding mastery, his tongue teased between her sweet, plump lips, their tongues initiating a sensuous dance.

He paused long enough to raise his head and said to the driver, "We'd like to stop by the Salon before heading to the airport." Tristian touched the switch to bring up the privacy panel between them and the driver.

The limo slowed in front of The Wycked Hair Salon. Tristian stepped out of the vehicle and offered his hand to Hannah. She reached for his hand and bounded out of the limo. Her face, flushed with excitement, made Tristian smile. He skipped the entrance to the Salon and held the door open to The Krystal Unicorn as chimes announced their arrival. Rainbows bounced over the walls and glass display cases when the cut crystals swayed in the windows from the fresh breeze provided by the open door.

"Oh Tristian, you did come to our grand re-opening." Angie squealed rushing forward to throw an arm around his neck.

"You look a hell of a lot better than the last time I saw you." Tristian returned the hug, never letting go of Hannah's slightly moist hand. He smiled wide as Hannah glanced from Angie to Bruce then swept over the rest of the group. He released Hannah's hand and wrapped an arm around her waist, pulling her forward. "This is Hannah Shaughnessy." Tristian nodded toward Angie. "And this is my sister, Angie, who chose to tie herself for eternity to the cause of all our trouble—" Lowering his voice, he jerked his head toward Bruce. "The Western Hemisphere's Territory Overlord, my boss, and the source of all of our trouble."

Angie immediately enveloped Hannah in a hug. "So, this is the woman who tamed my big brother."

Hannah blanched, and red patches bloomed on her

cheeks. "I wouldn't say that." She peered down at the floor then shifted her gaze shyly over at Tristian.

"Oh, I would, and he's a better man for it," Angie said batting her eyes at her brother daring him to retort.

Not pushing my buttons today sis, in fact, I think those days are over. Tristian's voice wafted through his sister's mind, a smirk on his lips.

A slow wicked grin spread across Angie's face. *Oh, boyo you have no idea.* She replied in kind.

Hannah's gaze scanned from Angie to Tristian a puzzled expression on her face.

Bruce stepped forward, hand extended. "I'm Bruce, the trouble to which Tristian referred, and the boss that has made him a very rich man. It's a pleasure to meet you, Ms. Shaughnessy."

She gave him a nervous smile. "Please, just Hannah."

"Hannah, are you enjoying your visit to our historic city?"

"Oh yes. At least I was, until... I'm not used to this type of intrigue. But now that it's safe..."

"It's never safe..."

Tristian frowned and motioned toward a petite woman with jet-black hair, tipped in bright blue arranged in spikes over her head. "This is Willow, my sister's life-long best friend. They're business partners." He made a sweeping motion around the store. "And own The Krysal Unicorn. Willow's parents live next door to the family house in Maine."

Hannah nodded and grinned. I'm so glad to meet you. Tristian has told me so much about you and your family. Do you get home often?"

"Not much. Work keeps me pretty busy. But I've

got some news that will rock my parents' world. The kind you have to tell in person. So, guess I'll be seeing them soon." Willow looked at Angie and grimaced a little. "And my fiancé lives here. He's an artist," she said proudly.

"Fiancé?" Tristian nearly choked on his own spit. "But you're just…"

"Really glad you're not my brother." Willow dissolved into a fit of giggles joined by Angie.

Glancing from Willow to Angie, he saw a broad smile spread across her face. He was sure it was due to his being blindsided by this announcement.

"We were going to discuss a double wedding when you arrived," Angie said gleefully.

"A double wedding?" He involuntarily looked in Hannah's direction, then caught himself. "Who's getting married?" It must be catching; he'd considered, even wondered about asking Hannah to marry him. But there was no way his sister would know.

Oh, big brother, you need to keep your thoughts shielded better. Angie giggled, as her thoughts whisking through her brother's mind had the desired effect. *Your secret is safe with me, for the time being.*

Shock registered in Tristian's eyes as they flew open wide, then narrowed to slits in a threatening look.

Fear not brother. "Bruce asked me to marry him, and Willow's Caleb proposed to her, so naturally it will be a double wedding. You'll get an invitation as soon as we iron out all the details."

Bruce extended his hand to his long-time employee and soon to be brother-in-law. "Settling down, huh?"

Still, shell-shocked, Tristian nodded and clasped Bruce's hand.

Taking advantage of the situation, Bruce said, "Maybe it would be a good idea to stick around and let Angie and Hannah get acquainted. Willow too. I can make the apartment available a while longer."

Tristian shook his head. "We gotta get back and check on things at home." When he switched his gaze to Hannah and found her frowning, he cleared his throat. "But we'd like to return in a couple of weeks. Will that work?"

Nice save big brother. She has changed you. Angie's amused voice floated through Tristian's mind.

He shot her another warning glance. *Still my pesky little sister. Somethings never change.* Tristian shook his head.

Hannah's frown faded, and the corners of her lips curved into a bright smile.

"Sure. Sounds like the wedding will be sooner rather than later." Bruce slid his arm around Angie's waist and pulled her into him, brushing a kiss across her forehead in a rare show of public affection. "Let us know when you're ready to return. We'll send the jet for you."

Tristian gritted his teeth and tamped down a simmering flame of anger. *I've got to get used to this, Angie made her choice and is happy.* He gave a wan smile. Seeing them together, he hated to admit Hannah was right. "We gotta get going." He strode to the door, tugging Hannah behind him.

Holding the door open Hannah and Tristian said their goodbyes. Hannah promising to return soon. About to step into the limo, Tristian pulled up short. "Go ahead and get settled, I've got to talk with Angie before we leave. It wouldn't be right…"

Hannah nodded and slid into the seat. "I understand. I'm going to give my sister a call while I wait. Brandy will stave off my parents for a while." She pulled out her cell phone and dialed her sister's number.

"Good idea." Tristian sprinted back to the shop, yanked open the door and chimes sounded. "Angie, could I have a couple minutes of your time?"

"Sure, big brother." She remained next to Bruce, his arm around her.

"In private? It won't take long."

"Okay." She wriggled out of Bruce's grasp, led the way to the shop's office, and closed the door. "What's so important? I've got guests and customers out there for our—" The look on Tristian's face curtailed her rant.

"I should have told you years ago, and I'm so sorry." Tristian, hands behind his back, paced the floor, stopped, and gazed out the little window for a beat and took a deep breath. *What a mess.* When he returned to face her, he held her by the shoulders for a second then tugged her to him. "Please don't hate me."

She twisted her head to look at him, wrinkled up her nose and forehead. "I could never hate you. You gave up your dreams to raise me. Don't be ridiculous. But you are scaring me, so out with it."

He sucked in a breath, let it out slowly. "Our parents didn't die in a car accident. The coven was attacked the day we arrived for my induction celebration. It was an only brother left of a demon clan that Dad had terminated. The demon went looking for revenge and exacted it on Mom and Dad and most of their coven. The only reason I escaped is that I was in the basement helping Corra gather dishes, getting bowls, and making out with her when they arrived. And the demon clan didn't know Dad had a family until Mom came to his defense. I saw it all through my mind's eye. I froze, couldn't move. Couldn't get there in time." He hung his head, then dared to look in Angie's shocked face as she drew away from him.

She chewed on her bottom lip, anger flashed in her eyes, and she was silent for several beats. Tears gathered in her eyes and slid down her face, dripping from her jaw spilling on her new blouse. Yet she didn't move to wipe them away.

Finally, unable to stand it any longer, Tristian cradled her chin in his big hands and wiped the tears away with his thumbs. *She was so small. All I wanted to do was protect her.* "I'm so sorry, Ang." He took it as a good sign that she didn't pull away from him. "Say something."

In a halting voice, she began. "You were wrong not to tell me. I understand why you did what you did. When you attacked Bruce with such venom, I figured something more was going on. I was prepared for you to be angry, but to try to kill him. Endanger me? You were out of your fucking mind with rage. Strange for a man who'd never shown much emotion. I questioned Willow, Bruce, and others, but no one said anything. Then Tobi repeated the things you mumbled while unconscious."

"Yeah, I apparently spilled a lot of secrets during that time."

One corner of her mouth turned up in a half-smile. "I pieced the puzzle together and concluded it had something to do with our parents' death. Bruce told me what he was and what you did for a living before we ever got serious."

Tristian narrowed his eyes at Angie. "I should have been the one to tell you."

"Yes. You should have, but you didn't. I was afraid to go to you and ask with such strong feelings for Bruce racing through my body. He actually told me to go ask you. Bruce didn't want to tell me. But I can be persuasive." She quirked an eyebrow. "I was shocked beyond belief, at first. We talked at length about you keeping me a secret from him, just as Dad kept his family a secret from Bruce. That went a long way to explain why you were so willing to take up Dad's profession. The money was good and you had to support me. Of course, he didn't realize that. Figured you were out for revenge. Bruce wanted to circumvent your efforts through Paul's training. He owed it to Dad. Paul did a good job."

"Died doing a good job," Tristian said vehemently.

Angie shook her head. "Tristian, you've spent your entire adult life carrying burdens on your shoulders that were not your fault. Things happen. You made some bad choices, but for good reasons."

"So, what you are telling me is that you knew what happened."

"Not exactly until today, but close enough. I was planning to pay you a visit after you got home and clear the air. I'm glad you decided to handle it this way." She raised up on tiptoe, pulled his head down, and kissed his cheek. "Hannah's quite a woman. She's not going to put up with your shit." Angie laughed. "Don't let her get away."

"I don't plan to. Glad I came back. I didn't want to ruin your wedding with the truth. And I'm not going back to Maine yet. I have a surprise for Hannah. If your mate will agree."

"Oh, he'll agree." Angie breathed on her fingernails and rubbed them on her blouse. "What do you have in mind?"

Tristian laid out his plans, and she squealed with glee. "Hannah will love it." Angie grabbed his hand and tugged him toward the door, then skidded to a sudden stop, turned to face her brother. "I love you. But promise me no more secrets. They're deadly."

With a smirk, he said, "You got it. I've made the same promise to Hannah. Except for my assignments. She doesn't want to know."

"Understandable. But remember she is your confidant and will always have your back. Not that we all won't, but your relationship is different. Now let's go tell Bruce your plans."

"Angie, let me handle this, please."

"Okay, but don't muck it up."

Tristian strode out behind his sister. "Hey boss, the company jet might be gone a wee bit longer than anticipated. We're not going straight back to Maine. I hope you don't mind."

Bruce raised an eyebrow at Tristian's cockiness and glanced at Angie, who discreetly shook her head. "Okay, but make sure the pilot files a revised flight plan."

A puzzled Tristian stood in front of Bruce for a couple of beats, his mouth a gape. *Not the reaction I expected.* Then the light dawned. "She told you telepathically before we came out here."

Bruce smiled and winked. "I'll never tell."

Tristian grinned and headed for the door, grabbed

the handle, and turned back to the group. "Willow, this Caleb is the same one I met when you took me to dinner?"

"Of course. How many Caleb's do you know?" Willow shot back, with everyone murmuring in agreement.

He chuckled and waved exiting the door.

Once inside the limo, he proceeded to give Hannah a blow-by-blow description of everything, with one tiny exception, their destination.

"Well, I'm glad everything went well, and Angie was rescued without irreversible trauma. It will be good to get home." She sighed and relaxed against the smooth, white leather seats of the jet. The fresh lilacs in attached vases on the wall filled the plane with a pleasant aroma.

"About that." Tristian grinned outrageously.

Chapter Fourteen
Planned Detour and a Tropical Retreat Turns Stormy

Once they were settled inside the plane, Tristian twisted in his seat to face her. "We're not going home yet." The corners of his mouth turned up in a devilish grin.

"Where are we going?" A puzzled expression crossed her face as she shifted her attention from the window to him.

"It's a surprise, but I guarantee you are going to love it. It's a long flight, so..."

"When we arrive, I'd better call Ma and Da. And what about my boss? He's going to have a fit. How much longer will I be gone?"

"A week or so. Did you have a nice chat with your sister?"

"I did." Hannah grimaced. "I told her I was seeing someone; that's why she had such a hard time catching me at home."

Tristian frowned. "I'd rather you didn't..." He caught the spark of defiance in Hannah's eyes and reconsidered his reply. "Temporarily, I'd rather you keep our relationship under wraps, for now. I trust you, but I don't know your family. As you discovered, my line of work is—can be—dangerous. Not only for me but those closest to me. Protecting you, I can handle.

148

Anyone else—out of my area." He shook his head.

"Oh, I know. I didn't tell her your name or any information. Just that I was seeing someone, and I'd fill her in if it turned serious. Believe me, the last thing we need is her showing up on my porch, unannounced. She'll do exactly that, if I don't tell a little of what is going on."

"Isn't she going to want to check me out at some point? That's when it could be difficult, as I explained to you." He extended his hand, stroked her thigh.

She brushed his hand aside and turned to watch out the window.

"Hannah. We discussed all of this."

"I know, but my family is close, and we always keep in touch. Don't make me choose between you and them." She rested her head against the seat and continued to stare out the window.

More complications. How in the hell do people make a relationship work? He rubbed his eyes with thumb and forefinger, blinked a couple times, and closed them. The last few days had been difficult, to say the least. Leaving this conversation until they landed would be best. Resting his head against the seat, he drifted in and out of sleep, checking on Hannah frequently until she pushed her seat back and covered herself with a blanket.

He hadn't considered her family in the equation. Of course, she had a sister, brother, ma and da but were there anymore? Were they gryphons too? Sure they were. He shoved his fingers through his hair. Ireland is a land of myths, legends, and magic. Would keeping his identity a secret be problematic? A dad is always going to want to know how a suitor plans to support... *Aw shit...* He had so many sources over there, it would be impossible to keep a low profile. Unless...her family knew she worked in security, couldn't talk about her work. He'd claim the same. As long as he and Hannah stayed on this side of the pond, everything would work out fine. He could deal with her sister. Checking on Hannah again, her regular breathing indicated she was asleep, so he drifted off to sleep again.

Tristian jumped at the sound of the flight attendant's voice as she woke him. "We'll be at our destination within the hour, sir. Thought you'd like to know." He nodded and yawned, checked his phone for messages. There were none. He'd let his team know he would be out of the loop for a few days and left Ruben in charge. Bruce and Owen knew his whereabouts. He would check in with them periodically as required. This vacation with Hannah was just what he needed, though he'd taken more time off in the past couple of months than in his entire career. Relationships take work.

When the jet touched down at the Lihue Airport and taxied to a stop, Hannah's eyes blinked open. She covered a yawn with her petite hand and stretched. "So, are you going to tell me where we are?"

Tristian got to his feet and offered her a hand. "Nope, when you step off the plane, you'll know." He snickered as he moved her ahead of him while he reached for their stowed luggage. He nudged her with his elbow. "Day one of the tropical adventure."

Hannah hurried to the door of the plane and stepped out onto the stairs. A dark-skinned man waited on the tarmac next to a gleaming white SUV with a couple leis in his hand.

Tristian followed behind her and nodded at the

man. "Right on time! Thanks."

"Welcome to Kauai," the man said in a cheerful voice, keeping a blank expression on his face. He draped a beautiful purple and white orchid lei around her neck. He grinned and offered one to Tristian. "Sir, it's been a while, thought you might like…"

"Very funny, Daewon." Tristian leaned to the side waving the yellow and orange lei away. His gaze met hers, and he motioned to the man. "This is Daewon Tamaloa; he takes care of my property when I'm away. Daewon meet Hannah."

Her eyes rounded. "You own property here?"

"Yes."

As Daewon held the door open, Hannah snatched at the ring of flowers. "Oh, I'll take that one too." She inhaled deeply. "Heavenly."

Daewon chuckled and held the lei over her head, dropping it around her neck. "You look very festive ma'am."

"Oh, it's Hannah."

He cut his gaze to Tristian. "I've already got the rest of your luggage; ready to go?" Daewon asked.

"Yes, we are."

Tristian waited for Hannah to settle into the soft buff-colored leather seat of the vehicle. He scooted in beside her. "You hungry? We could stop somewhere and grab a bite."

"That's not advisable, sir. Kachina has lunch ready at the house. She spent most of yesterday getting the house ready for you. Did grocery shopping too."

"That's was nice of her." He wrapped his arm around Hannah's shoulders and leaned back against the seat.

Daewon glanced in the rearview mirror, surprise now etched on his face. "Yeah, I told her you were coming, but you didn't mention a guest. Knowing Kachina, she'll have bought and prepared enough food to feed an army."

"She usually does."

"Oh, by the way, we're having a big luau this evening. You're welcome to come."

"Maybe. We'll see how things go."

"Really? My wife won't believe..." His gaze met Tristian's in the rear view as he raised an eyebrow. "Never mind." He cleared his throat, turned the key in the ignition and his attention straight ahead on the road."

Tristian fingered a red curl along Hannah's face. He smiled at her murmured oh's and aw's as lush vegetation and tall trees blurred past the window. "It's green like back home, but much warmer. The breeze from the partially lowered window blew the curl out of Tristian's fingers, and she turned to smile at him. "My hair is a mess after the long plane ride, and my brush is packed. Didn't know we'd..."

He combed his fingers through her hair. "I think it looks just fine." Cupping her chin, he gently turned her toward him, brushed his lips over hers. "What would you like to do first?"

The vehicle slowed following a winding driveway up to a house with large bay windows facing the ocean, a porch ran the full length of the front. On it a swing and four chairs with matching blue and yellow swirled cushions occupied space between the windows.

Hannah sucked in her breath as she exited the SUV, her fingers twined in Tristian's. Walking up the path, the sun shone on the oval stained glass inset in the door depicting a bright fantasy scene, with a dark cloaked figure in the bottom right. "Is that you?" She pointed to the bottom of the glass.

He glanced at her then the door and cackled. "No, well, never really thought about it. Meant to show even in a mystical carefree world, danger lurks."

"You." She giggled and ran her finger over the glass. "It's warm to the touch, and there is something else."

"A protection spell is woven in the glass. Surprised you could feel it." He unlocked the door, stepped inside, and waved a hand over the alarm panel.

"I have many talents." She shot him a saucy smile and sashayed by him only to stop mid-stride and stare at the rooms before her. A dark leather and cream sofa sat against one wall, with a matching lounger a few feet away. Carved wooden end tables graced one edge of the couch and beside the chair, large brightly-colored floor pillows were scattered in front of a fireplace. The circular staircase wound its way to a second story loft. It was an open concept with the kitchen separated from the living room by only an archway and breakfast bar and stools. A short petite woman with miles of shiny black hair whirled around and started toward them. She paused and looked from Tristian to Hannah, her gaze landed on Daewon as he brought the luggage in behind them.

"I didn't know you were bringing…who's…you never…"

"Kachina." Tristian strode forward and hugged the woman. "Now could you finish at least one sentence?" He laughed, releasing her, and squeezed her shoulders one more time before turning to Hannah. "This is—Hannah—she's become an important part of my life. Hannah, Kachina is Daewon's wife and keeper of my castle."

Kachina finally found her voice. "I guess so—in all the years."

"Things have changed," Tristian said in a firm voice and pointed to the loft, hesitated then jerked his chin toward the floor. "Daewon put those bags at the bottom of the stairs. I'll see to them later."

"It's no problem." He sprinted up the stairs with suitcases in hand then returned.

"If you two are having a luau this evening, you better get back home and tend to it. I've got things handled here. I really appreciate your help." Tristian looked around the kitchen at the spread Kachina prepared and let out a low whistle. "You fixed all this for me? Did you expect me to bring an entourage?"

She shrugged then put hands on her hips. "I certainly didn't expect—"

Daewon ambled over to his wife and threw an arm around her shoulder. "After all these years, we never know what to expect."

"You're welcome to grab a bite before you go home."

"Sounds good. I haven't eaten all day. Too busy." He reached out and scooped up a Hawaiian Sweet Roll, added pork, and took a large bite. His wife glared at him.

He shrugged one shoulder. "What. He offered." His expression clouded over for a beat then he beamed. "Guess what? They might come to the luau tonight."

His wife's glance shifted from her husband to

Tristian. "Well, there's a first time for everything. You two will have a grand time. Unless."

"I said maybe."

"Oh, it's sounds like fun. We'll just take a little nap and be good to go." Hannah's effervescent attitude and smile were contagious.

Tristian nodded. "We'll probably see you tonight." Thinking back, he couldn't remember ever going to one of their luaus, though he was always invited. In fact, usually he stayed to himself, this place was his sanctuary, a place to unwind, relax without interruption from anyone, and he liked it that way. *Almost anyone.* Yet, he was elated at the thought of taking Hannah to the luau. *Huh?*

Daewon smirked. "We'll leave you to your nap." He wriggled his eyebrows at his wife and grabbed her arm, tugging her toward the door. "See you tonight."

As they walked out the door, Kachina whispered, "What if she comes?"

"Shhhh…I bet he can handle it." Daewon stopped, pivoted, and tossed the keys to Tristian. "Almost forgot. You'll be driving yourself this trip?"

"Yep." Tristian reached up and caught the keys, turned to see Hannah narrowing her eyes at him.

"Is there something I should know?"

He took her hand and led her up the winding staircase. "I never pretended I was a monk. There have been—several women, but none mattered. They were well aware of that. Until you."

She stiffened and yanked her hand out of his when they reached the top of the stairs. "How many are several?"

Tristian rolled his eyes and blew out a breath. "I

enjoy women and didn't see a reason not to indulge. It was a release for me after grueling assignments. That's all."

"Am I—"

His eyes steeled; he reached for Hannah and took her mouth with a savage intensity. Her lips parted in surprise, and his tongue thrust inside taunting, teasing, tasting. She struggled for a moment then succumbed to his domination, curving into him. His mouth softened, the tip of his tongue traced her full lips. He nibbled on her bottom lip, felt her heart thunder against his chest, her pulse race. He enjoyed arousing her. Raising his mouth from hers, Tristian gazed into her eyes. "No woman has ever mattered to me, except you. Now, I don't want to visit the subject again."

"What if we meet some of your conquests?"

"I'll handle it. You can look them in the eye and know I'm yours. I've seen that domineering look you have. Use it." Nuzzling into her neck, he inhaled her warm fragrant scent and let his hand slip to cup her butt cheek, pressed her against his excitement. "How about that nap?"

She slithered against him. "You have too many clothes on."

"As do you." With a quick flick of his hand, they were both naked.

Chapter Fifteen
Commitment Decisions Can't Wait Forever

Muted orange, yellow, and red spread across the wall as Hannah opened her eyes. The sun's reflection sank low in the sky as its warm glow seeped onto the hardwood floor. She rolled against Tristian and breathed a kiss on his bare chest. "If we are going to make the luau, we better get up."

"Huh? Oh...yeah, the luau. Positive you want to go?" His strong arm snaked around her waist, fingers feathered along her soft skin, caressing, teasing.

"Is that all you think about?" she teased.

"Yes, when I'm with the sexiest woman alive." He brushed his lips over hers. "But if we must get up, we must. Daewon seemed quite pleased that we would be there."

"Kachina too. Don't socialize much. Do you?"

"No." Tristian pushed up to a sitting position, sliding her into his lap. "If you're sure," he said in a low sensual rumble.

In answer, she wiggled out of his arms and stood beside the bed. "What should I wear? Didn't pack for the beach."

"What you have on is fine with me."

She picked up a pillow and tossed it at him. "You don't want the whole world to see me naked, do you?"

"You've a point." He swung his feet off the bed

and sat on the edge. "I guess I could have told you where we were going, but that would've spoiled the surprise." Sitting quietly for a moment, while his gaze wandered over her, he shifted and snapped his fingers. Colorful Hawaiian sarongs, bikini sets, and short outfits covered the bed, along with two pairs of sandals. "That should keep you in clothes until we can go shopping." Tristian picked up a sarong in aqua, with yellow and orange florals. Held it up for her to see. "This would be perfect for the luau." He cleared his throat. "If you like it."

Eyes rounded, she stared at the clothes on the bed, then glanced at the turquoise sandals on the floor. "You've quite an eye for style. Those strappy sandals match the dress perfectly. Normally, I like to pick out my own clothes, but…" She stepped to him and threw her arms around his neck. "The clothes are perfect. Thank you."

"And you will have a chance to do that. But right now, we're a bit pressed for time." He picked out light tan shorts, his favorite Hawaiian shirt that happened to match her dress and slid his feet into worn leather sandals. "I'm ready."

She blew raspberries at him and shimmied into the sarong, surveying herself in the mirror. "Fits great. How did you know?"

He cocked an eyebrow. "Really? I've had my hands all over you and…"

"Never mind." She interrupted. "You use magic more than most. Aren't there rules?"

"Magic is a necessary part of my job. I risk my life to keep the magic stabilized in a mortal world and the creatures from tipping the balance from good to evil. If

I use a bit more than most for personal reasons, not gain, the effect on me is less because of the perils I endure to keep it safe. Does that make sense?"

"Sort of." She brushed her hair and put on the sandals. "I'm ready. How do I look?"

"Delectable."

She swatted at him and grinned. "You are different here. I like the fun, carefree Tristian."

"A combination of circumstances causes that effect. Don't get used to it." He slipped his arm around her waist and guided her to the door, stopped to set the alarm, and closed the door behind them.

****

Walking through the door at Daewon and Kachina's house was like being thrown into a blender without warning. Tristian scanned the area, seeing several familiar faces, his arm tightened around Hannah. When a short, stocky man with black hair, who appeared just a bit tipsy, clasped him on the shoulder, Tristian paused, hand fisted, then glared at him. The man removed his hand immediately and shuffled away.

Beaming, Daewon waved from across the room and pushed his way through the crowd. "So glad you actually made it." He shook Tristian's hand and kissed Hannah on the cheek. "Drinks are over there." He pointed in the direction of the tiny kitchen. "Snacks are out on the patio. That's where everyone is." Motioning for them to follow him through the crowd, he wound his way to the kitchen.

Hannah laughed and smiled. Tristian's arm remained tight around her waist as they maneuvered through the throng of people dressed mostly in traditional Hawaiian garb.

Once in the kitchen, Daewon turned grinning like a Cheshire cat. "What'll it be? Wine, beer, soda, mixed drinks, we got it all."

"I'll take one of those micro beers." It had been a long time since he'd drank socially. He always preferred to be in control and prepared for anything. But tonight felt different.

"Red wine, please," Hannah said. Her body bounced to the rock and roll music blaring from a set of speakers out on the patio. "Dance?"

"Used to…" He surveyed the dance area outside as a petite hand with blood red nails snaked around his waist.

"Oh, he can dance, and that's not all." She peered out from under long dark lashes. "Don't let him tell you different." A tiny woman with jet black hair to her waist, a white orchid arranged above her left ear snuggled up to him. "How long you here for?"

"A while," Tristian said in a clipped voice.

"I see you're busy tonight. How about tomorrow?" She reached up, ran her fingers up his neck, and through his hair, then ran the tip of her tongue around her red lips.

He circled his fingers around her wrist, removed her hand from his hair, then untangled himself from the grip of her other arm around his waist. "Coral, things have changed. Hannah is my permanent companion." He tightened his arm around Hannah, nuzzled below her ear, and brushed a lingering kiss across her cheek.

The woman's eyes went wide. Her full lips formed an "O." When her gaze shifted from him to Hannah and back, in an awed voice Coral purred, "You're off the market? She took you…" Her eyes narrowed, and she waved her hand with polished nails in a dismissive gesture. "She meets—all your needs?"

He raised an eyebrow and gave Hannah a smoldering look, then cut his gaze back to Coral. "More than. So yes, I'm off the market."

"We'll see how long that lasts," she snarked, turned, and flounced toward the door, stopping only a beat to glance over her shoulder at him. "You know where to find me when you change your mind." She latched on to a tall good-looking man, his Hawaiian shirt unbuttoned, well-muscled chest bared, and she slithered against him. As they made their way outside, she paused several times to peer at Tristian while whispering to several other women in passing.

"Well, that was interesting," Hannah said. "Popular, with the ladies, huh?"

"Never led you to believe I was celibate." A sensuous smile curved his lips as he twined their fingers and sauntered toward the dance area. *Let's see just how turned on I can get you.* He twirled her into his arms and undulated to the beat of a Latin Salsa. To his surprise, she shimmied and shook her assets stirring his blood as he had hoped to hers.

She batted her eyes at him as if to say, two can play at that game. He nodded, up for the challenge.

Hannah's sexy salsa moves kept the men's attentions. Tristian snickered, that display should keep Coral at bay. Rather than being jealous, he rather liked the looks she got from the males, especially since he was the one taking her home.

Before the dance ended, the other women took back their men's attention with a good-natured sensual dance competition. When the music turned to a more traditional Hawaiian beat encouraging a hula contest, he drew her into his arms moving to a secluded area where he took her mouth with a fiery possession. She returned his kiss of passion even as he raised his mouth from hers. "Better get back to the party, don't want to draw attention."

She snorted. "Too late, you already had everyone's attention, especially the women with your dirty dancing display."

Waggling a finger in front of her face, he gave her a wicked grin. "Oh, babe, it takes two to tango or rather salsa." Chuckling, he grasped her hand and ambled back to where the food was being served.

Hannah filled her plate with Kalua Pua'a, a bit of Teriyaki Chicken, and baked sweet potato. Tristian piled his plate high with baked Mahi-Mahi, chicken long rice, and taro rolls. Both avoided the Poi but sampled the Lomilomi Salmon.

The crescent moon hung overhead, a few thin clouds floated across the sky as the torch flames wavered in the breeze. As the night wore on, the party-goers became rowdy. Tristian found Daewon and Kachina in the kitchen watching a weather warning on the television. "Great party, the food is fantastic. Afraid we need to call it a night, going hiking early morning."

"See what you've been missing all these years?" Daewon chided then returned his attention to the weather warning. "They said that tropical storm was going to miss us, but now, it's headed straight for us, landfall after midnight. Guess we'll have to wrap the party up early."

Tristian looked out in the back at the shoving match between a couple men and raised a brow.

"Thanks again for the invitation." He jerked his chin toward the altercation. "You might want to monitor your guests a bit more closely."

"Shit." Daewon dropped the tongs in the sink and raced out the door. "That's enough. You're going to pay for the damage, and you two are outa here." With the help of a couple of large men, Daewon escorted the unruly guests out of sight.

Kachina rolled her eyes. "Time to cut off the alcohol." She threw an arm around Hannah and grabbed Tristian's shoulder. "Thanks so much for coming."

"Our pleasure," Hannah said.

Tristian gave the woman a quick hug then touched his hand to the small of Hannah's back guiding her toward the door.

"Might want to keep an eye on the weather," Kachina called after them.

"Will do," Tristian said, just as the wind gust caught the door and slammed it behind him.

Glancing at the sky, he shook his head. "Hard to believe there's that kind of storm brewing." He opened Hannah's door and waited for her to settle in the seat before closing the door and moving to the driver's side.

After arriving at the house, Hannah toed off her shoes. "How about a moonlight stroll on the beach?" She wiggled her toes. "I like the warm sand on my bare feet."

Slipping out of his sandals, he followed her to the back door, noting the breeze had died down. Seeing how antsy she was, he said, "You go on ahead, I'll be right there." Grabbing a beach blanket from the closet, he sprinted out the door to catch up with her.

She paused, stood on tiptoe, and kissed his lips,

then ran behind a rock, tossed her clothes to him. With a whoosh of air, she was airborne. Powerful wings stroked as her gryphon form soared into the star-strewn sky. Tristian spread the blanket out over the sand, stretched out with his hands behind his head, and watched her effortless flight.

When the wind whipped up again, Hannah gracefully landed on the sand beside him, tucking her wings and batting her huge blue eyes. With a blur of copper, she shimmered morphing into human form. She snatched at her neatly folded dress, but he was faster and held them out of reach.

"I like what you have on." He got to his feet and pulled her to him, wrapping his arms around her, he dropped her sarong. She ducked and grabbed her dress quickly shimmying into it.

"I am not walking back to the house naked for your benefit." Hannah huffed.

He captured her breath as he covered her mouth with his then murmured against her lips, "Your teasing me is done." In one smooth movement, he swept her into his arms. She slid her arms around his neck as he carried her back to the house. Large raindrops plopped on the ground around them. With a thought the door opened, and he closed it with his foot. Gently he lowered her to her feet, caressing his lips across her damp cheek, down her neck, and trailing kisses lower.

His hand moved to the back of her neck untying her one shoulder strap allowing the top of her dress to slide slowly to her waist baring her beautiful firm rounded breasts. He leaned down caressing her breast, sucking gently first one nipple then the other. A deep groan rumbled from his throat.

She leaned her head back and moaned softly. The wind driven rain pounded against the window.

Cupping her face in his rough hands, he tilted it up, their gaze met. "Hannah, you are so beautiful. You take my breath away."

Without hesitation, she reached for his shirt, already unbuttoned, sliding it off his shoulders and tossed it on the floor. Thunder rumbled outside, a few beats later a loud crash. "I thought Hawaii didn't have thunderstorms. Do you have anything to do with this?"

"With the storm, no. Hawaii does have thunderstorms with a tropical depression. Not to worry, I've magical protection surrounding this house." He snickered nuzzling her neck while reaching around her back and untied her sarong. It slid down her curves and pooled at her feet. *I've never had a conversation like this while making love. Another first.*

"Amused?" She reached for his zipper, he tried to playfully bat her hand away, but she was having none of it. Pulling the zipper down slowly, the pants slipped over his hips, her foot pushed them to the floor, where he kicked them out of the way.

Caressing the skin of her thigh, his hand trailed slowly to the crotch of her moist panties. Fingers curled around the edges feeling her heat, and he tugged the panties to her ankles. She stepped out of them.

As his lips traced a sensuous path to her ecstasy, she moaned and slipped her fingers inside his waistband, stroking then slowly slid his underwear to the floor. Completely naked, he gathered her into his arms and carried her to the whirlpool tub. In one fluid movement, he slid into the tub with her. They continued to explore, to arouse, and pleasure each other as the warm fragrant water pulsed around them.

Lightning streaked across the night sky as thunder continued to rock the beach house. Stepping out of the tub, Hannah toweled off and slipped into a black lace teddy that left nothing to the imagination. Just the way he liked it. Tristian slowly slipped into the black silk bikini briefs she enjoyed him wearing. Usually, he was all about getting her naked, but tonight it was about enjoying each other, not just satisfaction.

Hannah smiled seductively as she curved her body against him, her lips pressed firmly to his. They moved to the bedroom and lay on the bed mesmerized by the storm through the wall of windows facing the ocean. Waves crashed onto the white sand beach sending sprays of mist high into the air.

Lovemaking began slow, tongues teasing and tasting, hands touching, caressing, exploring, and arousing intimate sensations. The sheer, raw, primitive power of the storm surrounded them fervently fueling needs and desires.

Kisses were hot, deep imitations of their bodies intent and desires. His lips moved from her luscious mouth to her breast, tongue teasing and gently stroking while his other hand massaged her most intimate parts then he slid down.

She arched against him. "Oh…Tristian…Please."

His fingers slipped under the teddy into her heat and caressed until she softened, melted, ready to make love for the first time. The commitment wasn't as scary as life without her. *Tonight, I'll take her completely and make her beg for more. Tomorrow can take care of itself. With a wave of his hand, the teddy and briefs disappeared.*

Hannah moaned wrapping her long beautiful legs around his, "Tristian, please I want to feel you inside me."

"Patience…my love…soon. If you are sure. Let's just enjoy each other for a little while longer," he murmured against her ear.

"I've never been surer of anything in my life," she whispered against his lips.

A flash of silvery lightning filled the room making her moist skin shimmer as he hovered over her. Thunder rocked their room once more as he grasped her hips and thrust into her slow and easy at first then hard, fast and deep. The strobe effect of the lightning flashes caused a sensation of slow motion.

The storm directly overhead now, as the rain beat against the roof. The wind shook and bent the trees outside the windows. Lightning pierced the night sky, again and again, followed immediately by rumbles of thunder that shook the walls around them.

Feeling her shiver beneath his hands, "It's okay sweetheart; we're safe." He gathered her into his arms tighter, her hips arched against him.

"Oh Tristian," she moaned, "take me, NOW." She screamed, ripples begin from her center caressing, and stroking. One final thrust into her quivering depth and their shouts of ecstasy were lost in the thunder rolling around them.

Panting, chests heaving, he savored the immense satisfaction as contentment and peace flowed between them. Wrapping his arms around Hannah, he spooned against her, legs tangled together he fervently hoped this had not been a mistake as sleep overtook them.

When Tristian opened his eyes, the bright sunlight

streamed through the gaps in the curtains warming the room. Insects buzzed outside the screened windows opened halfway. Hannah leaned up on one elbow, her soft cornflower blue eyes watching him intently. "Good morning," she purred. "What a fantastic night."

"My exact thoughts." He leaned up and brushed his lips over hers.

She eagerly returned the kiss as her stomach gurgled loudly. Embarrassed, a giggle escaped her lips. "I guess—I'm hungry?"

He grabbed her up and draped her across his body moving sensually imparting exactly what he was hungry for. "Me too, but not…"

Hannah nuzzled his neck, teased the hollow of his throat with the tip of her tongue and breathed a kiss there. Her stomach gave an extended growl.

"Okay, okay, guess we better feed you." Tristian snickered and kissed her lips once more before sitting up, still unable to take his gaze from his beautiful woman. *What to do about the commitment? It would have to be addressed soon.*

They spent the next several days playing tourist. Tristian drove the Na Pal Coast Highway to show Hannah the dramatic cliffs and pinnacles. Then they spent a couple days on the beach under trees in lounge chairs catching up on email and business.

Hannah packed a lunch for a hike up to Sleeping Giant Ridge. On Kauai's East side between Wailua and Kappa, the Nounou Mountain range stretched toward the sky, also known as Sleeping Giant.

As they got closer to the range, Tristian stopped the vehicle and got out pointing to a ridge. When Hannah stepped out and joined him, he said, "If you use a little imagination, it looks like a human figure lying on his back. Hawaiian legends claim a giant was tricked by villagers into eating a lot of rocks hidden in fish and poi. Sleepy from the meal, the giant took a nap and hasn't woken since."

Squinting, Hannah shaded her eyes with her hand and stared at the ridge for several minutes. "I don't."

He eased behind her and curled his hand around her waist, then rested his other arm on her shoulder, pointing forward. "No imagination?"

"I do so have a lot of imagination." She followed the direction his finger pointed and tilted her head, "Oh...oh...I see now."

Taking the opportunity while her head tilted, he brushed his lips over her cheek and kissed her nose. "Let's get going, the Nounou Trail will take us to the top of Sleeping Giant. It's a scenic two-mile hike, and we can eat lunch there."

"Provided the giant doesn't wake up. I didn't pack enough to feed him." She broke into gales of laughter.

Back behind the wheel, he followed Halelilo Road in Wailua to the trailhead, where they climbed out of the vehicle. He strapped on the backpack with lunch and headed up the trail.

After the fun filled day, they returned home and showered. Tristian slipped into light green swim shorts, and Hannah wiggled into a red bikini. He grabbed a bottle of wine. She arranged cheese and crackers in a dish. They strolled down the beach pausing at the lounge chairs arranged beneath a group of trees. Easing down onto one of the chairs, Tristian wrapped his arm around her, and they enjoyed the spectacular sunset.

When the moon rose, Hannah walked toward the

water. "Up for a moonlight swim?"

"Of course." Taking her hand, he waded into the water beside her. He enjoyed moonlight swims and relaxing on the beach with her more than he ever thought possible. With Hannah in his life, it was easier to understand why his father took the chance to marry and have a family. Somehow, he had to find a way to make this work.

The day before leaving the islands, he drove the Waimea Canyon Drive on the west side of Kauai. "This is Hawaii's answer to the Grand Canyon in Arizona."

"I've been to the Grand Canyon once with friends," Hannah said. "On a smaller scale, this has the same panoramic views of crested buttes, rugged crags, and deep valley gorges, but the colors and the ambiance are different. The Grand Canyon feels ancient—it's hard to describe almost sacred in areas."

Tristian continued down the main road and pulled off at Waimea Canyon Overlook. Hannah stepped out of the vehicle and sucked in a breath at the views of Kauai's dramatic interior. He stood behind her, leaned over taking a strand of her hair coiling it around his finger and whispered against her ear. "Beautiful, isn't it?" After they returned to the SUV, he followed the road into the mountains, ending at KoKee State Park. Out of the vehicle's console, he tugged a wrinkled map and handed it to her. "We have several trails to choose from. Where would you like to start?"

She reviewed the map and pointed to the Kalalau trail along the Napali Coast.

"That's an eleven-mile hike. But we have time to do the first two miles, which leads to Hanakapiai Beach and has amazing views of Kauai's North Shore."

"Good enough," Hannah added to her growing photo collection of Kauai as they hiked the trail. Upon returning to the vehicle, she took her shoes and socks off. "I feel like I've hiked the entire island over these two weeks." She wiggled her toes and relaxed against the seat.

"You probably have. It's the best way to see Kauai since ninety percent of the island is inaccessible by road. That's why I like it."

Arriving back home, Tristian suggested they spend their last evening on the beach watching the sunset and finish their final bottle of wine. Hannah nodded in agreement.

Daewon would pick them up before the crack of dawn and drive them to the airport where The Wycked Hair's private jet would be waiting. This trip had confirmed Tristian's feelings, now he had to figure out how to make it all work.

Chapter Sixteen
Homecoming to Unexpected Guests and Problems

Carefully, Hannah picked her way up the stairs to the private jet and felt Tristian's mood change as he walked beside her. The carefree, fun man she'd spent the last two weeks with was gone. Laptop in hand, he was somber and thoughtful, with an air of foreboding mixed in. Holding her laptop in one hand, purse slung over her shoulder, she followed him into the plane. *I should have discussed our relationship situation before we left the islands.*

She touched his hand as they settled into the roomy leather seats for the flight home. Turning to her, a smile curled his kissable lips. The man was sex on a stick when he wanted to be, but now it was only a companionable smile. She could feel him at war with himself again, as his professional persona took over. Learning to live with both Tristians would take some doing, but she was up to the task. If only he'd let her.

The decision to consummate their relationship had been the toughest thing she'd ever done. Tying herself to a warlock for life, whether he committed to her or not, may have been the worst decision she'd ever made. Still, she could only hope that he'd come around. Telling her parents would not be easy. Her sister—that was entirely different matter. As children, she'd been Brandy's confidant. When they reached adulthood, she'd always told her sister everything and vice versa. Brandy would know if she held anything back. What was she supposed to tell her? That she'd fallen in love with not only a warlock, but an assassin for the Demon Overlord of the Western Hemisphere. *Yeah, that would bring Brandy running.* The last call Hannah had made to Brandy went to voice mail, so Hannah left a message about leaving on vacation and would call when she returned. *The coward's way out.*

Usually, they talked at least once a week, more often depending on what was going on in their lives. It had been nearly a month since…

As if Brandy felt her turmoil, Hannah's phone chimed an incoming text message from her sister. "Where the hell are you?" Hannah bit her lip and glanced over at Tristian bent over his laptop working. His forehead creased in concentration.

His gaze met hers giving her a slight grin. "Anything wrong?"

She shook her head and he returned his attention to the laptop. Her fingers skimmed over the phone texting back. "On my way home from Hawaii. I'll call and tell you all about it tomorrow." Brandy texted back. "U better, Ma & Da are worried sick. Need to call them also."

"K" she typed in then held the phone to her chest and sighed. *Time to pay the piper.* A tear trickled down her cheek.

Tristian reached up and wiped the tear away with his thumb. She didn't know how long he'd been watching her, but his eyes were clouded with concern as he twisted in his seat to face her.

"No secrets," he said as a firm reminder.

Still holding her phone, her hand came to rest on her lap. Glancing at her phone, she raised it up again. "It's my sister." Hannah paused and pursed her lips. "And Ma and Da. Haven't talked to them since D.C. Brandy knows something's up. She has a talent for knowing these things." Raising her gaze to meet Tristian's, she said, "I've got to tell her about us."

Tristian frowned. "Okay—tell her you've met someone special."

Hannah rolled her eyes. "Yeah, that will work. She'll want to know all about you. I wouldn't put it past her to fly out to Misty Harbor unannounced to meet you."

"That would be a problem. Right now, Angie and Willow want you back in D.C. Bruce is chomping at the bit for my return. Apparently, the reports filed while I was gone are…problematic."

"I can't—I won't—alienate my family. Not even for you. Nor will I lie to them. Then there is the little matter of my job, the citizenship test. My life doesn't revolve completely around you."

Tristian glowered at the computer screen, closed it and raked his fingers through his hair. "I'm well aware of that. But as far as your family is concerned, it's too dangerous to drag them into to my—our world. I'm still working out how to keep you safe—your extended family… I can't. Not yet."

She stiffened, clenched her teeth. "So, what then?"

His fingers tapped lightly on the top of his black laptop. "Tell them about us. Tell them you don't know where the relationship is going yet. And you don't want to jinx it by divulging too much."

"That's a lie. Our relationship has gone a lot farther

than that, and you know it. So will Brandy."

Tristian unfastened his seatbelt, pushed up from his seat, and paced. On the second pass, he paused in front of her, blew out a breath, and plopped in his seat. Shifting, he faced her and took her hands in his, gaze locked on her. "Okay, how about you tell Brandy I've asked you to attend my sister's wedding. That alone should tell her we are serious. Let her know you are nervous about it and will be leaving soon. Remind her you have the citizenship test to take the day after tomorrow. Suggest that when you get back from the wedding, she should come for a visit."

"Really?" Can she visit? You'll meet her?" She eyed him suspiciously.

His devilish grin was back, making her feel more at ease. "Of course. By that time, I hope to have worked out a few changes I'm considering with Bruce. No promises, but it's a start. Right?" Tristian's gaze flicked over her cheeks, her eyes, and lingered on her mouth.

She moistened her lips with the tip of her tongue. "I hope so. My sister is tenacious and protective."

"Oh, I have no doubt. But you're the same with those you love. I can see it. Family trait?"

"Probably." She drew her bottom lip through her front teeth. "It just might work, for now. But Ma and Da."

"Same story, go ahead and tell them I took you to Hawaii to relax. If what I do for a living comes up." He paused. "We'll say I work security and can't talk about my job. Compare it to your cyber security. Imply they understand things like that. Most people won't admit they don't."

"Jetting off to Hawaii with you will tell them our

relationship is serious, without telling them about the wedding. I have to tell them you are not one of us. Trust me, they'll ask."

"I can't believe that'll come as a surprise to them." He stroked the couple days' stubble on his chin with his thumb and forefinger. "If a gryphon was what you were looking for, you'd stayed in Ireland."

Her eyebrow quirked up, and she gave him a hard stare.

"Look, I've traveled the Western Hemisphere for years on business. Dealt with numerous paranormal creatures but never ran across a gryphon. Until you, I thought they were mythical creatures." He shrugged and opened his laptop. "You proved me wrong."

Hannah grinned, opened her laptop, and wrote an email to her sister. Giving her enough information, Hannah hoped might satisfy her, so Brandy wouldn't bombard her with questions that she couldn't answer. Finished, Hannah closed the laptop and snuggled against Tristian, her eyelids drooping.

When the plane touched down in Misty Harbor, Hannah stepped out onto the stairs of the plane and glanced around in the crisp night air. She spotted Tristian's sports car parked under a nearby light. "How'd that get here?"

He smirked winding an arm around her waist. "Magic."

She raised an eyebrow and gave him a dubious stare. "Yeah, right."

"I asked Sean to leave it here on his way home. Figured we'd arrived late, didn't want to inconvenience him."

"So, you had him go out of his way to drop off

your car. How did he get home?"

"Rena, his wife, is my housekeeper. I imagine she followed him here and picked him up." A knowing grin spread across his face. "Sean sure loves to drive that car." He shrugged. "I like to keep my employees happy. That's one thing Bruce and I agree on. Good help is hard to find. Treat them good, hopefully, they'll be loyal."

"That would be important in your line of work." Hannah trotted over to the sports car, reached for the handle as Tristian slid his hand under hers, and opened the door.

"I don't see why you can't wait for me to open the door." He held it open while she slid in, then closed it quietly.

When he folded himself in the driver's seat, she smiled at him. "Too independent for your likes?"

His eyebrow winged up as the car rumbled to life. "Obviously not." He touched the gas, and the vehicle sped down the road. "But Dad always insisted on opening the doors for Mom and Angie. Part of being a gentleman, he always said."

"Okay, I see your point." She jerked her head to the right. "Hey, you missed the turn to my house."

"I wasn't going to your house."

"Well, it's not up to you. I want to go home. I need to study for the test tomorrow and…"

"You don't have any food in the house. I can help you study, but I don't think you need it. In D.C., you had everything down pat. Anyway my house should be fully stocked, if we want a bite before we go to…"

She groaned. "My fridge is going to smell to high heaven."

Waving a hand dismissively, he turned up the road to his home. "Not exactly. When we left for Hawaii, I had Rena pop over to your cottage and clean out the fridge."

Jerking around in her seat, she stared in disbelief. "Without my permission and you don't have a key?"

"Don't need one. Rena is half demon and witch."

"But still it's my cottage, you need permission to... You had no right." *Pick your battles. That's what Da always said.* Her temper vibrated, but she kept her mouth clamped shut in a thin line. Now was not the time to start an argument. The discussion about privacy would have to wait until her brain was alert. *Besides, he had a point the fridge would stink horribly.* She grimaced wrinkling her nose. *The deed was done. I'll make sure it wouldn't happen again.* Her jaw popped as she covered a yawn with the back of her hand.

At Hannah's less than pleased expression, he said, "It was my fault you left in a hurry with no idea how long you'd be gone. Sorry about that. But then our impromptu vacation, I thought you'd appreciate not coming home to that mess."

"True, but you need to respect my privacy." She gave him a withering look. "A locked door in my world means you have to ask permission to enter, not barge in with magic because you want. Understand?"

"Got it." He nodded and squinted at shadows moving across his porch.

"You just expect me to spend the night with you?" she asked incredulously.

"I've learned not to expect anything where you're concerned. Don't know about you, but I'm exhausted, so a snack and bed sounds pretty good."

"Yes, I guess it does. Tomorrow…"

"I'll take you to the cottage, if that's what you want." His gaze flicked from her to the porch.

"I'd like to be well rested for my exam."

"Understood." Tristian turned up the driveway to his home. The porch light was on, and two individuals were seated on his Adirondack chairs. He pinched the bridge of his nose. "This is an unexpected turn of events."

Hannah, who was watching out the window glad to see familiar surroundings, followed his gaze. "Oh…it's Willow…and who's the young man with her?"

"That would be Caleb, her fiancé. A better question is why are they on my porch at…" He glanced at the digital clock on the dash. "…Two o'clock in the damn morning?" His voice held a hint of irritation.

"Bet we're about to find out." When the car stopped in front of his house, Hannah waited patiently for Tristian to open her door. *What a pain.* Taking his hand, she stepped out of the car. He turned abruptly and strode toward the door.

"To what do I owe the pleasure." He extended his hand to Caleb first, then gave Willow a nod. "Got your days and nights mixed up?"

"We didn't expect you home 'til tomorrow."

"Obviously." Tristian unlocked the door, stood to the side, waved the luggage into the house, then looked from Willow to Caleb and back. "So, are you spending the night? Or…"

"Guess we better go to Mom and Dad's house." Willow said with such reluctance that Hannah sidled up to Willow and asked, "What's wrong?"

"I can tell you what's wrong," Tristian said

grumpily. "Birch and Freesia are not as understanding as anticipated."

"Sort of," Willow admitted.

"Come on in. We'll put the coffee on and hash this out. Unless you just want to spend the night and settle it tomorrow."

At Willow's hopeful expression, Hannah nudged Tristian into the kitchen. "Why would her parents object? Birch and Freesia are her parents. Correct?"

"Yes. Because Caleb is a Satyr. Mixing bloodlines in the magical world is frowned on to say the least. Things are changing, but…" He scooped coffee in the maker, filled the pot with water, and poured it into the reserve, then quickly slid the pot underneath.

"So, there is a problem with warlocks and gryphons?" she whispered, opening cupboards looking for mugs.

He huffed out a breath. "No…not exactly…hell, if a demon overlord can take a witch for a mate, anything is possible." He shoved his fingers through his hair. "But as Bruce's position afforded him leeway, you bet mine does too." Tristian pointed to a cabinet where he kept the mugs.

"I see." She opened the cupboard door and pulled out four mugs, set them beside the coffee maker.

"No, you don't." He hesitated for a couple beats. "One problem at a time. Let's take care of Willow and Caleb, so we can get to bed. Okay?" Opening the refrigerator, he pulled out a covered dish with a note, read the note, and glanced at the covered tortilla warmer on the counter.

"Maybe best if I go on up to bed? Got a long day tomorrow." Hannah sighed.

"Suit yourself, but you're the one that asked what's wrong." He shot back. "And you'll miss out on the best enchilada casserole in the world." Holding the dish up, he looked at the microwave, then passed a hand over the container. The mouthwatering aroma wafted from the dish as steam rose around the edges of the lid.

She eyed him speculatively. "And you couldn't tell Willow was upset?"

He shrugged. "Sure. But I don't stick my nose where it doesn't belong. In my business, that will get you killed." Dark liquid streamed into the glass pot and the aroma of freshly brewed coffee mixed with enchiladas filled the kitchen.

Hands on hips, she glared at him. "I see through that tough façade you project."

"Okay...yes I knew she was upset, and I planned to address the issue, hopefully in the morning—if necessary—But obviously, that isn't going to work." He waved the food under her nose, set it on the table, along with plates and silverware.

Hannah threw up her hands. "I give up. Good thing my test is late tomorrow afternoon. I'm starved." She paused and poked her finger in his chest. "And you are going to help me do one last quick study."

"Of course." He winked at her, filled the mugs with coffee, and put them on the table.

"Hey, did Rena leave her enchilada casserole for you?" Willow said gliding into the kitchen, Caleb followed.

"Yep," Tristian said smugly, waving to the kitchen table. "So, the real reason you are camped on my porch is revealed." Waggling a finger at them, he said. "You two owe me." He glowered at them and pulled the chair out for Hannah. By way of introduction, he said, "You know Willow, but her young man—" Willow glared at him. "Oh, I'm sorry, Caleb is her fiancé." Tristian added emphases to the last two words. "Which is the second reason we found them on my doorstep."

Caleb stretched out his hand, and Hannah took it. "Nice to meet you."

"I'm sorry to crash your homecoming. We thought"—he paused a beat to look at Willow— "Tristian would be alone," Caleb said with a chagrined expression.

Willow elbowed him in the ribs. "Caleb."

"So, this was planned. You want me to smooth things over with your parents." He cut his gaze to Willow, then to Caleb. "What does your family think of Willow?"

"They love her. Our family is a mixed group, I'm a throwback from a union that was kept under wraps for years. So, my marrying a fairy is no big deal. Now who performs the ceremony and where is another thing entirely." He shrugged.

"Birch and Freesia are aware?" Tristian scooped up a huge bite of enchilada, blew on it, and popped the tasty morsel in his mouth. Picked up a tortilla and rolled it up.

"Not exactly." Willow shifted uncomfortably in her seat. "We didn't get a chance; they knew what he was when we walked through the door. Dad didn't—"

"It's been a rough patch for your parents, what with my—well, it's been rough. So, your unexpected announcement was probably the last straw. Tomorrow things will look diff—"

A loud knock sounded at the door. "Shit—now

what." Tristian pushed to his feet, crossed to the door, and yanked it open. He stared at Birch. "Of course—Come on in." After Birch strode in, Tristian stuck his head out the door. "Where's Freesia?"

"Home," Birch said firmly. He sniffed. "Rena's enchiladas?"

"Yessss. There's plenty. Have a seat. Shall I call Freesia?"

"No. Not yet." Birch took a sudden interest in his shoes. "I flew off the handle this afternoon, though I was provoked; my wife saw it differently."

Tristian waited until Birch's gaze met his. "Old man... Remember the heart wants what the heart wants—shit, you told me about Angie and Bruce? And the advice you dished out?" He paused for a couple beats. "Well—right back at you."

"I know. But you didn't listen, just…"

"Yep. And we all know how that ended. It looks a bit different from the other side, huh?" Tristian clasped a hand on Birch's shoulder. "Caleb is a good guy. He loves your daughter. I could see that when I first met him."

"Yeah, that's what Freesia said." Birch peered at Tristian for a couple minutes. "You've changed."

"Doubtful. Call your wife, enjoy Rena's enchiladas, then take your family home and work it out, so we can get some sleep."

"Now there's the Tristian I know." Birch smirked.

"It's going to be a spectacular double wedding, you know," Tristian added.

"So we've been told," Birch said.

"Oh, so Bruce has been in contact with you too?" Tristian took a drink of his coffee.

"No, Angie called for Willow, I—said a few things—then, yes, Bruce got on the phone. We had a discussion. Here I am."

Tristian threw his head back and roared with laughter. As he sobered, there was a light tap on the door. "Freesia, come on in." She peeked her head through the door. Tristian motioned her in. "Join the party." He pulled another chair from his office, rolled it up to the table.

"I'm so sorry Birch barged in," Freesia said in a quiet voice, she sniffed.

"Yes, it's Rena's enchiladas. Fix yourself a plate."

Her eyes wandered over to Hannah. "Who…"

"Oh, I'm sorry. This is Hannah. Hannah, Birch, and his wife Freesia. Now no more questions. When I have something to announce… I'll do so."

Hannah shook her head and glared at Tristian then switched her attention to the couple. "You were out in the yard last time I was here. Nice to meet you."

Birch raised an eyebrow. "Same here." He shook her extended hand.

Freesia gave her a quick hug and whispered in her ear.

"Hey, no secrets. Remember," Tristian said glaring at Hannah.

"No secrets. Girl talk," Hannah retorted.

Freesia laughed. "She's got your number, Tristian."

Hannah was the last to finish the food on her plate. She pushed up from the table. "Nice to meet you all. But tomorrow is a busy day for me, so I'll say my goodnights and head to bed."

Tristian got to his feet as a mischievous grin spread across his face, lit up his eyes. "Would you like to know where you are sleeping tonight?"

The group still seated at the table chuckled, and Willow said, "We can take a hint. Differences will be settled at Mom and Dad's house." She glanced at Tristian. "Thanks for everything. Goodnight. We can show ourselves out."

Tristian nodded, wrapped an arm around Hannah, tugged her against him. "So, my bed or the guest bed?"

"Does it matter?" She giggled, breathing in his spicy, masculine scent.

"Nope, I can join you in either. But my bed is bigger," he said seductively.

****

The sun was high overhead when Tristian opened his eyes; his gaze wandered over a naked Hannah cuddled against him. His fingers feathered along her breast as he wrapped her in his arms.

Her eyes blinked slowly open, then rounded. "Oh my god, what time is it?" She bolted upright in the bed.

"Relax, it's only a little past twelve. Plenty of time." He brushed his lips over hers.

She pulled away, shoved at his arms encircled around her and jumped out of bed. "You promised to quiz me. Now I barely have time to get dressed, grab breakfast, and an extremely quick review."

"You know that stuff backward and forward. Breakfast is ready, just have to warm it up and put coffee or tea on, whichever you desire. That gives us time for a nice shower." He waggled his eyebrows.

"No way. No time for that. Don't you ever think of anything else?"

"Murder and mayhem, but you changed all that." He rolled over and sat up. "So basically, it's your own fault."

"Ohhhh...I don't have time for this." She rushed into the bathroom and locked the door.

He smirked. *I'll have her tonight. No way she's going back to her cottage if I have anything to say about it.*

Chapter Seventeen
Changes are a Fact of Life—But We Don't Have to Like It

Tristian dropped Hannah off at the cottage to pick up her car. When he returned to the house, he reviewed the paperwork filed in his absence and called Bruce on a secure line. The phone rang only once.

"It's about time you checked in," Bruce said.

"Wanted to review the reports before I called you. I'll get the paperwork straightened up today. Hannah has to catch up with her work before we head in your direction. A few days at the most. Unless there is an immediate problem."

"No problems. I want to go over a few things with you. The wedding is going to be held at my parents' place in Tahiti."

"Oh... Not sure that's a good idea."

"The guest list is small, and they will meet at the Salon, go through the portal. But we need a team to remain there around the clock until everyone returns. Angie along with my parents would like you, Hannah, Willow, and Caleb to spend a few extra days there before or after the wedding."

"What no honeymoon? It figures..." Tristian muttered.

"Don't start. We are going away later in the week. Want to make sure everyone gets back okay, and no rumblings before I leave you in charge for a month."

"Me…? I don't want that responsibility," Tristian argued.

"You have Hannah now to think about. We're going to make a few modifications to your job responsibility to fit your change in life status and mine. I have Angie to think about too."

"Things are just fine."

"You may still get the final call, but only under dire circumstances. You've trained your team leaders well. It's time they take on some of your responsibilities as you take on part of mine. We'll talk about it when you get here. Wanted to give you a heads-up, so you can blow off steam there rather than here."

"Not going to happen."

"Make no mistake, it is. I'm still your boss and make the ultimate decisions. Is that clear?" Bruce said in a commanding voice.

"Crystal." Tristian disconnected the call. "Shit." He'd considered delegating some responsibilities, even decided to broach the subject with Bruce. But…being told he would do it, didn't set right. In addition, he was expected to take on some of Bruce's responsibilities. *When hell freezes over.*

For several hours, Tristian poured over the reports making corrections where needed. He sent notices to those who completed them as well as the final reports to Bruce. Disgruntled, he wandered the house, slipped into sweats and running shoes, then sprinted down the jagged trail to the beach.

After an hour or more, physically exhausted, he thought the door open and trudged up the stairs to shower. Maybe Hannah wasn't coming back tonight. Did she decide to stay at her cottage? His mood darkened as the full moon rose in the sky.

No sooner than he pulled on jeans and stretched out on the bed, gravel crunched as a car made its way up the driveway, stopped in front of his house. He peered out the window but knew it was Hannah. Trying to slough off his thunderous mood, he jogged down the stairs, opened the door as she was poised to knock. He swept her up in his arms and kissed her as if she'd been gone for months, rather than hours.

"Wow, love that greeting." She wrapped her arms around his neck.

"Been knee deep in paperwork since I returned to the house. Not fun." He whirled around with her before putting her feet on the ground. "How'd the test go? You passed with flying colors. Right?"

She paused to grin at him. "Yes. I did. A perfect score. Swearing in ceremony will be in a few weeks. I'm late because I had to talk with Brandy, kinda fill her in about us. Otherwise, she was headed here on the next plane." Hannah grimaced. "She might yet."

"That would be a big problem. Especially since we'll be leaving town shortly." He paused and blew out a breath. "I knew you'd pass." He kissed her again. "Good, so we'll be back in plenty of time. And work?"

"Well, we reached a compromise. Boss wasn't happy about my taking more time off, but we worked it out. Have to pay to have a secure line installed at the cottage, so I can work from there."

Tristian cocked his head to one side. "Cheaper to just move in here. You can use my secure line for free. I guarantee it will meet any standards your company requires."

She stroked her hand down his arm and around his waist. "I'm not ready to make that move yet. Besides, until we leave for D.C., I'm going to work at the office as usual."

"According to your... How about a walk?" His temper vibrated at the end of its tether. *Not ready... Is she playing with me, waiting for a commitment? I can't, not yet. Soon?* Anger and frustration closed in around him. "Gotta go. Join me if you want." He bolted out the door and down the driveway. Not much energy left to expend, he ran a circuit around the area, slowed to a walk before heading toward home.

A dark shadow fell across cliffs as a winged creature soared through the starry sky backlit by the full moon following his trek. A burst of wind cooled his sweat drenched skin as he eased onto the bench behind the house. He sucked in a breath as Hannah, in gryphon form, glided into the glade and shimmered into human form a few yards from him. She bent down and shimmied into a silky halter dress from Hawaii she'd left out and ambled to his side, her fingers tracing the sinewy muscles on his bare back.

"May I sit down?"

He motioned her to sit, unable to find the words to express his feeling of awe at that moment.

"Care to tell me what's bothering you?"

"Nothing," he snapped.

She slid next to him, reached up with her hand, caressing his cheek then running a finger along his chin, she turned his face toward hers. "That's a pretty serious expression for nothing. Problems at work? Or with me?"

"Both," he growled. "Bruce wants to…change my job responsibilities."

"But weren't you considering some changes of your own, when you returned?"

"Yes, but he wants to leave me in charge while they take a honeymoon. I'm not suited for that."

"You could be," she whispered against his ear.

"No. I'm not."

"Okay. What's bothering you about me?"

"I thought—I want you to—" He ran his fingers through his hair, rubbed at his neck. "I'd rather you stay here with me, not at the cottage."

She chewed on her bottom lip. "We don't have to make a decision right this minute. I'll stay tonight. Tristian, you have to understand our relationship goes against everything I believe in." She held her hand up as he started to object. "Don't misunderstand, I don't regret my decision, being with you feels right. Nonetheless, my family, my sister… How am I going to explain a male voice in the house, should she call, not to mention if she pops in unannounced? I won't lie to her."

"I'm not asking you to. I'm fine with things the way they are, and before you disagree. I'm working on…"

She held her hands up. "I had a wonderful time, don't spoil it. I'm sorry your day sucked. How about we put off any decisions until we get back from the wedding. Until then, my nights are yours, but if I want to spend one alone at my cottage, you'll understand. I'm going into work as long as we are here."

He blew out a breath and stood, then paced around the bench. "The art of compromise is not my strong suit."

A sly smile played around her lips. "You underestimate yourself. It's easier to be given an assignment and complete it. You have the tools or your teams would not have held their own while you were gone."

"That's just it. The paperwork was a mess."

"So...teach them the way you want it done. You have the skills. I saw them when you tried to teach me to surf in Hawaii."

He grinned. "You never did stand and ride a wave."

"Only because my balance is lacking. Not due to your teaching." She laughed. "Besides, I don't like sharks."

Waving a hand dismissively, he noticed the orange glow in the east. "Let's go to the diner, have breakfast, then I'll drop you off at your cottage." *For now.*

"Great plan."

****

Over the next few days, Hannah put in a lot of hours at her job, leaving Tristian time to work up an outline for his team demonstrating how to complete reports properly. He had plenty of time to mull over what she'd said, and the changes Bruce wanted to make.

Tired of paperwork, Tristian stood, raked his fingers through is hair. Hannah had chosen to spend the last few nights in the cottage, exhausted from long hours at work. Tonight, he wanted to see her. Willow and Caleb were leaving early tomorrow for Washington D.C. to prep for the wedding. He snapped his fingers and strode out the door.

Freesia was on her knees, hands buried in the dirt of their garden. Birch had just joined her when Tristian strode over to their yard. "Good afternoon."

"Good afternoon to you too. What brings you over here?" Birch looked up holding three nice ripe tomatoes, eying Tristian in jeans, no shirt or shoes.

He ignored Birch's stare. In Hawaii, he'd gotten used to going shirtless, barefoot, or wearing sandals. It was a far cry from his usual attire. "Since Willow and Caleb are leaving in the morning, I thought we could have a cookout tonight. I'll throw steaks on the barbecue, add baked potatoes and…"

"Oh, that's a wonderful idea," Freesia said peering up at him. "I'll make the salad, got lots of fresh veggies and whip up a dessert. What time do you want us over?" She got to her feet, wiping her hands together to get the dirt off.

"Hold that thought. I want to call Hannah and see what her schedule looks like. She's been spending a lot of time at work recently."

Birch raised a brow and exchanged a knowing look with his wife.

Tristian pulled out his cell phone. "That's enough. It's not what you think. Hannah wouldn't want Willow and Caleb to leave without a chance to say goodbye." He tapped the #2 button on his screen and held the phone to his ear. After the fourth ring, he started to disconnect the call when Hannah answered, her voice frazzled.

"Hi, Trist. What's up?"

"Hi, I'm standing here with Birch and Freesia. We're going to throw steaks on the grill since it's Willow and Caleb's last night. Wondered if you could get away this evening to join us?"

She blew out a breath, "Man, I am swamped. Boss threw a bunch more files on my desk after I told him how long I would be gone for the wedding."

"Shouldn't have told him, yet." Tristian tried to keep his voice light. "Well if you can't come, I understand. I'm sure everyone else will too." Disappointment dripped from his voice.

"I was in at four this morning trying to get a good start on the files." She paused for a couple beats. "I'll be there. What time?"

"About five-thirty-ish. Will that work for you?" He glanced over at the Coppervales. Their heads nodding in unison.

"I'll do my best. Want to go home and change, then I'll be over. Gotta go." She paused for a moment. "Miss you lots."

"Me too." Hannah ended the call before he could offer to pick her up. Which was in his plan as well, but at least he would see her tonight. Shrugging, he stuffed the phone in his pocket and grinned.

"Very well done." Birch clapped his hands together. "You know she saw right through you?" He laughed.

"Or at least we did," Freesia said gleefully. "I never would have believed there was a woman alive that would tame you. Nice I was wrong."

Tristian shot her a dark look. "Tamed? I don't believe anyone has tamed anyone. I am not a wild animal to be tamed."

"Oh, son, you are sadly mistaken. But..." Birch paused at the footsteps headed in their direction, turned to see his daughter and Caleb striding across the lawn hand in hand.

Raising her hand in a wave, Willow called out. "Tristian, you haven't scared Hannah off already?" Grinning wide, Willow hugged her mom and dad, started to swing an arm around Tristian, thought better of it.

Caleb extended his hand. Tristian shook it. "Looks like things are better than the last time I saw you two," he chided.

"Yeah well, strong will seems to run in the family." Freesia gave a sideways glance at her husband. "But the heart wants what the heart wants."

Willow raised her arms, palms up, and shrugged.

"So I've been told." Tristian grimaced and shoved his hands in the front pockets of his jeans. "I need to get cleaned up, take the steaks out of the freezer, and straighten up the house a bit. Come on over when you're ready."

By the time Hannah arrived, Tristian had steaks on the grill, the table set with salad and iced tea, thanks to Freesia and Willow.

"Wow, nice spread," Hannah said walking through the living area into the kitchen. "Hi, ladies and Caleb. She grinned seeing Tristian glance over his shoulder at her through the open sliding glass door.

Leaving the grill in Birch's capable hands, Tristian sauntered inside. "Glad you made it." He caught her up in an embrace and kissed her soundly. "I've missed you." Grabbing her hand, he led her outside to the covered patio and grill area, off to the left of the veranda and garden.

"The steaks are done medium. Anyone want well done?" Birch waved the spatula toward the smoking grill. He turned back to the barbecue, picked up a long fork, and poked it into the foil wrapped potatoes. "Yep, they're done too."

Freesia brought out a platter and handed it to Tristian. "Better check those steaks, his idea of medium is pretty rare," she whispered as a conspiratorial smile curved the corners of her lips.

"I heard that," Birch retorted, placing a steak on the platter for Tristian's inspection.

He cut through the steak. "Perfect."

Birch smirked at Freesia before she disappeared into the kitchen. He piled the remaining steaks on the platter.

Hannah took the plate from Tristian. "Want me to bring another for the potatoes?"

"Sure. The platters are in the cupboard to the right of the microwave, top shelf.

Freesia bustled by waving her hand. "It's already taken care of. Everyone go on inside. Dinner is ready." Her lips twitched as she hip-checked her husband when he picked up the potatoes from the white-hot coals with tongs and set them on the plate.

"Hey, you nearly made me drop one." He grinned affectionately, took the plate, and gave her a little nudge toward the kitchen. "I got this."

"Let's eat." Tristian led the group into the house where Caleb stood watching Willow fill the glasses with water and ice. "You're hired. Rena needs a little help around here."

"She'd have your head if she heard you say that," Freesia said glaring at him.

Tristian's hands when up in a gesture of surrender. "You're probably right." He held the chair out for

Hannah while the others gathered around the table.

The conversation was light. Tristian's mind wandered replaying his discussion with Bruce, then on to the task of getting Hannah to spend the night. By the time he'd forked up the last bite of baked potato and popped it into his mouth, the others had finished dinner.

"Coffee and tea outside on the veranda?" he suggested.

"Sure. I made a cheesecake topped with strawberries, drizzled with chocolate. You're not going keep it all to yourself, Mr. Shandie," Freesia said.

"Wouldn't dream of it. Thought we'd give dinner a chance to settle." He unfolded his tall frame from the chair and padded toward the kitchen. "Coffee or..." His cell phone buzzed in his pocket. "Hold that thought." Yanking his phone from his pocket, he frowned at the screen and walked into the living room put the phone to his ear. "What's up boss?"

"We have a situation that may need your attention."

"Now?"

"Unfortunately, yes. I'd like you to fly back with Willow and Caleb tomorrow morning, rather than next week as originally planned."

"Okaay," Tristian said pensively.

"Fill you in when you arrive." Bruce disconnected the call.

Tristian glared at the phone, then shoved it in his pocket with a heavy sigh and returned to the kitchen. When he entered the room, Hannah shot him an inquiring look.

"Something's come up. I have to leave tomorrow with Willow and Caleb." His gaze held Hannah's. "Any chance you can accompany us?"

"Absolutely none. I promised my boss I'd be here this entire week."

Lips drawn into a thin line, his gaze turned stormy, then his features softened as he became aware of Birch's almost unperceivable shake of his head. Tristian shot Birch an irritated look.

"So, Hannah will come with us next week?" Freesia asked.

"Yeah, Bruce w—will send the jet back for you. Unless..." Having learned years ago not to take anything for granted where Bruce was concerned. He reached into his pocket, pulled the cell phone out. "Call Bruce." Phone to his ear, he walked out the front door.

Bruce picked up on the first ring. "Tristian?"

"Yeah. Checking to make sure you'll send the jet back for Hannah, Freesia and Birch—next week."

"Of course."

"Thanks." The call disconnected. Tristian flexed his fingers from a fist and returned to the house. *This is why a personal life and my professional life won't mix. Dividing my attention could be deadly.* He stalked into the house. "Yes, Bruce will send the jet next week for the rest of you." He frowned at the recent turn of events.

Willow danced from one foot to the other. "We can't have a bachelorette party or activities without my matron of honor and Angie's bridesmaid." She looked brightly at Hannah, who blushed slightly.

"Who me?" Hannah's eyes rounded in surprise.

Freesia drew in a sharp breath. "Me?"

"Yep. Angie got dibs on Hannah. So Mom will be my matron of honor." Willow twirled on one foot, her arms flying out from her sides. "This is going to be the best wedding ever." She stopped abruptly and flung her arms around Caleb's neck. "I love you."

He blinked at her a couple times then smiled glancing around self-consciously. "Me too."

Tristian stepped back to observe the happy chaotic scene playing out before him. Joy was the last thing on his mind.

He'd only taken a couple strides toward the door when a gentle hand caught his arm. "Tristian why are you leaving tomorrow?" Hannah asked concern clouding her eyes.

"I told you, something…" he said more terse than intended.

"I know what you said. Are you being sent on assignment a week before the wedding?"

"It would appear so. Trouble doesn't take into consideration life plans," he growled.

"Seriously?"

"Well, the demon overlord doesn't call me in to play cribbage." His voice belayed his thunderous mood.

Hannah fisted her hand on her hip. "Don't be condescending with me." Her voice sharp at first softened. "Should I be worried?"

"What kind of question is that?" He hissed. "You know what I do. Bruce didn't give me the specifics. I'll find out when I get there."

She laid a hand on his shoulder, slid it down his arm. "You'll call me?"

"Expect the worst and I'll be back when I can." He ran his fingers through his hair leaving the front standing up in tufts. "This is why relationships don't work for me." He tried to jerk free.

Hannah tightened her grip on his wrist, glanced back at the others who all had stopped talking and were staring at them. "Let's take a walk in the gardens." She glanced over her shoulder and said, "We'll be back shortly to enjoy a piece of that delicious cheesecake. So, don't think you get to eat it all either."

"I'll cut and serve the cheesecake on the veranda, so don't be long," Freesia called out cheerfully.

Once in among the flowers, Tristian stopped and turned to face Hannah. "You go on back to your job. If everything works out, I'll call you and see..." He rubbed the back of his neck.

"Tristian—take a breath and listen to me." She shook his arm making sure she had his total attention. "Other than being whisked away in the dead of night, I'm new to this side of your world. I don't know what to expect when you're called away. Don't distance yourself from me."

"You don't understand."

"That's a cop out. I am aware you have to be completely focused when on assignment. I'm not asking you to change anything. Only that you let me know what's happening when you're able."

"That's just it. The element of surprise is an absolute. Your phone is not secure enough for such communications. The fact that I have a significant other is a liability and puts us both at risk."

"I get it. But we agreed, one step at a time and see where it leads. Nothing has changed."

"Everything has changed," he insisted. "My sister has aligned herself with the Demon Overlord, my boss. They're getting married. I'm tangled up with a woman—a gryphon—and I don't know how to keep her safe. My boss wants to change how we do things…"

"You don't like change," she completed for him.

"Okay, I'll give you that."

"I can take care of myself. A gryphon is a formidable foe, with magical powers you have yet to see." At his raised eyebrow, she shook her head. "I'll be careful, but you concentrate on what you have to do."

Tristian searched her face looking for…hell he didn't know what. He'd never known a woman like her. He couldn't let her go. Tilting her chin up, he took her mouth hungrily. Her lips parted in surprise, his tongue thrust inside exploring, soothing, teasing. Her arms slid around his neck as her body curved against him, returning the kiss with wanton exuberance. Eyes closed, he enjoyed the moment then whispered against her lips. "Stay with me tonight." Reluctantly, he opened his eyes to find her gazing up at him.

She held his gaze for a beat and nodded.

Brushing his lips over hers once more, he shifted to wrap an arm around her waist and started toward the house. "Better get a piece of cheesecake before they eat it all."

Chapter Eighteen

A Reprieve from All Things Evil—Never Lasts Long

After saying their goodbyes to the Coppervales and Caleb, Tristian took her in his arms. Her knees felt weak as his hard chest pressed against her sending jolts of desire to her core. He moved them toward the double chaise on the veranda.

"Not here," she murmured against the pulsing hollow of his throat. Unable to help herself, she breathed a lingering kiss there, her tongue tasting along the ridge of his collarbone.

Tristian sucked in a breath. "No one can see." He pushed her peasant blouse off her shoulders, his lips trailed across her jaw, along her neck to the swells of her breasts. Reaching around her back, he flipped opened the catch of her bra. Her firm breasts tumbled out into his waiting hands. The rough pad of his thumb circled and teased her nipples. She shivered as moisture gathered between her legs.

She reached for his shirt worn open halfway down his sculpted chest and unbuttoned the remaining buttons. Her fingertips caressed the contours of his pectoral muscles, reached up and slipped the shirt off his shoulders. His earthy, spicy scent filled her nostrils and she inhaled deeply, holding onto his biceps as he lowered her to the chaise. She reveled as his muscles tightened and released beneath her fingers. His raw masculine strength was an unbelievable turn on. Commitment or not, she intended to make him hers, one way or the other and nothing else mattered.

His warmth radiated over her as he hovered above her. She released the button on his jeans and lowered the zipper, his remaining clothing disappeared along with hers.

"No fair," she squealed her eyes drinking in his hard-naked body. Tingles raced up and down her spine as his smoldering gaze raked over her. Yet, mischief glittered in his eyes as she held his gaze reminding her of the Tristian in Hawaii. The man she'd fallen in love with, but his darker side…now that was a challenge— and if she admitted it—a turn on as well. What was it about bad boys…scratch that…men? There was nothing boyish about this Adonis.

All thoughts flew from her mind as his warm hands began a slow caress over the curves of her body, exploring, teasing, touching. *Ohhh God.* His mouth devoured hers, and his fingers slipped into her heat. She arched against him, wanted so much more. He spread her legs with his knees and knelt between them. Desire spun out of control as she reached down, felt him smooth and hard in her hand, fingers wrapped around him.

Tristian groaned and thrust against her. "You're going to kill me, woman."

His fingers reached the sweet spot at her core, and she moaned crashing over the edge of ecstasy, her fingers digging into his back. She should have been embarrassed at her lack of control, but she wasn't. It seemed so long since Hawaii and his intimate touch...had ignited her.

Gasping for breath, she slowly traced her lips with the tip of her tongue and grinned. "But what a way to go."

A seductive rumble rose from his throat then he shifted and slid into her. His eyes widened when she arched up to meet him with deep, quick thrusts of her hips. She snickered. "You're in so much trouble." She wound her leg around his and raised up on one elbow just enough to off balance him. When the time was right, quick as a wink, she wound her leg around his and tugged it out from underneath him, rolling him onto his back. "I like it on top," she purred.

While surprised, he seemed thrilled as she ground her hips down on his, he arched up repeatedly finding the rhythm that brought her to the brink again. She threw back her head and howled with pleasure. When her eyes came back in focus, a smug smile curved his lips. "Now that's something new. My gryphon is part wolf?"

She had only a second to ponder the "my" thing, before he cupped her neck and brought her lips to his, tongue parted her lips, thrust inside matching the motions of his hips. All at once his arms tightened around her, his breath coming in gasps, he tensed and let out a long, throaty growl.

She lay cradled in his arms wrapped tightly around her waist pressing her back to his chest, exhausted, but sated. "Can we go back inside yet?" she asked. Heat crept up her neck spread across her face as she felt his answer rather that heard. "Fast recovery rate."

"It's a perk, besides I've been thinking about you all day"—he cleared his throat—"all week and about the things I wanted to do to you when we were alone." Tristian licked his lips.

Peering over her shoulder at him, a sensuous smile curved his lips. She twisted in his arms, slid her leg over his rubbing her center against him. "Have your way with me…sir." She giggled, teasing his nipples with the tip of her tongue. Scared shitless about his assignment tomorrow, about explaining this relationship to her parents, her sister, and wondering which Tristian would return to her. Hannah shook her head to dislodge such thoughts. All that mattered was tonight.

He moved with the grace of a panther stalking his prey as he got to his knees and slipped his hands down the inside of her thighs, spreading her legs, leaning into her. *Mine.* Surprised by his thought floating through her mind, she tried to keep the connection open, but as in previous times, it snapped shut without warning.

The few glances into his mind had come at times when they were alone, intimate, but she wasn't sure he was aware of the connection. It was a subject she intended to discuss with him, but now was not the time. His warm breath heated her core. She relaxed under him and gave into the delicious sensation of his moist lips on her, his warmth penetrating her body and soul. Yep, she was in trouble. There was no turning away from this man. His ministrations brought her to the brink over and over. Finally, he filled her, waves of ecstasy throbbed through her, then long surrendering moans escaped his lips. She smiled, kissed his cheek softly as he rolled to his side spooning with her, slipping into the sated sleep of lovers.

Sometime during the night, he must have carried

her into the bedroom, she didn't remember, but she awoke in his bed to the sounds of him moving around in the dark room. Her skin cooled without his warm body in the bed beside her. All her insecurities bubbled to the surface, she shoved them away determined to stay in control of her emotions. *I'm a strong, confident woman in love with an impossible warlock. What a mess.*

His warm breath caressed her face as he leaned over and kissed her on the cheek. Then trailed his lips to her mouth covering it, his tongue tracing her lips then slipped inside. Raising his mouth from hers, voice husky he said, "I'll see you in a week." And he was gone.

Muffled voices rose from outside, car doors opening and closing then a hum of an engine as the vehicle eased down the driveway to the main road. She rolled over and sat on the side of the bed as a single tear slipped down her cheek. His robe lay at the foot of the bed, she wrapped it around her, pausing to inhale his scent, earthy with a hint of spice. She rolled up the sleeves and tied the belt around her waist. How she loved his scent lingering in the plush robe.

Slipping her feet into soft slippers, she padded down the stairs. Searching the couch, beside the chairs, she finally found her purse and took out her phone. She plopped onto the couch and tucked her feet up under her. Staring at the device for several long minutes, she straightened, then tapped the screen and said, "Call Brandy."

Her sister answered on the first ring. "Hannah, everything all right?"

Hannah brushed the tear from her cheek and

sucked in a breath. "Yes, of course. Wanted to let you know, I passed the citizenship test. So, moving to Colorado should be in my future."

"That's great. We need to celebrate! I've got quite a work load for the next couple weeks, got couple of rangers out, but I can fly out afterward," Brandy said excitedly.

"That would be great fun. But I'll be leaving for the wedding in a few days. Can we do it later?"

"Later, not now, that's all I hear. You're hiding something, Hannah. What have you gotten mixed up in? Are you in trouble?"

"No. Nothing like that. I'm fine, I promise. It's just that I have a pile of work to get through before I leave. There isn't time for anything else. When I get back, we'll make arrangements to get together, and I'll introduce you to him."

"Does him have a name?"

"Of course." Her phone pinged with another incoming call. "Brandy, my boss is on the other line. I've got to take his call. Love you. Talk to you soon and I'll tell you all about him, the trip, our plans, then we'll make arrangements for you to fly here to meet him. Fair enough?"

"Yeah, sure. But I'm going to hold you to it," Brandy warned.

"I'm sure you will. Gotta go." Hannah disconnected the call.

****

The couple hour flight from Maine to Washington D.C. seemed much longer to Tristian than usual. Anxious to have his meeting with Bruce over so he could get on with this assignment. His thoughts kept drifting to Hannah all warm and fragrant in his bed this morning. He shook his head vehemently. That was an indulgence, he couldn't afford. Leaning back in his seat, he closed his eyes. A long way off, he heard someone call his name.

"Tristiaaan." A woman's voice drew out his name. "Oh, there you are. Want a bagel?" Willow asked seeing that she now had his attention. "What were you so deep in thought about? Or do I want to know?"

Caleb caught her arm and pulled Willow back in the seat, clicked the belt. "Sorry about that. I think the wedding is affecting her like sugar does most people."

Tristian sat up straight and twisted in his seat to see Willow still holding a bagel with cream cheese out to him on a plate. His stomach growled as he accepted the plate from her and took a bite. "In answer to your question, you don't want to know," he growled. Settling back into the seat, he glanced at his watch. *We'll be landing soon.* He took another big bite. *Hannah is probably on her way to work.*

As the plane taxied down the runway, Tristian recognized The Wycked Hair's limo waiting on the end of the tarmac. He released the seatbelt and was first off the plane. Willow and Caleb ran to catch up with him. Their luggage was carted to the limo and loaded into the trunk.

"What's the big hurry?" Willow asked trying to catch her breath.

"Nothing," Tristian said in a clipped tone, folding his tall frame into the limo followed by Willow and Caleb.

Willow chattered nonstop about nothing and everything. He tried to tune her out, but her happy chatter was hard to ignore. Glaring at her, he exited the limo and yanked open the door to The Wycked Hair Salon. The stations were full, and people milled around outside the shared doorway into The Krystal Unicorn.

His gaze lifted to the glass-enclosed mezzanine where Bruce's office was located. The place looked deserted. At a light tap on his shoulder, he whirled around hands fisted in front of him.

"Easy there, guy," Owen's smooth voice warned. "Bruce is in The Krystal Unicorn with your sister." No sooner had the words left his mouth than Angie came flying out of the door, crossed the polished floor, and flung herself into Tristian's arms.

Her momentum knocked him back a couple of steps. "Hi, sis."

"Hi, yourself." She dropped to her feet, backed away, and gave him the once over. "Wow, you look great. Hannah is good for you."

"Isn't she," Willow chimed in waiting her turn to hug Angie, her best friend.

"Oh, I think a Hawaiian vacation had something to do with that too." Bruce's voice boomed from behind Angie. "Good to see you, Tristian. Thanks for coming. Sorry about the timing."

"Yeah, the timing sucked. But what can you do?" Tristian's frown melted into a half smile as he looked at his sister who beamed up at him. "You'll make quick work of this assignment and get back in time to attend the pre-wedding activities." She grinned at her brother then switched her gaze to Bruce.

"As I told you, Angie, I haven't briefed Tristian yet. It's at his discretion and that of his team how they want to handle it."

She peered at him her lower lip stuck out in an exaggerated pout. "You—"

Bruce interrupted her. "Don't you and Willow have wedding things to discuss?" He glanced around. "Where's Caleb?"

"We dropped him off at the gallery. Said he had business to take care of and he'd meet me at the apartment. Why?"

"No reason." Bruce turned his attention to Tristian. "Let's go on up to the office and discuss the situation."

Tristian nodded, stopped at the drink bar to fill a mug with steaming coffee, took a sip, sighed. "Delicious as usual. Got anything else to eat around here?"

Pausing to wait for Tristian, Bruce smiled. "Tobi brought up fresh bagel's and donuts earlier."

After another gulp of coffee, he said, "Lead the way." And he shadowed his boss up the stairs two at a time. Bruce held the door to his office open for Tristian and closed it behind them.

Chapter Nineteen
Surprise in the Scottish Highlands

Bruce walked across the office and stood behind his desk. "Have a seat." He waved a hand toward the navy and maroon leather chair in front of the desk. Picking up a large file, he slid it across the desk to Tristian. "We have a situation in the United Kingdom. The Legion Commander of warrior angels has asked for our assistance. More in an observing than fighting position, at the time we spoke. As you know things change. Stefan from the Vampire Council will be meeting you with his team. There are vampires on the ground as well. Word has it that this will be his last assignment for the Council."

Eyebrows shot to nearly Tristian's hairline. "What do you mean last assignment?" Surely, he wouldn't be asked to terminate an ally.

"He's been released by Lady Rose. His service to her and the Council is at an end. He's free to seek other living arrangements and jobs." Bruce tented his fingers and leaned back in the chair.

"That isn't usually the way those things end," Tristian said warily holding Bruce's gaze.

"Well… I assure you it is this time. There was some kind of arrangement between Lady Rose and Stefan when she first contacted him as a rogue vampire. I don't know all the details."

"Wow, that's got to be a first." Tristian shook his head and eased back in the chair.

"As I said, things are changing. You'll leave at first light tomorrow through the portal in the basement. But that's not the only reason I called you here." Bruce blew out a breath and sat up straighter angling his head toward Tristian. "Angie and I will be leaving for an extended period of time a month or so after the wedding. I want you to handle things in my absence." Bruce paused.

"Me—take on all your responsibilities—for how long? What if I'm needed in the field?"

"You'll send in one of your team leaders and his crew." Bruce said matter-of-factly. "We've had our differences. But I trust you to make the right decisions in my absence. My father will be your backup, if necessary, but I don't see that happening."

"You expect me to stay here?" Tristian bristled.

"At first, so you get a feel for the position. Later I see no reason why you can't control your teams and assignments from Maine. The only difference is you will be orchestrating the action, rather than leading the teams. You've trained your top leaders well, it's time they executed the missions."

"But I'm a hands-on kind of guy."

"Were. Things change—for both of us. I have your sister to consider. And you—Hannah, her family, and a family of your own—someday."

"Wait—Hannah and I are—"

"Yes? Don't deny your feelings for her. Everyone can see it. With your head elsewhere, you are too great a risk in the field. That's not a bad thing. We evolve, so do our relationships."

"So, you're taking me out of the field entirely?" Tristian shoved up from the chair and paced the floor, pausing at the window to stare out. Part of him was relieved. This made things easier with Hannah. But he was an enforcer, responsible for his life and those of his men. What if he sent them into a situation that...? "No."

"Yes, after this unique assignment. Apparently, this is the last of a long-standing battle between the angels and dark demons who have wreaked havoc on the financial markets of the British Isles among other things. Originally, their target was world financial markets. However, due to divine intervention, the demons stopped in their tracks. But the hidden agenda didn't come to light until it too late and the vote took place withdrawing the UK from the European Union. Utter financial chaos ensued worldwide for days."

Tristian shifted in his seat, fingers gripped the chair arms as his interest grew.

"The Warrior angels were able to win the battle in the Scottish Highlands using the mists to travel to the past and return to present day. Unfortunately, while that was ongoing, the dark demon's influence in the United Kingdom was devastating, though they couldn't get a foothold in Scotland. When their subterfuge came to light, it was too late."

Tristian opened his mouth to speak, but Bruce held up a hand to silence him.

"Let me finish. Now the angels have rooted out the primary actors and destroyed them. The vampires involved have been neutralized. Except for a few high-ranking creatures that were probably calling the shots and are on the move, time slipping through the highland mists. Latest intel has them trapped in present day somewhere in the Scottish Highlands where Nathanial and his legion are holding on, but barely. He needs your help to magically contain them in present day while he and his warriors surround and capture or kill the holdouts.

Stefan is there, in the event their intel is wrong and vamps are embedded in the demon's ranks. You're to refrain from entering the fray unless invited by Nat, the legion commander. Any questions?"

Tristian returned to his seat and remained silent for several minutes, mulling over the information, playing scenarios out in his mind. "I understand the assignment. Will someone be at the portal when we arrive in Scotland? Or are we on our own?"

"As you know, battles are unpredictable. You'll be porting to the outskirts of the highlands. From there it's your call."

"I want to take most my team leaders on this assignment. I'll leave a couple with teams to handle whatever wedding duties you require. Guard the portal here and in Tahiti until we return. The teams staying behind will be experienced enough to handle any trouble that should happen in our absence."

Bruce nodded. "We can further discuss your new position and duties when you return."

"Oh, you bet we will," Tristian said pointedly. "I'm not comfortable taking over your duties for any amount of time. Diplomatic negotiations are not my strong suit, and you know it."

"That isn't up for discussion. You'll learn." Bruce's voice was curt and left no room for discussion. "How tasks will be transferred is what I meant." He diverted his attention to the computer screen, indicating the meeting was over.

Tristian remained seated glaring at his boss. "Owen is better—"

"Owen is not an enforcer. He doesn't have experience in directing teams that you have, or evaluating situations and acting immediately." Bruce lifted his gaze from the screen. "This discussion is at an end. Prepare your teams. Let me know who is accompanying you and which teams will remain here. That is all."

Tristian spun the chair around and shoved to his feet. "Yes sir," he spat out and strode to the door, yanked it open and sprinted down the stairs. As he strode toward the entrance, Owen called his name from the front counter. Tristian whirled around.

Owen tossed him an envelope. "Reservations for you and your teams are in the usual place. I understand you promoted Terra. I've set her up in her own room. Will she be going with you or staying?" At Tristian's stormy expression, Owen added, "I only asked so I know how long to reserve her room."

"She will be heading up the team staying here. In case of trouble, I trust her abilities."

"Do you expect trouble?" Owen asked, raising an eyebrow.

"No, but believe in being prepared. Daniel and his team will be in Tahiti at the portal."

Pushing through the Salon door, Tristian paused on the sidewalk, then waved the limo away. He needed to walk off his temper before dealing with his team in the hotel where they'd stay the night. Abruptly, he turned toward the glass door to The Krystal Unicorn. A closed sign hung in the window, there was no one inside. Glancing up and down the sidewalk, he magically passed through the glass and stood inside the shop.

Pride swelled inside him at his sister's accomplishments, even though she'd pledged her life to a demon. He shrugged and walked to the telephone, checked the network. As he suspected, the connection was through the secure network of The Wycked Hair Salon. As he touched in the numbers to his home office, he fervently hoped Hannah had stopped by his house on her way home, on the off chance he'd try to contact her. The phone rang only once.

"Hello?" Rena's voice answered.

"Oh, it's you." He couldn't hide the disappointment in his voice.

"Who'd you expect your cyber ops sweetie?" She giggled. "You'd be right. Hang on a minute, she's right here."

"Hi. I just stopped by for a second, wanted some of the leftovers from last night. I forgot to take them with me," Hannah said carefully.

"It's all right. I wanted to hear your voice. Nothing to worry about. I'll see you soon."

"Really?"

"Yes. Really. Take care of you."

"Always. You too."

"Bye." He disconnected the call and felt much better. Yep, everyone was right, he was a goner. His steps were lighter as he made his way to the hotel strategizing in his head team plans for tomorrow. Going over those plans with the team would have to wait. Everyone had turned in for the night by the time Tristian arrived at the hotel.

After a fitful night, Tristian's eyes blinked open at the first golden rays of dawn peeking through the space below the curtains. He dressed quickly, shaved the day and a half blond stubble off his face, and stepped into the shower. When he exited the bathroom toweling his hair, Ruben still snored softly in the bed across the hotel suite. Shaking Ruben awake, Tristian said, "Get the others up and ready. I'm going out for a few minutes."

He knew he shouldn't but unable to help himself, he called Hannah's cell. It rang once and went to voice mail. She'd turned the phone off for the night. For some reason, that irritated him, though he'd told her he wouldn't call her cell because of lack of security. After listening to her soothing voice tell the caller she was unavailable and to leave a short message. Tristian spoke in a soft voice. "See you soon. Take care." He disconnected the call. A simple message that would mean nothing to anyone but to her. Smiling he leaned one shoulder against the wall and gazed out the floor to ceiling window at the end of the hallway.

Orange fingers spread across the dusky horizon as a few cars made their way up the street, headlights still on. The sidewalk was deserted as he turned on his heel. Sprinting up the stairs, he walked the hall to his room and yanked open the door. His team was assembled in the room peering expectantly at him has he strode in and closed the door. After going over the detailed plans, the men exited the hotel and climbed into the waiting limo. It was a short drive to the Salon.

Tristian touched his hand to the security panel in the back entrance of The Wycked Hair. A distinct click and he pulled the door open. The men clattered down the stairs behind him. At the bottom, he was surprised to find, several plush chairs scattered around the room. Glass top tables were arranged between the chairs, a coffee bar and little refrigerator on the far wall. A far cry from the last time Tristian was down here. Had it not been for the slight magic pulse from the corner he'd picked up on only because he'd used it before, a creature without special talents would never know the portal was here. Kudos to Bruce.

All was quiet as Tristian and his men made their way to the magic gateway. With a wave of his hand and a silently muttered reveal spell, the portal swirled into view, pulsing in a full spectrum of blues with a silver center. In hushed tones, the men confirmed instructions once they reached the other side. Tristian was the first to pass through the portal.

He stepped out into the misty countryside of the Scottish Highlands. The unexpected thud of a body hitting the ground and a groan had Tristian fading into the bushes as he disguised the portal with wave of his hand.

Fog swirled so thick across the meadow that he could barely make out a dark form in the distance. The creature brandished a sword over a crumpled figure on the ground. When the sword started its downward slice, Tristian cast a spell dissipating the mist. A concussive force flung the sword out of the shocked demon's hand. Furious, the creature's loud roar reverberated off the rock faces.

The figure writhing on the ground was a warrior angel, singed from head to toe. Blood gushed from a wound in his side, leaving a dark red stain on the ground. The next second, the demon rushed at Tristian.

He raised his hand and sent an electrified ball of fire toward the advancing demon. The flaming ball hit the creature directly in the chest, electrical current shot across its limbs as it doubled over, howling in pain. A crack sounded from behind, and two of Tristian's team shot flaming arrows toward the demon as Tristian lobbed another concussive wave of magic knocking the flaming demon against the rocks.

The smug satisfaction Tristian usually felt after neutralizing his prey didn't happen. *Huh?* Instead a sense of relief spread through him. Gray and black ash rained down as the demon succumbed to his injuries. The enforcer flicked pieces of ash from his black duster as an eerie silence settled around him. *So much for staying out of the fray.* He shrugged and turned toward his men, eying the previously writhing angel, who now lay quiet.

"What the hell?" Ruben bellowed running toward his team leader.

"Damned if I know." Tristian rushed to the fallen warrior, bent down checking for signs of life. "He's still breathing." Kneeling, he placed his hand over the still body. A copper light glowed between his hands and the prone warrior. He didn't have the strong healing power of his sister, Angie, but he had to try. The last thing he needed was a dispatched seraph on his record.

The angel's eyes flickered open. In a halting voice he said, "Was waiting for you—" He gasped for breath. "The darkness called to me—I couldn't battle—too weak—" His eyes closed and head lolled to the side.

"Shit. Don't you dare die on me," Tristian bellowed and increased his efforts. A coppery aura enveloped the angel, his heartbeat strengthened, color returned to the warrior's face. Tristian got to his feet, wobbling a bit as one of his men steadied him.

"You all right?" Ruben asked.

"Yeah. Just give me a minute." Tristian straightened and drew in a couple deep breaths. *This healing shit sucks.*

The mist whirled and thickened, what appeared to be three warrior angels appeared beside the fallen one, swords in hand pulsing with a white-hot power. After surveying the scene, the first one stepped forward. "Tristian?"

"Who wants to know," Tristian demanded, shoving up the sleeves of his duster preparing to launch poison darts from his wrist gauntlets at the intruders, angels or not.

Swords still at the ready, the angel replied, I'm Nathanial Cross, the legion commander. "What happened here?"

Easing his stance, Tristian lowered his arms. "Not sure. But apparently, your boy was attacked before we arrived. If we'd arrived a split second later, he'd be singing to the choir, so the speak." Tristian smirked, knowing he was out of line but didn't really care. "What the hell were you doing leaving one man alone? These highlands reek of magic and time spinner spells." He straightened his black duster and brushed his hands together, his dark gaze demanding an answer.

"This sector was cleared several hours ago, and Caden was left to wait for your entourage's arrival." The commander shot back glancing around warily. "Wasn't there supposed to be an envoy from the Vampire Council with you?"

Tristian shrugged and glanced around. "I'm sure

he's around here somewhere. Never misses a chance to…"

A tall figure, with long black hair, stepped out of the trees, dressed in a full-length black duster. "That would be me. Stefan Talltree, assassin for the Vampire Council." He swung out of his coat a long handled, jewel encrusted, double headed ax and leaned on it. "Looked like the warlock and his team had things in hand when I arrived. So, I waited." He nodded to Tristian. "Nice job."

"Nice choice of apparel," Tristian snarked.

"Yeah, handy for carrying concealed weapons. Don't you think?"

"If you two are finished with the mutual admiration society." Nathanial frowned and glanced at his men. "Catrell, take Caden above, have someone tend to his wounds. Meanwhile, the rest of you with me."

"Wait a minute. My orders are to observe unless needed. Are you calling us to action?"

"No. I hope not. But as you encountered, it's been a difficult battle over the past few months. I hope this is the final confrontation. My other warriors are just mopping up what I thought was the last of 'em. They're battle weary and ready for some well-deserved R&R."

"Huh…missed one," Tristian chided. He immediately held his hand palm up in a gesture of surrender. "Sorry, it's the adrenalin still talking."

"Your boss told me you could be difficult, but that you were the best," Nathaniel said.

Tristian opened his mouth, then closed it again. Stefan smirked and stepped beside Tristian. "What will you have us do?"

The legion commander gave a wave of his arm and

they all found themselves on a smoking blackened stretch of land covered in piles of ash and the stench of death all around."

"Okay then," Tristian said glancing around uneasily as the mist closed in. "Don't like being out in the open like this."

"Blend into the background. Use your magic ability to sense if there are any other dark demons lurking around. I believe we are done here. But…as you aptly put it—we missed one." The commander grimaced.

"When we first arrived, there were traces of time spinner magic, protection, and anti-detection spells. But here," Tristian paused for a minute then shook his head slowly, "I don't detect any magic other than what you're using to keep the time spinner magic at bay." He turned to his team loosely gathered in a semicircle around him. "Do any of you?"

The men shook their heads. "Not here. But they could have escaped—wait—didn't you say in our briefing that these guys…" Ruben glanced at the commander and his warriors. "The time spinner magic of the highland mists had been closed down, and we were to back up that magic to make sure it held?"

"Yes, insofar as I know, the magic held," Nathanial said thoughtfully. "I guess only time will tell for sure."

"Do you have a divine clean up team?" Tristian snickered under his breath. Somehow, the thought of a person cleaning up the black and gray ash reminded him of a child's movie Angie used to love to watch. *I'm losing it.* He shook his head, took a step back, and met the commander's icy stare. "Or do you want us to magically clean up this mess?" Tristian spread his arms wide and turned in a three-hundred-sixty-degree circle. "Can't leave it this way, even in magic infused Scotland."

"I'd appreciate your assistance. Dispatching a team to clean up takes more time than we have. Our legions are spread thin with the condition the world is in right now."

"I can arrange that, but you'll need to stay and cover our backs while we infuse our magic with your residual magic, and that of the land, to mop up this mess."

"Understood."

"When we are finished—there will be a debt to be repaid."

The legion commander raised an eyebrow, frowned, opened his mouth as if to say something.

"Or we can leave and let you arrange your own cleanup crew," Tristian said shrugging.

Chapter Twenty
Work Will Take Your Mind off the Worry—Not

A large travel mug of tea sloshed in one hand, a backpack full of files and notebooks slung over her shoulder, Hannah rushed out the door of her cottage, tossed the pack on the back seat, and climbed into the SUV. Last night had been a nightmare of gargantuan proportions, codes on the latest security patch failed on customer accounts. She needed another pair of eyes to review the programming, and there were none to spare. Half the team was in Colorado reviewing the needs of the new building. The other half had gone out for a drink or home, and she didn't have the heart to call them back in. After a jog around the building's perimeter despite it was after midnight, she'd finally cleared her head. Upon her return to the building, she'd found the glaring code error, corrected it, and ran another test which was successful. In the wee hours of the morning, she'd driven home in a fog and stumbled into bed, failing to set the alarm.

Jerking straight up in bed, she stared at the clock in horror. She was late for work, no time for breakfast, and she'd not heard a word from Tristian since before he left for his assignment. Tired, irritable and worried didn't look good on her, as she glanced in the rear-view mirror. She froze, taking another peek in the mirror. *Shit.* A pale face with a sprinkling of freckles across her nose and high cheekbones, barely visible light red eyelashes and pouty lips with little color stared back at her. She'd failed to put any makeup on this morning and looked like a corpse.

Tires squealed as she turned into the parking lot of Shadow Hawk Cyber, jammed on the brakes, and coasted into a space. She grabbed her purse and spilled the contents on the passenger seat. Her cell phone clattered to the floorboard while she searched for mascara, at least. A sigh of relief passed her lips as an almost empty bottle of foundation, black mascara, her favorite shades of blue eyeshadow pack, rose lip gloss, and powder blush tumbled onto the seat.

She dabbed on foundation to cover the freckles she'd disliked as a kid, hated as an adult. One more glance in the mirror and she applied light blue eyeshadow, carelessly swiped on black mascara to long thick lashes, brushed on lip-gloss and a bit of blush. Hurriedly, she stuffed everything back in her purse.

Leaning across the seat, she stretched out and scooped up the phone, accidentally touching the screen, which lit up with a missed call from an unknown number at four this morning. *Telemarketers are out of control.* Before she hit the delete button on her phone, she paused, it was a D.C. number, and they'd left a message. Curiosity got the better of her, and she retrieved the message. Tristian's deep resounding voice comforted her frazzled nerves. "See you soon. Take care." *He was all right. At least he was at four this morning.*

Pressed back against the seat, she blew out a breath. *I can't do this. Work these ungodly hours, and...* Her determination not to worry about him had failed miserably. Even though he'd survived all this time and was one of the best in his field, adding her to his equation changed everything, and she knew it. *Thinking like this was not helping.*

She blew several strands of hair from her face, grabbed her stuff, strode into her office, and closed the door. Almost immediately, a soft knock sounded on the door as she dropped her backpack and purse on the desktop.

"Come in," she said irritably, slid open a drawer, and shoved her purse inside. Dumping the files from her backpack to the top of the desk, she divided them into two neat piles. She pursed her lips and peered at the intruder.

A short wisp of a woman with dark brown hair and huge brown eyes, hidden behind wire-rim glasses peeked in, a steaming mug of coffee in hand. "Hey, don't bite the messenger. Sorry, we kinda abandoned you last night. Boss reamed us all this morning. You didn't leave here until three a.m.? At least that was the last swipe of your card in the security system."

"Sounds about right," Hannah said her words clipped. "Sorry. Didn't mean to take out my mood on you. Rough night and woke up late, lots to do."

"It's all good." She smiled. "Boss said your work last night was ingenious. The team had spent several days trying to work out the bug before he laid it on your desk."

Clearing his throat, a slight built man dressed in a red-striped polo shirt, board shorts, and high top sneakers peered over the woman's head. "Good job, Shaughnessy. Transfer your remaining files to the team. They can handle things until you return."

"But I'm not scheduled to leave for a couple more days," Hannah protested fearing he was going to let her go.

"I know, but—" He glanced at Shelia then out into the common area where several people were chatting and drinking coffee. "The time off is well-deserved. All I ask is that you check in periodically in case we have a problem these geniuses can't solve." He said sardonically jamming his thumb over his shoulder. "When you return, I have a new government R&D project I want you to head up."

"But I'm working on the civilian side. I have several customers depending on…"

"Your top security clearance came through. You've been promoted and will be relocating to Colorado in the next eighteen months," he said, a smile curving the corner of his mouth. "Congrats." With a wave, he turned on his heel, shoes squeaking, and sauntered into the common area. In a flurry of activity, the others picked up their cups and headed to their offices.

Hannah plopped down in her chair and stared at Sheila who still stood in the doorway, holding her mug.

"Well, he kinda spoiled my moment." She pouted. "Anyway, there's an email on your computer with all the details. Congratulations Hannah. Have a good time on vacation." She gulped down her coffee. "I'll be in my office if you need anything." Sheila turned to leave and paused. "Oh, if you don't mind, could you make notes on each of the files and bring them into my office before you leave. I'll distribute them."

Nodding, Hannah signed into the computer, clicked on the email icon, scrolled to an email marked private, opened it and read—and reread the communication. A wide smile spread across her lips as she pumped a fist in the air. "Yeah."

She knew Sheila would sift through the files and take the premiere accounts for herself, though she lacked the drive and talent others on the team possessed. Then she'd dole out the rest of the files. But Hannah didn't care, she'd been promoted to her dream job with a salary to match.

Her first inclination was to call Tristian, but he wasn't reachable. So she dove into her work, making careful notes on each file. By the time she reached the last file, she looked up and pinched the bridge of her nose. The sun was sinking behind the hills. Coworkers laughed and talked as they passed through the common area outside her office. Getting to her feet, she stretched her arms above her head and rolled her shoulders. "I'm out of here," she declared to no one in particular.

Picking up the stack of files, she pushed through her office door, stopped, and called out to the others, hoisting the pile in her arms a bit higher. "These are my remaining customer files. I'll just put them on Sheila's desk, and you can take your pick. When she headed toward the woman's office, several team members followed her murmuring thanks and well wishes. With a flourish, she set the files on Sheila's desk and turned to face everyone except Sheila. "See you when I get back. Danny has my cell number, and I'll be checking in on a regular basis if you need something." With a wave of her hand, she returned to her office, gathered her things, and nearly skipped out to the parking lot.

Inside her vehicle, she pulled her phone out of the bag. "Call Brandy." After several beeps, the phone rang, then went straight to voice mail. "Hey, sis. Got a promotion, will be definitely moving to Colorado in the next eighteen months. Going to meet the hot guy's family. Will talk at you later. Tell Ma and Da I'm fine, and we'll talk soon."

She breathed a sigh of relief. Her first spontaneous thought was to call her sister, as it had always been. But as the phone rang, misgivings of the info her sister had a way of wheedling out of her kicked in, so leaving a message was exactly right.

She drove directly to Tristian's home, parked in the driveway, hopped out of the vehicle, and paused for a beat at the bottom of the stairs leading to his house. Then she turned and sprinted to the Coppervale's yard where Freesia was kneeling on the ground weeding her garden. The older woman glanced up, her lips twitched as Hannah skidded to a stop a few feet away.

"Well, that's some entrance. You look like you are about to burst." Laughing Freesia pushed to her feet, she brushed her hands together removing most of the dirt and straightened making sure her wings were tucked. "Spill it."

She snickered at Freesia's movements. There was no one around to see, even if her wings weren't tucked. "I've been promoted and allowed to leave early on vacation." Out of breath, she gulped in air and couldn't wipe the smile from her face.

"That's wonderful." She paused almost putting her finger to her lips, then yanked it away. "I'll have Birch call Bruce and see if he'll send the jet earlier."

"Have Birch do what?" The door banged behind her husband who sauntered down the path to where they were standing.

"I've been granted leave early, and I got a

promotion," Hannah crowed. "I will be going to Colorado, to head a team for R & D on the government contract for Shadow Hawk Cyber."

"That's great." Freesia hugged her, while giving Birch a sideways glance. "Your sister lives in Montana, right?" He returned her look, a little crease dug its way across his forehead.

"Yes, I tried to call her, but it went to voicemail, so I left a message that I would call her later." She whirled around heading back toward her SUV. "I'm going to run home and pack, in case we are able to leave early."

Birch took his phone from his belt clip, touched the screen, and peered at Hannah. "I'll call Bruce and let you know—"

Freesia interrupted, "When you return for dinner tonight." She picked up her gardening tools and put them in the basket resting on the lawn.

Glaring at his wife, he nodded. "It might be best for you to pack, then plan on spending the night at Tristian's place since Bruce usually makes decisions and acts on them rather quickly. No guarantees." He waggled a finger at Hannah then walked a short distance away.

"Sounds like a plan. I'll be back in time for dinner." She stopped to call over her shoulder. "Oh, by the way, what time is dinner?"

"Whenever you get here, dear," Freesia said with a twinkle in her eye.

Sitting in her vehicle seat, Hannah watched the two faeries glide across the grass hand in hand, in serious conversation. They looked back over their shoulders at her a couple times then gave a wave before Birch opened the door and followed Freesia inside the house.

She settled back in the seat and started the engine. Then it hit her, *what would Tristian think about me moving to Colorado? Long distance relationships were difficult at best, with Tristian... Oh god..."* As that thought circled through her mind, the cell phone in her bag rang. She yanked the device out of her purse resting on the passenger seat and checked caller ID. Sucking in a long breath, she blew it out slowly and touched the screen putting the phone to her ear. "Hi, sis."

Chapter Twenty-One

A Surprise Compromise Leads to Confessions of the Heart

Tristian stepped out of the portal into the basement of the Salon and heaved a heavy sigh. Pausing he waved his hand to close and conceal the portal entrance. He surveyed the updated furnishing and aesthetics in the room, then relaxed into the nearest lounge chair and stretched his legs out in front of him, rubbed his eyes with thumb and forefinger.

The rest of his team had ported to Shaughnessy's in Ireland, a favorite watering hole with his men. They'd have twenty-four hours before he required them to report and take on the wedding assignments. On previous assignments, he would have relished the time at Shaughnessy's, but today the meeting with Bruce hung over his head. He wasn't in the mood. The R & R offered by pubs didn't interest him since Hannah had strolled into his life. Sure a brew or socializing with his team had its benefits, but again, not in the mood. He pulled his phone out of his pocket, texted "Done." And laid his head back on the chair and closed his eyes. *I'll call Hannah in a minute...*

Footfalls on the stairs had Tristian jerking straight up in the chair.

"There you are." A soft lilting voice crooned. "I felt you arrive a couple hours ago, but when you didn't

appear upstairs, thought I'd better check things out."
Angie's gaze floated over him. "Rough assignment?"

"Naw—I've had worse—didn't go exactly as
planned."

"Bruce is waiting in his office for you. He was on
the phone when I left to check on The Krystal Unicorn,
then make a detour here."

"I'm going to head over to the hotel, get some shut
eye before meeting with Bruce. We don't seem to see
eye-to-eye lately, and I don't want to say something, I
won't regret. So best to take my tired ass to the hotel,
adjust my attitude before embarking on a war of words
with your mate."

His sister eyed him with amusement, then
speculation. "I'm not sure that's an option, with the
wedding and all."

"I'm sure Terra has everything handled."

"Bruce is sending the jet for Hannah, Birch, and
Freesia at first light tomorrow." She shrugged.
"Apparently, Hannah's boss let her leave early, but I
don't have all the details."

He yawned wide. "In that case, I'm out of here."
Getting to his feet, he'd taken only a couple of steps.

"Not even going to report in?" A deep voice
boomed from the stairway.

Tristian rolled his eyes and dropped back in the
chair. *Shit.* "Unless things have changed, I have twenty-
four hours to report. A week to file a written report
unless the urgency of the matter requires differently.
And it doesn't." Tristian grumped. "I let you know the
assignment was done. That should be sufficient until
tomorrow."

"Not worried about the assignment. We need to

talk."

Shoving to his feet, he took several steps toward the stairs. "Believe me, the last thing I want to do right now is talk to you about a change in job duties and responsibilities. Your damn angel left one warrior to guard the portal, who by the way nearly lost his eternal life if we'd not arrived when we did. One warrior. That's plain irresponsible."

"Things go bad in battle. You of all people are aware of that," Bruce said good-naturedly while wrapping an arm around Angie's waist. "What I have to say will only take a few minutes then you can sleep on it."

Resigned, Tristian returned to the sofa and plopped down. "Let's get this over with. I don't want your job, even temporarily. I like being out in the field. I hate paperwork. You need to find someone else to cover when you want to disappear to dally with my sister."

Angie glared at Tristian, but she said nothing.

Bruce frowned, his normally dark amber eyes whirled with a tinge of orange. Voice deadly calm he said, "First and foremost, I'm your boss. Second, there is no one else I trust to handle things while I am gone. Owen will be here to help you, but he doesn't have your expertise, and he has The Wycked Hair on his plate. I've watched you negotiate several tricky situations. You have the tools to do the job."

Tristian narrowed his eyes and opened his mouth to protest, but Bruce held up a hand and continued.

"Killing is not your only talent, regardless of what you want others to believe. Finally, what your sister and I do and when is none of your concern." His features smoothed, eyes returned to normal and voice took on a more conversational tone. "The phone conversation I just finished with Nathanial, confirms my decision. To hear him tell it, you walk on water, and that's saying something from a legion commander of warrior angels." Bruce raised a brow. "Nathanial owes us one?"

Tristian snorted shifting from one foot to the other waiting for Bruce to step out of his path to the stairway. "Yeah, well his carelessness nearly cost the life of one of his warriors and put my team in a precarious situation coming out of the portal. I figured that was the least he owed us. The demon was neutralized, but…"

Firmly planted in front of the stairs leading to the main floor, Bruce continued, "We can go over your new job description in my office now before Hannah arrives mid-morning tomorrow. Or do it after she arrives. Your choice. Either way—" Bruce raised an eyebrow and shrugged. "The outcome is the same, only you'll have less time with her. I'm told the bridal party has a spa afternoon planned for tomorrow. The next day, you, Hannah, Birch, and Freesia will accompany Angie and me to Tahiti. From that point on—discussions will be of the wedding, nothing else."

"Fine. Let's get this over with. I'm beat." Tristian's shoulders slumped, and he blew out a breath..

Bruce's brow quirked up as he leveled his gaze at his employee. "Always this tired after an assignment?"

"Of course not. But when healing powers are required and then magic to clean up the battle scene, it's a different story. Not normally the duties of an enforcer."

"Angie is the healer," Bruce said.

"She is, but I have the latent power as well. Don't use it often. But didn't want an angel expiring on my watch. Bad for the reputation."

Bruce looked thoughtful then pinned his gaze on Tristian again. "Your father didn't have the healing power?"

"No, it comes from Mom's side," Tristian confirmed. "Now how about we stop with the twenty questions, and take care of business so I can get some shut eye."

With a quick kiss for Angie, Bruce released her, turned on his heel, and took the stairs two at the time to the first floor. He strode across the Salon floor giving a quick nod of acknowledgment to Owen, at the counter, and bounded up the stairs to the mezzanine. He waited at the entrance of his office for Tristian to enter and closed the door behind them. "Have a seat." Bruce motioned to one of two sleek leather chairs arranged in front of his desk.

The office looked different from the last time Tristian remembered. The glass top desk and white leather chair with chrome accents were the same, but the matching white and maroon leather chairs arranged on the other side of the desk were new, as was the art on the walls and an Irish crystal lamp hanging over the desk. Angie's touches, he smiled and settled on one of the new chairs. It made a new leather sound as he sat.

Rather than sit in his desk chair, Bruce eased in the one next to his enforcer and picked up a file from the desk, handed it to Tristian. "What I have in mind is for us to work as a team. You take over policing the problems as they arise. Assign a team to handle the problem and the leader will report directly to you. As you have to me all these years. I'm going to step out of the way and let you handle it once we agree on the parameters you will operate under."

Tristian surveyed his boss warily. "That leaves you to…"

Bruce leaned back in his chair, tented his fingers and eyed Tristian for a beat. "To be more active with the other Overlords and Council heads. Not that it's any of your business. We'll be keeping an eye on trouble spots and try to step in before chaos reigns, innocent lives are lost, or mortals take notice of us. It's going to be a cooperative effort. The angel legions will be involved as well."

Tristian flipped through the file pausing at an incident report.

"This is a plan we've been bouncing around for a while. The recent situation you encountered brought to light the necessity of communication and cooperation. I'm not saying there won't be times you'll need to get physically involved, but your team leaders are competent to handle most situations on their own. Wouldn't you agree?"

"Yes, or they wouldn't be working for me," he said flatly. "Do I need to be here? Or is it possible to work from Maine?" *Maybe this won't be so bad after all.* He relaxed in the chair. There was no denying that Hannah in his life had made a difference in his thinking and approach to assignments. Not that Angie hadn't, but it was different.

"While Angie and I are gone after the wedding, you'll need to handle things from here and anytime you are covering for me. After that, if I'm here, you can work from Maine. We can meet up once a month and compare notes. Sound good?"

"Yeah, worth a try." Tristian conceded, letting out

a jaw-popping yawn, shifting in his seat trying to keep from falling asleep.

"Great. I'd like to review the duties you'll perform while I'm gone. But I'd rather do it when you are more alert. Say early tomorrow morning? You can surprise Hannah when she arrives."

"I'll probably call her before I go to sleep," he mumbled..

"Make sure the line you talk to her on is…"

"I'm well aware of security procedures," he snapped shoving up from the chair, tossing the file back on the desk. "Tomorrow then."

Bruce stood and walked Tristian to the door. "The car is waiting to take you to the hotel."

"I can wa… Thanks." He considered walking, it wasn't that far, but he was so damn tired.

Arriving at the hotel, he kicked off his shoes, pulled his shirt over his head, and took the cell phone out of his pocket, glancing at the screen. "Call home." The phone rang several times then rolled into voice mail. *She must be at her cottage packing.* He considered calling her cell, but after the welcome in Scotland and the upcoming wedding, it was safer to wait and see her tomorrow.

*****

The next morning standing in front of Bruce's desk, Tristian stared darkly at the two-inch thick file folder Bruce shoved across the desk.

"This has all my contacts, the calendared meetings, my passwords for the computer, Salon, and disk for entrance into my apartment. You'll be staying there in my absence. It's more secure, and everything you'll need is at your fingertips. The computer in the apartment is networked with this one." He gestured toward the screen sitting on his desk connected to the main computer.

"Great," Tristian said with less enthusiasm than being handed a dead fish.

Tugging open a drawer, Bruce pulled out a thin laptop computer, set it on the desk, and reached to the floor producing a sleek black computer bag. "All of my business will be handled on this computer. I realize you have your own, but this one is set up on my secure network giving you access to all my business contacts and info you will need operating from other locations."

Mouth set in a thin line, Tristian picked up the file, flipped through it, then took the laptop and slid it into the computer bag. "Is that all?"

"I want you to review that file this afternoon. Sign onto your new computer, and we'll run tests to ensure everything works as designed before we leave. My network team assures me everything is good to go, but…"

"Understood. But I'd like to talk this whole thing over with Hannah, before—"

The corners of Bruce's mouth turned up in a knowing smile.

"Oh, wipe that smug look off your face."

Bruce raised his arms up in a gesture of surrender, lips twitching.

"Hannah loves her job. Maintaining a long-distance relationship is problematic at best—if not impossible." His forehead creased as a look of displeasure spread over his features.

A light knock on the door and Angie poked her head in. A wide Cheshire cat smile spread across her face as an "I told you so" look flew between her and Bruce that irritated the hell out of Tristian.

She crossed the room, brushed her lips across her mate's lips, and whispered something, then turned her attention to her brother. "The limo picked up Hannah, Birch, and Freesia at the airport. They should be here with thirty minutes. Thought you'd like to know—brother before we whisk her off for manicures, pedicures, and general girl stuff."

"Thanks, sis." He'd disguised his magic signature upon arrival this morning to keep his presence a secret in order to surprise Hannah.

"Of course." Angie winked and flounced toward the door. She paused at the entrance and turned. "Bruce, Owen needs to talk to you when you get a chance."

Bruce nodded and got to his feet. "I better see what Owen needs. Make yourself comfortable, review the file." He strode through the door and sprinted down the stairs in his usual fashion. A habit Tristian previous considered unprofessional for the Territory Overlord of the Western Hemisphere. But what did he know, probably made people feel at ease around him, which was a point Tristian hadn't considered until recently.

He grabbed the file with a grunt and strode over to the couch, plopped down. He sifted through the papers, committing to memory the people and numbers he might need. Then he separated them into piles according to importance and returned the documents to the file. When he waved his hand over the folder, it reduced to a size he could conceal inside his jacket pocket.

Hannah's magic aura swirled around him, a feeling that pleased and excited him. Grinning wide, he glanced through the glass walls of the office to the Salon below. Hannah and Freesia breezed through the door talking and laughing, followed by an animated Birch obviously entertained by their conversation. Angie greeted them with a hug. She led the group to the lounge where the coffee bar and fresh pastries were available for staff and customers.

Fresh coffee and a pastry is just the ticket. He bounded off the couch and yanked open the office door. Silently descending the stairs, he took a sharp right at the bottom and wound up a few feet from the arched entrance to the lounge. Hannah was blowing on her cup of tea. Birch poured coffee into Freesia's cup then his own. Angie gave him a sidelong glance then turned back to the group.

Tristian sauntered in, pausing in the doorway, and sniffed. "Hey, leave any of that Hawaiian fresh brewed coffee for me?"

Hannah whirled around, dropped her cup. It shattered on the floor, and tea flew everywhere. Oblivious to the mess, she ran to him, wrapped her arms around his neck, and claimed his lips in a tantalizing kiss.

He crushed her against him reveling in the feel of her body curved into his, returned her kiss hungrily, then trailed his lips along her jawline, buried his nose in her neck inhaling her vanilla and raspberry scent, not giving a damn what anyone thought. He'd missed her.

When someone cleared their throat, he raised his head to look at her and grinned. Grasping her around the waist, he swung her easily to his side. "Well, is there?" He ambled into the room.

Angie glanced around then swept her hand in the

air, the broken cup and hot liquid disappeared. Birch poured coffee into a large mug and handed it to Tristian while Freesia, grabbed a cup, tossed in a raspberry vanilla tea bag and poured hot water. Hannah took the steaming cup and mouthed "I'm sorry" to Angie.

She made a dismissive hand gesture and smiled.

Leaning over, he whispered against her ear. "Let's take a walk." Then moved toward the door.

Hannah nodded. "We'll be back in a bit."

"You have her back here at one o'clock sharp, you understand—big brother," Angie instructed. "Willow and Caleb will be here by then and the guys are taking Bruce out for a—"

Birch caught her gaze and gave a slight shake of his head. She shrugged. "Well—I'm not sure what, but you are included, and I am taking possession of Hannah for the afternoon."

"We're doing what?" Bruce eyed Owen who'd just walked into the room and abruptly did an about face after sending Birch a conspiratorial grin.

Chimes sounded as the front door of the Salon opened. "Nothing boss. Gotta go, customers." He scooted out the door ahead of Hannah and Tristian.

"Remember you two be back here in three hours, or heads will roll—yours," Owen said over his shoulder.

Tristian pushed the heavy glass door open, looked up and down the sidewalk filled with people rushing to their next destination. The last thing he wanted to do was share her with the world. What he wanted...

She slipped outside under his arm, drew in a breath, and blew it out slowly. "Awww, fresh air."

He quirked an eyebrow, let the door close with a

whoosh, slung an arm around her shoulder. "D.C. air is not exactly what I'd describe as fresh."

"Depends on what you are comparing it to." She wrinkled her nose. "The Salon has a chemical smell to it today. Did you notice?"

"Yeah, when I entered the main floor from Bruce's office. Wasn't like that earlier. Probably because they're busy doing several hair colorings and nail sets. Owen needs to turn up the filtration."

Hannah slid her arm around his waist, tucked her hand in his back pocket as they walked down the sidewalk in front of The Krystal Unicorn.

He shot her a devilish grin; she in turn gave his butt a little squeeze. At the end of the building, he tugged her into an alcove, trapping her against his hard body and the brick wall. He covered her mouth with his. Her lips parted in surprise, and his tongue slipped inside teasing, tasting until she shoved at his chest with both hands. He raised his head to see fire in those beautiful blue eyes.

"What are you? A horny teenager? Pulling me into a niche in broad daylight for a make out session?"

He shrugged. "Works for me." The corner of his mouth turned up in a sly grin.

She huffed out a breath. "It doesn't work for me." Her lips twitched in an attempt to keep a snicker at bay. He saw right through her.

"Okay, let's go back to my hotel. Don't tell me you don't want me, after your sneaky attempt to feel my ass."

Red patches bloomed on her cheeks. "You're absolutely incorrigible. Besides, we don't have time for a romp in the sack."

"Oh, we could." He wiggled his eyebrows. "A little magic, a little whirl of time, and we have all the time in the world." He nibbled at her neck.

Her eyes rounded, and she stared at him for a beat. "What do you mean? Can you manipulate time?"

"Forget it, killjoy. How about a walk in the park? I'd like to discuss a few things with you." He grasped her hand, returned to the sidewalk, and pulled her toward the curb.

She dug in her heels and refused to move. "I want an answer."

A man dressed in a business suit nearly running down the sidewalk frowned at them and swerved as he hurried past them. "Watch where you're going."

Ignoring the man, Tristian tugged at her again. "People in hell want ice water too. Not going to happen. Are you coming or not?" She jerked her hand free and followed reluctantly.

Most of the park benches were full. Parents watched their children play on the playground. Couples sat close to each other talking softly. Hannah spied an unoccupied bench at the far end of the park and made a beeline for it. Tristian sprinted along behind her. She stopped in front of the bench, then took a few steps to the side to smell the roses in bloom in one of the many flowerbeds that skirted the perimeter of the park.

"You'll love this park when the cherry trees are in bloom," he said, settling onto the bench. "Bruce wants me to cover for him while he and Angie take a mini honeymoon after the wedding."

She lifted her head and peered at him. "You will be staying here then?"

"Yep, guess so. I tried to reason with him. Bruce

has this idea in his head that I should manage the assignments rather than execute them." Tristian shook his head. "I'd rather…" He paused as a couple strolled by in front of them hand in hand.

"He must have a lot of faith in you, especially after all that has transpired between you two."

"He has my sister's best interests in mind, but I don't like being—I'm a hands-on kinda guy. Always have been." He ran the fingers of one hand through his hair while he stared down at the other. "Until I learn how he wants things done, I'll reside in D.C. for the time being—staying in Bruce's apartment."

Hannah licked her lips, running her front teeth delicately over her bottom lip. "Oh—well, I have some news of my own." She eased onto the bench and scooted next to him. "My boss has offered me a promotion. That's why he let me leave on vacation early, and he was pissed at the other guys on my team."

He peered up at her. "Lucky you. Tell me about your promotion."

"My security clearance came through. He wants me to head up a Research & Development team for the government's new cyber security assessment." She paused for a couple beats. "I'll be moving to Colorado with Shadow Hawk Cyber."

His head jerked up as the muscle in his jaw worked overtime. "When?"

"I was getting to that. Not for at least eighteen months. I may have to fly out there once in a while to oversee setting up our work environment. But that's all."

"That's going to make things difficult. I was hoping you could stick around here for a while until

Bruce and Angie get back."

"I was granted a month's vacation, plus two days." She grinned. "Will they be back by then?"

"Maybe. He hasn't said how long they'll be gone." Tristian stood, paced in front of the bench. "I don't see how…"

Hannah got to her feet, caught his arm with her hand, slid it down to his hand, and entwined their fingers. "One day at a time, remember. Don't get all wazzed out before we have all the details."

Lips set in a thin line, he nodded settling back on the bench, tugging lightly on her arm to join him. "So, what is this new job going to entail?"

She beamed. "It's been a while since I've been privy to the top security stuff, but I believe it will be assessing and creating code to strengthen the government's security on sites. Also evaluate events where national security could be at risk, such as the Olympics. All the data that zooms back in forth is ripe for a hacker to fudge the outcome of the competitions. Anything is possible."

Her eyes lit up when she talked about her job. He couldn't ask her to leave it, but how could they make this work. Colorado was a hell of a long way from Maine or D.C. He didn't—couldn't—see a way through. *One day at a time. I'll try to give her that—for a while.*

Chapter Twenty-Two
Bachelor Party Fiasco and Girls Night Out

"Well, it's about time you brought her back," Angie chastised her brother. "Have a couple hours of fun?" she asked eyebrow raised, a knowing look on her face.

He gave Angie an "eat shit and die look" before one last glance at Hannah and strode to where the men were waiting.

Blood rushed to Hannah's cheeks. "Far from."

"Oh, girl you got to learn to control that blush or you'll leave no doubt what you've been up to." Angie giggled, grabbed Hannah's arm. "We're going to start with pedies, mannies, and finish up with having our hair done. Then off to Tahiti tomorrow." She twirled around once and pointed to chairs lined up along the wall. Willow waved, already settled next to her mother, feet in the tub. To her right, two empty chairs awaited them. Angie took the chair next to Willow. Hannah gave one last look over her shoulder at Tristian and climbed into the chair beside Angie, hesitantly sticking her toes into the warm swirling water.

"Don't worry, they're taking Bruce out to dinner to discuss male things," Angie said airily, patting Hannah's arm. "Now spill, where did you two disappear to? And what on earth have you done to my brother?"

Willow snickered. "I was about to ask one of those questions."

Both women peered expectantly at Hannah. Even the woman doing the pedicure on Freesia slowed her work to give Hannah a sideways glance.

"I have no idea what you are talking about. He's still the same difficult, stubborn, protective, wonderful person." Her hand flew to her mouth. *I've said too much.*

Gales of laughter flowed from Freesia, Willow, and Angie. "No...no...we're talking about my brother, Tristian." Angie managed to say in between fits of laughter. "And don't let him hear you say that." She sucked in a breath between giggles, made air quotes with her fingers. "He is a tough, hard as nails, domineering enforcer." Angie shrugged. "We all know and accept him for what he is even though a few of us have glimpsed a softer side." Her gaze searched Hannah's face. "Oh no."

"What? What's wrong?" Hannah asked peering at the others who looked aghast.

"You're in love with him," Angie said in a whisper. "Does he know?"

"Don't be ridiculous. We enjoy each other's company. That's all." Hannah felt the damn heat rise in her cheeks again. *I've got to get a better handle on my reactions.*

"No, nope." Willow shook her head. "I know that look. Angie had that same expression when I confronted her about Bruce. Now look at her, mated to a demon overlord, and her brother's boss. What a tangle. From the looks of things, it's about to get a whole lot worse."

"Yeah, that kiss at the Salon, it wasn't a fling kiss," Angie said solemnly.

"Aw, leave Hannah alone, she's good for him," Freesia said waggling a finger at Willow and Angie. "Stay out of it. Let them work it out. Now, what about the bridesmaid dresses?"

Angie waved a hand in a dismissive gesture. "They're all ready, with a bit of magic woven in. We'll check the final fitting at the event location." She frowned at the nail tech who seemed a bit too intent on their conversation.

The woman who'd been doing Hannah's pedie returned with fresh towels. Patted her feet dry and helped her out of the chair. "Manicures next ladies, follow me."

They all trouped into the back of the salon where four nail techs were waiting. Once the women settled, Angie grinned at the others, her eyes sparkling with mischief and waved her hand. "Spell to make sure they"—she nodded to the nail techs—"don't overhear anything, as I did out in the Salon." Then she turned to Hannah. "Did Trist tell you his job position is changing?"

"Yeah, we touched on that." Hannah pressed her lips together.

"Isn't it great?" Angie bubbled. "He won't be in the thick of things anymore. He isn't getting any younger. It's time the young blood he's trained for years takes on some of the responsibility." She leaned back in the chair and pointed to the light lavender nail polish and a floral design for her nails.

"Yes, but he seemed to enjoy keeping the peace." Hannah winced. "If that is what you call it."

Angie quirked an eyebrow. "That's putting it mildly. You do know exactly what he does?"

"Of course. When mortals police their world, people sometimes die, but that doesn't make them assassins," Hannah said testily.

Angie opened and shut her mouth, then blew out a breath.

Freesia glanced over at Hannah. "We all know what Tristian does is necessary in the magical world to keep things in balance. What's bothering you, girl?" Her kind eyes stayed locked on Hannah's.

"Nothing—" Hannah's gaze wandered over each of the other women. *Do I dare confide in them? Oh, how I wish I could talk everything over with Brandy. What a mess. I have to talk to someone.*

"You know, Caleb's family had no problem with us getting married. But when we told them a retired demon overlord would perform the ceremony, they got all squirrelly. Why who is marrying us makes a difference, I'll never know. But we're working it out. They've agreed to attend the ceremony," Willow offered.

Hannah smiled weakly at the attempt to make her feel better.

"No one said the life we lead would be easy. But is it worth loving the men we do?" Angie said a resounding, "Hell yes." Chorused by the rest of the women.

Except for Hannah. This was all so new, danger was a turn on at first, but now, a whole lifestyle centered around looking over her back. She blew out a breath. *What kind of life is that? What have I done?*

Angie put a hand on her arm and rubbed softly.

"You'll get used to it."

"Oh, it's not what he does. I've known that about him since shortly after we met. It's now we have added pressure. He will be in D.C. or Maine. I'll be moving to Colorado in the next year and a half. I got a promotion. My dream job really." *And I can't tell my family.*

Angie's eyes went wide. Willow's hand flew to her mouth, and Freesia smiled knowingly.

"A small detail to work out over several months." Freesia waved a hand dismissively, shifted in her seat to face Hannah. "The one thing I know about Tristian is he'll move heaven and earth for those he loves. And believe me, he loves you. He may not have said it yet; he's a complicated male, to say the least. Where his family is concerned, he has a heart of gold. And if any of you tell him I said that, I'll deny it to your face—Angie."

Her hands flew up in a gesture of surrender, then zipped her lips, motioned throwing away the key, and giggled. Holding out her pinky finger to swear. "We all know that about my brother." She paused a couple of beats. "Well, maybe not Bruce—yet. But he will, he's family too now."

"What are we twelve?" Freesia said with a laugh, she curled her pinky finger around Angie's.

A single tear trickled down Hannah's cheek. "I sure hope you're right." She wiped the tear away with the back of her hand. The nail tech working on her thumb frowned and pointed to the table. Hannah obediently returned her hand to the soaking dish. *What have I done? Tied to a warlock for all eternity. Would he commit? Could he?* Her gaze traveled to each of her new friends. If they only knew.

****

Tristian led the way into the private room of an Italian restaurant housed in a renovated townhouse in D.C., one of Bruce's favorites. Owen, Caleb, Birch, Bobby, and Ruben settled around the long polished cherry wood table. Bruce took his place at the head of the table. He rubbed his hands together. "I'm starved." Glancing at Tristian kicked back relaxed at the opposite end of the table, Bruce surveyed the others. "So glad you didn't opt for a bar or strip club. I'm way past that behavior these days."

Bobby sent a sidelong glance to Ruben with a snicker. Tristian caught the exchange and cleared his throat. *They better not have done what I think they've done.* Two of Tristian's best team leaders, single with a taste for exotic females frequented D.C.'s nightlife when in town. Their actions were no different than he or Bruce had indulged previously. Power and money brought anything you desired, especially here. Having enjoyed the fare in Scotland and Ireland, he hoped the men satisfied their craving and would conduct themselves appropriately.

A tall, raven-haired beauty dressed in a black clingy dress with a low neckline sashayed into the room holding dinner and drink menus. Tristian had explained the event for this evening to the proprietor of this establishment, Nicoli, and requested female servers. He figured just because you are on a diet, there's no reason you can't peruse the menu. The first entree was tantalizing. After ordering, he leaned back in his chair and watched the parade of beautiful women strut in with drinks, meals, and flirt outrageously with Bruce and Caleb before undulating out of the room.

His boss eyed him suspiciously. "I assume you arranged all this for mine and Caleb's benefit?"

"Noo, not really. I only requested female servers to celebrate your upcoming nuptials," Tristian said with a grin. "I think we've all benefited from the menu." He shifted in his chair. Bruce laughed as the other men at the table ogled the women.

"Angie and Willow are secure enough in their seductive qualities to be okay with this little display." Tristian took a deep drink of his red wine, the third glass this evening.

Birch frowned at him.

Caleb who'd remained quiet for most of the evening seemed relieved. "I hope you're right. Willow and I don't keep secrets. I wasn't sure how much trouble this little foray was going to cause."

Bruce cleared his throat and peered at Tristian. "But will Hannah? You realize she will hear about this one way or the other."

Tristian waved his hand in dismissal. "They weren't brushing against me and flirting."

"To hear you tell it," Bruce warned eyebrow raised.

"Besides, I'm not the ones... Never mind."

"Watch yourself, Tristian," Bruce warned. "Don't want the wine saying anything you'll regret."

While the staff cleared away the dishes, lingered close to the guests of honor, and refreshed the drinks, Bruce and Tristian set out the assignments for the next few days. But he refrained from mentioning the actual event and specifics.

When each server leaned over and placed the dessert plates on the table, Ruben reached out and curled an arm around his server, pulled her into his lap, and mentioned his prowess of enjoying desserts, not on the table. Bruce and Tristian stood at the same time, sending warning glances in Ruben's direction. The woman, who seemed to enjoy the attention, shoved up and sauntered away mumbling something about "a little fun."

Chastised, Ruben sent Bobby a concerned glance. Tristian watched the exchange again and stood. "Ruben, Bobby, could I see you outside."

"I'm not quite finished with—" Bobby stopped mid-sentence at the sharpness in Tristian's voice, the scowl on his face. "Yes, sir."

As the three men walked toward the door, it burst open with a bevy of scantily clad women. Tristian whirled around to see Ruben and Bobby grinning, hands freely roaming over the newcomers.

Tristian glanced at Bruce who had his head in his hands to cover a smirk. When Bruce raised his head up, an amused expression spread across his face. "Gentlemen, we appreciate the thought, but I'm going to call it a night."

Caleb quickly echoed Bruce's sentiment and Tristian seethed. Bruce put his hand on Tristian's shoulder. "Let it go, let them have their fun."

"They were specifically instructed no strippers and no strip joint. That's insubordination." He headed toward the two men.

"And you've never defied my instructions," Bruce said, grabbing Tristian's arm.

"That's different."

"So is attacking your Overlord. Let it go." He released his soon to be brother-in-law and strode toward the door.

Tristian stood still for a moment, sauntered over to the men. "Enjoy your fun now. You'll be providing security for the place of business the next week."

"No, you said we were going to Tah—" Bobby slurred.

Tristian cut him off. "Things change, especially when you don't heed my instructions." He turned and strode toward the exit.

Bruce leaned against the doorframe and nodded approvingly. "Come on guys, bet we got beautiful wenches in our chambers," he said in his best Scottish brogue.

"Poking fun at the recent assignment?" Tristian asked, sauntering out of the restaurant with the others.

Bruce shrugged. "Not exactly. Thank you for an entertaining evening. The food was wonderful, the decorations titillating. A bit of advice, rein in that temper before you move into your new position."

"Seems to me a few short months ago, you wore a temper and womanized with the best of them," Tristian shot back with a grin, shoving open the heavy wooden door. It groaned at the abuse.

"So true. Things change when you meet the right woman." He winked at Caleb then leveled his gaze at Tristian. "You'll rue the day you let her walk away." The limo driver opened the door and waited while Bruce, Birch, Caleb, and Tristian stepped inside.

The Wycked Hair Salon was dark upon their arrival. "I've got paperwork to finish up, so I'll bid you three good night." Bruce stepped out of the limo, instructed the driver to take the others home.

"I'm getting out here too. Need to let Terra know

her assignment has changed. She'll just be ending her shift." No sooner were the words out of his mouth than Terra strode out of the Salon.

She blinked in surprise. "Aren't you supposed to be out celebrating manhood or something?" she quipped.

"Something like that." Bruce waved his hand across the door, touched the alarm panel, and walked inside.

She watched Bruce enter the salon without further conversation and turned to Tristian. "Is something wrong?"

"No, he's got business to finish up before tomorrow. There's been a chance in assignments. You'll be handling the event location starting tomorrow morning."

"Really?" She paused, searching his face. "Thank you."

Expecting a barrage of questions that didn't come, pleased him no end. She'd turned into a great team leader. "Good night."

"Morning, sir," she corrected over her shoulder as she strode to the parking lot.

His lips twitched. The limo remained at the curb with the door open. "Take Caleb and Birch home first. I'll go back to the hotel last." Tristian glanced at Birch. "You are staying with Willow and Caleb?"

Birch nodded.

Tristian pulled his phone out of his pocket, touched the screen, a gruff voice answered on the first ring. "I need you to keep an eye on Ruben and Bobby. Make sure they report for duty at the Salon at five sharp."

"But... Yes, sir."

He disconnected the call, shoved the phone back in

his pocket. Deep in thought on the ride back to the hotel, he startled when the limo slowed to a stopped. Stepping out onto the curb, he paused to wave to the driver. "Night."

The driver nodded in acknowledgment as Tristian closed the door.

He pulled the phone out of his pocket, then glanced at the time displayed on his phone. *Too late to call Hannah and see where she landed for the night. I'd rather she be with me, but she is probably having a great time with the girls.* Inside his suite, he kicked off his shoes, took off the jacket and shirt, slipped out of his pants. *Clothes were overrated.*

Passing into the bedroom, he stopped in his tracks. The wine had dulled his senses, but there was definitely light breathing coming from his bed. In addition, slight movement from the left side of the bed caught his attention.

Chapter Twenty-Three
Magic Abound in a Tropical Paradise

Silently he crept to the bed, touched the form beneath the covers. An ear-splitting scream resounded through the room. Hannah kicked off the covers, hands fisted and jabbing, feet thrusting. Tristian leaped off the bed and stared at her, then guffawed loudly. He swept her out of bed into his arms and whirled around a couple times.

"I'm so glad to see you." Before she could form any words, he smothered them with his mouth, as he held her close, he felt her heart hammering in her chest and smiled.

She wrapped her arms around his neck and blinked up at him. "Fancy meeting you here," she murmured against his lips. He smiled.

"What about your girls' night out, afternoon out, whatever it was?" Tristian said a bit giddily, which is why he never drank much. He liked to be in control at all times. Tonight, he'd thrown caution to the wind, a dangerous thing for a person in his position. He eased her down on the bed, enjoying her lacy see-through nightgown. Running his fingers over her curves, he sighed.

"You've been drinking." She giggled. "Guess your party was more fun than mine. We had pedicures, manicures, facials, makeovers, and giggled a lot, which

I enjoyed. Never had a lot of girlfriends, just my sister. So it was fun to listen to them."

He lay down on the bed beside her, propped up on his elbow, head in his hand while the other explored her soft curves. "We had dinner at Bruce's favorite Italian place. I'd arranged ahead of time for the servers to be all female. Nicoli went out of his way to provide sexy eye candy for us, with a bit of a tease for Bruce and Caleb."

Hannah raised an eyebrow. "So you all enjoyed yourselves."

"Yes, a beautiful woman is a wondrous thing. But Bobby and Ruben had other ideas and waaaayy too much to drink when the strippers arrived." Tristian waved a hand.

"Strippers?" Hannah said in a low squeal. "Angie and Willow are not going to appreciate that. But I bet you did."

He shot her a scathing glance. "I made it clear when we planned the party, strippers were off limits. It was over the top. I shut it down. Bruce, Birch, Caleb and I left. But not before I told Bobby and Ruben their assignments moved from Tahiti to the Salon for the duration of the events."

"Don't you think that's a little—"

"No. They'd disobeyed my orders. That type of thing can get you killed in our line of work."

"Overreacting just a bit?"

"Absolutely not."

"Wasn't Bruce's bachelor party in a safe secure environment?" Hannah frowned. "It was secure?"

"Of course." Tristian rolled onto this back, flung his arm over his face. "Maybe… I—" He paused and rubbed his forehead, which was starting to throb.

"So, what happened to Ruben and Bobby?"

"I imagine they got laid."

"Did you know the women?"

"Hell no, I didn't know the women. I knew you'd be—"

She held up a hand. "Listen—I meant the guys are not in any danger being left with, um…unknown companions?"

"Oh, the women never would have gotten in the restaurant without the owner being familiar with them. The guys are fine." He winced. "Until tomorrow morning when Jake and Ian roust them for work."

"Sucks to be them." She scooted over, curled into him, sliding a leg over his. "These women, were they—did they—have an effect?" Caressing his chest with her fingertips, she slipped her fingers lower twined them in the hair below his abs and breathed kisses along his neck.

"What do you think?" He reached over and pulled her on top of him.

She giggled and kissed him, whispering against his lips. "I think going to Tahiti is exciting."

"I'll show you something else exciting." He reclaimed her lips and crushed her to him.

****

The next morning when they entered the Salon, Caleb and Willow, Birch and Freesia, and Angie were waiting for them. Bruce came bounding down the stairs from his office dressed in jeans, a polo shirt, and athletic shoes. "Ready to go?"

The group mock gasped and stared at Bruce.

"What?" He grinned. "I can do casual Friday too."

"Already sent the luggage with Terra and her team. She was thrilled with her assignment. The guys not so much." Angie snickered wrapping an arm around Bruce as he led the way to the basement. "Tobi will put the sign up Saturday night notifying the clientele we're closed the rest of Sunday and Monday due to water damage repair. She didn't book anyone for those days in anticipation of the event. The rest of the invited employees and guests not attending the celebration dinner will join us Monday morning for the afternoon wedding. Owen will come back and take them through. Will that work? That way Tobi and Owen are free to attend the rehearsal dinner Sunday evening."

"Sure. I've already talked with Owen about being the last to leave from the Salon. He knows to check everything, then cast a protection spell over The Wycked Hair and Krystal Unicorn before he passes through the portal," Bruce said.

"Bobby and Ruben have security duty while the Salon is closed," Tristian said. "I don't think it wise to leave the portal unguarded while the Salon is closed and so many coming and going."

"A good point, but it's disguised well, and there's never been a problem," Bruce mused.

Tristian frowned running his fingers through his hair leaving it standing in little spikes. "The last thing we need on your wedding day is a problem. Overlords, Council leaders of the magic realm, and their security all in one place, make me nervous."

"Then what do you suggest?" Bruce asked tapping his foot impatiently.

"I'd like to have a few of Bobby's team secure the perimeter of the building. Bobby and Ruben can switch off with a couple members of Ruben's team guarding the closed portal."

Bruce began to shake his head and before he opened his mouth Tristian held up his hand in a silencing gesture. "Before you say it, the measures may be overkill, but it will keep the vulnerability down to a minimum. I still don't like that Nat and his angels weren't positive that none of the dark demons escaped. We both know about being targeted for revenge. Nathanial will be attending the event?"

"Yes, he will be accompanied by his wife. Okay, security is your forte. We'll do it your way."

"Thank you." Tristian took Hannah's arm. "Ready whenever you are."

Angie beamed. "Sounds like we are all set. Let's go." Angie grabbed Bruce's hand and tugged him toward the activated portal.

He held her back. "Wait. You, Willow, Caleb, and I will go through first. I want to make sure there are no—complications. Then Tristian will bring Hannah, Birch, and Freesia through, making sure everything is secure and the portal is closed."

The guests will arrive Monday early morning, right?" Willow asked. "Caleb would like to greet his parents and bring them through. They're a little leery of all the power that could be here and—well, you know."

"Not a problem. But aren't they attending the dinner?" Bruce tilted his head to one side and peered at her.

"No, they didn't feel comfortable coming." Willow pursed her lips. "Caleb thought it best not to push them."

"Okay, we'll make sure they feel comfortable and

welcome at the reception. Angie and I will take the time to visit with them." He turned his attention to Caleb. "Will that be all right?"

"Oh, they'll come around." Caleb blew out a breath. "My marrying a faery was no problem, it was the double ceremony with the Overlord—you know. Then having the retired Overlord perform the ceremony at an undisclosed location was more than they could handle. At first, they weren't coming at all." He shrugged, hands in his pockets.

Bruce leaned over and whispered something in Angie's ear, then peered at Caleb with a winsome smile. "Don't worry. We got this."

Tristian snickered when he saw Caleb scoot close to Willow and whisper. "That's what I'm afraid of." By the smirk on Bruce's face, Tristian was sure his boss had heard too.

Hannah elbowed Tristian in the ribs and scowled. He pulled her close and kissed the top of her head.

When it was time for him to lead his group through the portal, he peered in then hesitated a fraction of a second. He'd never been to Bruce's parents' place. He didn't like unknowns regardless of how benign the situation should be. After stepping out into thick mist on the other side of the portal with his entourage in tow, it was deja vue all over again.

Bruce's booming voice came somewhere out of the fog. "Don't worry; it's Mother's magic protecting their estate. The mist will clear as we get closer to the house. "The limo awaits." He opened the door to a large white stretch limo, the bright blue interior lights cut through the curtain of fog and guided the group inside.

Within a few minutes, the mist gave way to a lush

tropical paradise. A bluish-gray and rose stone villa with a decorative gated courtyard sat nestled in the center of the greenery. A waterfall cascaded down the towering cliffs behind the villa creating a mist that floated above and behind the structure. The driver pulled the limo into a circular driveway stopping at the multi-hued stone path that meandered through the open decorative wrought iron gate and across the courtyard.

Several panels of stained glass depicting a large golden dragon frolicking with a variety of faeries, wood nymphs, and water sprites adorned the arched front door. Tristian sucked in a breath. "Wow, this is some place," he whispered in Hannah's ear. He looked over her head at the stunned expressions of the rest of the party.

Bruce and Angie ambled up the pathway toward a tall muscular man with silver streaked sable hair who stood in the entrance. Beside him, stood the most beautiful woman Tristian had ever seen short of Hannah. The woman had reddish blonde hair that hung in graceful curves over her shoulders, petite build, and bright blue eyes that seemed to dance when she smiled. *So, that is where Bruce got his looks.* The next second Tristian was confused by the magic signatures he was picking up. Obviously, the demon signature, reminiscent of Bruce's, must be his dad, but the other light, but powerful signature, he couldn't get a handle on. It worried him as he glanced around making sure everyone was accounted for. The strange aura had to be emanating from Bruce's mother.

Just then, she gave Tristian a brilliant smile as Bruce introduced the group to his parents, Andre and Matiah.

"So wonderful to meet you all. Come on in. We have refreshments and snacks on the veranda." With a sweep of her hand, she motioned them inside, across the entryway tiled in white marble veined with turquoise to the rich wood floors of the living area. A massive stone fireplace occupied one corner of the room, top to bottom. Tristian had only a moment to wonder about a fireplace in a tropical climate before being whisked out with the others onto the marble tiled veranda.

Spread across a long glass top table with copper accents were meat and cheese platters, sliced veggies, fresh fruit, crackers, bread and dips of all kinds in crystal serving dishes. A matching crystal pitcher filled with amber liquid sat in the middle of the table. What looked to Tristian like a mini fridge, but he bet is was one of those fancy wine coolers that held several wine bottles. Beside the pitcher were eight tumblers with ice, moisture trickled down the frosty glasses. Wine glasses sat at the end of the table next to several different types of desserts. Cloth napkins embroidered with tropical flowers and the initials A & M lay at end of the table closest to them with silverware fanned out alongside.

"Iced tea, anyone?" Matiah called out.

Now this is luxury. Next to this, my home looks... Tristian caught movement out of the corner of his eye as Hannah ambled to the railing.

She leaned on the smooth marble support looking out over lush vegetation and a winding pathway to the three-story waterfall crashing over the rocks. Tristian walked up behind her, caught her around the waist. "Spectacular, isn't it?"

"Awe inspiring. What a beautiful setting for a

wedding."

Matiah touched Tristian on the shoulder. "You two can explore the path and waterfall after you get something to eat." She stepped back and motioned them to the table.

Following Willow and Caleb, they picked up plates and sampled most of the food.

Bruce paused and pointed to sliced bread. "Don't miss the chef's coconut bread. It's one of Maeva's specialties."

"Oh yes, it's to die for," Angie said, adding a piece to her plate.

Once their plates were full, Tristian led Hannah to a double gliding bench between Bruce and Angie seated in the swing. Caleb and Willow shared a large lounge chair next to Freesia and Birch. Andre and Matiah finished out the oblong circle seating arrangement. Small teak tables set conveniently beside the seats.

"This is a beautiful place you have here," Freesia gushed, nibbling on the fresh fruit from her plate.

Birch nodded, chewing a piece of red tuna, staring at the torches on either side of the veranda, and continued down the path toward the beach. He swallowed. "Do you light the torches every night?" Raising his glass of iced tea, he motioned toward the path then took a sip.

Andre grinned. "They flame on automatically when we sit out here in the evenings, even if we don't meander down to the beach. Ambiance you know." He reached over and patted Matiah's thigh, giving her leg a little caress before letting his hand rest there.

Matiah smiled at her husband, then returned her gaze to the group. "Feel free to wander around, make yourselves at home." She pointed toward the waterfall. "There is a cottage nestled between the waterfall and the main house." She shifted toward the path. "Another one you can barely see peeking out before the path curves down to the beach. There is also plenty of room in the main house, and all are ready for guests."

Twisting in her seat, Hannah tried to get a better look at the cottage in the direction Matiah motioned. "Oh, I want to stay in the one by the waterfall," Hannah blurted, her hand flew to her mouth. "If no one else does, of course."

The group erupted into gales of laughter as everyone nodded indicating the waterfall cottage was hers.

"That's a good thing since that's where your luggage went," Matiah said and winked at Tristian.

Freesia and Birch took the bungalow on the way to the beach. Willow and Angie decided to stay in the main house where they could review plans and arrangements for the wedding and reception.

The arrangements suited Tristian. He liked the waterfall and the cool mist that wafted off the cascading water. Tropical climates were a bit warm for his taste, unless they were situated on the beach where there was always an ocean breeze. Finishing the last bit of red tuna marinated in a delicious and aromatic blend of lime juice and coconut milk, Tristian turned. Hannah scooped up the last bite of sauce on her fresh water shrimp and popped it in her mouth.

"How about we take a walk around?" He stood and helped her to her feet. "We're going to check out your beautiful piece of paradise. If that's all right with you."

Andre smiled and motioned them to the steps of the

veranda that ended at the path leading to the waterfall then wound around down to the beach.

"Where to first?" Tristian asked.

"The waterfall, then let's check out the cottage." She tilted her face up to his and whispered. "How about a moonlit walk on the beach?"

"Your wish is my command." He pulled her close and brushed his lips over hers. Walking hand in hand, they stopped in front of the water crashing off the cliffs. He closed his eyes letting the cool mist caress his face. His mind's eye opened to see Hannah smiling, her eyes blinking at the mist. But behind the waterfall was some type of path that led to rooms carved out behind rocks. *Interesting, there's more to this place than meets the eye. Surveillance? I'll quiz Bruce about it tomorrow.* When he opened his eyes, Hannah was peering up at him.

"Ready to take a look around the cottage?"

"Sure." Tristian held the door for Hannah as she passed through the entrance. Cream walls with lacy floral curtains waving in the breeze greeted them. The king-sized bed seemed huge in the room. Neatly folded at the foot of the bed was a patchwork comforter of tiny flowers on multi-color squares. Gauzy curtains hung from the canopy frame, tied back at the four posters that held up the frame. A small white wicker love seat, with light blue cushions, sat facing the double glass French doors which looked out at the waterfall. Hannah eased down on the love seat and sighed. "Isn't this beautiful."

"And cooler too." Tristian slid in beside her and wrapped an arm around her. They sat in silence for several minutes. Hannah leaned her head on his shoulder. He kissed the top of her head and laid his cheek on her hair, his finger curling several strands of her hair around it. *So soft.* He breathed in the fresh lemon and honey scent.

Red and orange streaked across the azure sky as the sun set. "If you want to go to the beach, we can get changed and head that way. Or we could…"

"There is plenty of time for that." She chuckled. "I need to get the wiggles out, if you know what I mean."

"Not really, but I still think other activities could help with that."

"You would." She chuckled.

"Hannah," Angie called walking the path toward the cottage. "I hate to interrupt, but we need to do a final fitting on the dresses. Only take a moment."

"No matter how old that girl gets, she has terrible timing." Tristian huffed pushing up from the seat.

Angie waved exuberantly at the glass doors, turned the handle, and poked her head inside. "I'll bring her right back." She started to flounce out with Hannah in her wake, then stopped and glanced back. "A little possessive, aren't we?"

She still knew how to push his buttons. "Get out of here," Tristian growled playfully.

By the time Hannah returned, the torches lit the way to the shoreline. A warm breeze ruffled Hannah's hair as they walked barefooted down the sandy path to the beach. Once at the water's edge, Hannah sprinted into the surf laughing and looking over her shoulder as Tristian ambled after her.

Catching up with her, he brushed the hair from her eyes and noticed tiny copper feathers sticking out at her hairline. He touched his finger on one. It was soft. "What's going on? You going gryphon on me?"

269

"Oh, probably. I need to—she stripped out of her bikini top and bottoms, then ran down the beach, shimmered and transformed. With a couple of beats of her rainbow-feathered wings, she glided over the waves.

Tristian leaned against a tall rock face and glanced up the path. *They were alone. She probably knew that.* He hitched a hip on an outcropping of rounded rocks and settled in to watch her soar through the night sky. *In love with a gryphon, who would have thought? Now what to do about it.*

Chapter Twenty-Four

Decisions, Decisions, a Surprise Guest, Change of Plans and a Heart Warming Scene No Matter Who You Are

In the wee hours of the morning, Hannah finally landed and shifted back to human form. Once they got to bed, Tristian tossed and turned for what seemed like hours. Finally, he got out of bed and quietly slipped out the French doors onto the deck. Settled into one of the chairs outside, he watched the massive waterfall enjoying the cool mist on his face.

Plants swishing and twigs snapping broke the silence of predawn. Lazily, he turned his head in the direction of the sounds, sensing his sister long before she appeared. Grinning, she stepped on the porch and plopped into the other chair. Her legs slung over the arm of the chair, while she leaned against the other one.

"To what do I owe the pleasure of your company?" Tristian snarked and remembered how their parents used to holler at Angie to use a chair as it was intended.

"I couldn't sleep. Did you see the shadow across the crescent moon around midnight? I tried to get a better look, but it disappeared among the cliffs. "

Tristian made a noncommittal noise and turned his attention back to the waterfall.

"So you didn't see it?" Angie persisted.

He couldn't lie to his little sister. "Yes, I saw

something cross the moon and night sky, but it was well after midnight."

"What do you think it was? You don't think it was a harbinger of bad things to come?" She nervously picked at the bottom of her dainty scalloped edge blouse.

Heaving a heavy sigh, he shifted in the chair to face her. "No, I'm sure it wasn't a harbinger of doom."

"Come on Tristian, spill it. You know more than you are telling."

"It's Hannah's tale to tell. So, you'll have to ask her."

"I knew it. She's some kind of magical creature." Angie bounced up from the chair and flounced to the railing, turned and leaned against it. "I thought that was her magic a couple times, but it was disguised so quickly."

"All ready for the wedding?"

She paused, putting her finger to her lips and opened and shut her mouth as if deciding whether or not to pursue the Hannah secret then sighed. "Almost. Which is why I'm here. I felt you up and around. Something bothering you?"

"Yes, the heat." He grinned over at her. "Nothing else."

"I like Hannah. She's good for you."

"I like her too, though she drives me crazy at times."

"Tristian—" She paused licking her lips and blew out a breath, returned to the chair gently putting her hand on his.

He glared at her hand then caught her gaze, held it. *When she was a little girl this is how she always* *wheedled h*er *way out of me and Dad.* "What do you want, Angie?"

She smiled sweetly. "Would you walk me down the aisle and give me away at the wedding?"

His eyes rounded, and he stared at her. "You want me to give my little sister away—willingly—to a demon?" He shook his head. "Not just a demon but a Demon Overlord and my boss?"

"Yes."

"You're asking an awful lot. I've accepted that you've made your choice. But…" He tented his fingers and waited for her tirade.

"But nothing Tristian Shandie!" She stood and stamped her tiny foot. "You know Mom and Dad would be happy for me. Dad would have welcomed the chance to walk me down the aisle. He'd recognize Bruce is a good man."

"Demon." His lips twitched.

She swiped at him. "And be happy for me. I love him, and he loves me. I know you see that." Hands on hips, she gave him a hard stare.

He returned her stare, unable to continue the ruse, he roared with laughter. "Of course, I'll give you away. You don't seriously think I'd let my little sister flounder her way down the aisle, trip, and fall flat on her face on her wedding day?" Sucking in a breath, he gave one final guffaw.

"Oh Tristian, you're incorrigible." She stood on tiptoes giving him a hug.

"So I've heard," he said in a bored voice.

Hannah's form in a silky robe appeared behind the glass. The French doors squeaked when she pushed them open. "What are you two doing out here?" she asked sleepily.

"Talking wedding. What else?" Tristian sniped.

"Oh, okay." She yawned again and stretched, dragged a chair from inside the cottage and sat next to Tristian, laying her head on his shoulder.

"Hannah, you scared the bejeebers out of me last night," Angie said.

"How'd I do that?" Hannah raised a brow, more alert.

"Flying around in the sky. You know only witches fly across the moon, and it's supposed to be full when we do." Angie settled into the chair.

"I'm sure I don't know what you are talking about." Hannah shrugged. "A little too much wine last night?"

"Nope. You're a sly one. Good at disguising your magic signature. But you're busted."

Hannah switched her attention to Tristian frowning.

Angie giggled. "No. He didn't say a thing, but your actions sure did. Guilty as charged."

Bruce came around the tall tropical foliage and stepped onto the porch. "Who's guilty as charged?"

Angie raised her hand then lowered it. "Tristian, he's incorrigible."

"So what's new?" Bruce blinked and blew out a breath. "Did he agree to give you away?"

"Of course."

A puzzled look on her face, Hannah slid her glance from Tristian to Angie. *What just happened?* she asked Tristian silently.

After a start, he gave a little shrug, wafting his words through her mind. *I agreed to walk Angie down the aisle. She saw your escapades in the night sky. They're going to find out soon enough. Might as well come clean. You know your secret is safe with my sister and her mate.* He rubbed his wrinkled forehead. *How long have you been able to communicate like this?*

Forever. It's a talent.

Tristian shoved up from his chair, leaned over, and brushed his lips over Hannah's, then turned toward Bruce. "Hey, got a couple minutes?" He stepped off the porch and walked toward the waterfall.

Bruce shrugged one shoulder, kissed Angie on the cheek, and followed Tristian. "Sure."

Stopping far enough away so the roaring of the falls didn't impede their conversation, Tristian pointed to the path slightly behind the waterfalls. "Where does that lead?"

Bruce paused for a couple beats. "Father's got an—operations—computer center carved out behind the rocks, where he keeps a finger on the pulse of the magical world and a bit more."

"Really. Retired but couldn't let go?"

"Not so much. Kinda of a safety net for them. Ask him for a tour. He'll happily do so. But I don't think that's what you wanted to talk about."

"Partly. You're right. Should I agree to the new position."

"I thought we'd hashed all that out. Refusal is not an option."

Tristian ignored his interruption. "What if I wanted multiple locations to work from? Would that be a problem?"

"Not while I'm in residence, handling things. But when you cover for me, as I said before, you'll need to be in D.C. at the Salon. You'll stay in my apartment rather than a hotel, for security reasons."

"Okay."

"Why all the questions? Taking up residence at a new location?"

"Leaving my options open. Never know what the future holds."

Bruce nodded. "I see." Before he could make further comment, Angie came bounding across the path through the lush tropical gardens. Grinning, Bruce caught her by the arms and gently lifted her off her feet, kissing her lips. The demon eyed his mate and bride-to-be with amusement. "How much caffeine have you had this morning?" He eased her down on her feet.

She fisted her hands on her hips. "Not enough. I told you she wielded magic. Couldn't pin point what kind. I was right," she crowed, turned, and glowered at Tristian.

Bruce gave a subtle eye roll. "When aren't you, my li'l witch? She who?"

Examining her perfectly manicured red fingernails, she buffed them lightly against the front of her blouse. "Well there is that," she cooed, smiling up at him, batting her long golden eyelashes. Then as if she'd nearly forgotten her important information, she straightened. "Anyway, Hannah, she's a—" Angie craned her neck surveying the surrounding area. "Gryphon. Isn't it great?"

"A what?"

She huffed out a breath. "You know—a gryphon. The not so mythical creature, part eagle, part lion with rainbow colored wings. Or at least hers are. Hannah is what I saw last night, and you hinted I'd had too much to drink."

He cocked an eyebrow. "Learn something new every day."

"That's it? That's your only response?" She flung her arms in the air.

"Well, I'd heard rumblings of the same when Tristian was in D.C. earlier this year. But discounted it."

"And you didn't tell me?" Angie demanded, color rising in her cheeks.

"Business dear." He patted her on the shoulder, leaving his hand resting a little lower. "We better get back to the house; Maeva will have breakfast ready." He glanced at Tristian. "Join us?"

His lips twitched to keep from grinning; he'd seen that look before from his sister, and Bruce was in for a tongue-lashing, overlord or not... "Let me check with Hannah, but I'm sure we'll be along shortly. She'll be starved."

Angie glared at Bruce, shrugged his hand off her shoulder. "See you on the veranda."

Bruce grasped Angie's hand, she flailed the other while walking sideways facing him chattering as they walked the path to the main house. When they arrived, a woman was setting a pitcher of orange juice on the table.

Tristian turned his attention from the veranda to his woman. Amused at that thought.

Hannah ambled down the path and met him halfway to the cottage. "We've been invited to breakfast," he informed her.

"Great. I'm starved." She reached around his waist and leaned into him, brushing her lips over his.

"Figured you would be." He smiled. Sharing his life with her was growing on him. He could do this and keep her safe. Would she accept his conditions?

Hannah glanced up the path and jerked her chin toward Angie and Bruce. "What's that all about?"

"You." He smirked and guided her toward the big house.

****

After breakfast, Tristian and Hannah meandered down the path to the beach. Hannah splashed along the water's edge ahead of him. When she stopped, she bent down, scooped up two handfuls of water, and flung it at him. In a flash, his hands wrapped around her pinning her arms to her sides. "A bit daring today?"

"Nope. Having fun. A little water never hurt anyone." She smirked. "Unless you'll melt or rust and I don't think there's a chance in hell of either."

He scowled and shook out his black polo shirt with silver threads woven through it. "It's salt water and leaves a white residue on my favorite shirt."

She eyed him speculatively. "It is a nice shirt. Shows off your sculptured upper body." She ran her fingers over his chest, slithered her body around his, her fingers slipped inside the neck of the unbuttoned polo. "But, I prefer you..."

"There you are," Bruce's voice rumbled behind them with a slight chuckle. "We apparently need to rehearse the wedding before guests arrive for this evening's dinner. The courtyard is all set up for the wedding, so Mother has decided to hold the rehearsal dinner aboard the Seraphim. He motioned in the direction of the seventy-five-foot blue and silver yacht moored in the middle of the cove, waves slapped gently at her sides.

"Okay, we'll be right up." Tristian swept Hannah into his arms and kissed her, whispering against her lips. "Hold that thought, we'll get back to it later. Maybe on the…?" he smiled seductively with a quick peek in the yacht's direction.

"I'm going to pretend I didn't hear that," Bruce said with amusement. "One other thing, after the rehearsal, I'd like you to go out to the Seraphim and make sure everything is ready for this evening. Tane, Maeva's husband, will oversee the additional help my parents have employed, but…"

Tristian eased Hannah's feet onto the sand, still keeping an arm around her waist. "Not a problem. The only other guests you are expecting outside the wedding party are Owen and Tobi. Correct? The wedding guests will arrive tomorrow morning."

"Yes, but I didn't plan on security for the yacht. Seems the size of this event is—I don't want to put my parents at risk after this is all over. Too many people know."

"Relax. I've got this. But what I don't understand is your mother's magic signature. She's not…

A mischievous glint in his eye, Bruce waved a hand dismissively. "She's an angel,"

"Most mothers are," Tristian agreed.

"No, I mean an angel, wings and all. She's keeping them under wraps while there are guests on the premises." Bruce grinned at the shock registering on Tristian's face.

He quickly schooled his features into a thoughtful expression. "A demon wed an angel? Well, that explains a lot."

"If you say so. Now back to the security." Bruce glanced toward the house.

"Oh, yes. There're a couple extra guys with Terra's team. We'll put them on the yacht tonight." He shot Bruce a sideways glance. "Not having a case of wedding jitters?"

Bruce straightened his shoulders and glared at Tristian. "Of course not. I've fought…"

"Matters of the heart are a different animal. At least that's what you keep telling me." He clapped Bruce on the shoulder. "I've got your back." He nudged Hannah forward with his hand at the small of her back. "Let's get the rehearsal over with, then I'll take a couple of guys and return to the Seraphim." He paused for a couple beats. "Will Hannah be needed after the practice wedding?" he asked with a smirk.

"You'll have to check with Angie. You know she's running the show." Bruce winced and muttered something about the whole thing being Tristian's fault.

"Hey, you're the one who took my little sister as your mate, a witch, and agreed to abide by our family traditions." Tristian's swagger was short lived.

Bruce pinned him with a dangerous look. "Don't push it." He turned on his heel and strode away.

"Way to go Trist. Piss off the groom at your sister's wedding." Hannah elbowed him in the ribs lightly as they wound their way up the path to the wedding venue. Once they crested the hill, Hannah's lips formed an O before she covered her mouth.

Tristian whispered, "Wow."

The whole courtyard and gardens in front of the waterfall transformed into a magical fairyland with twinkling lights over transparent umbrellas placed through the center of each row of tables forming a large semicircle in front of the waterfalls.

Bird of paradise plants bloomed over the rock wall between the falls and the garden. Flowering ivy peeked out through the nooks and crannies of the stones where tiny multi-colored lights glowed. In the middle of the wall, a wide archway rose up covered in climbing orange roses.

"Bet that's where Andre will stand presiding over the ceremony as the couples say their vows," Hannah whispered, then peered up at Tristian. "Why are we whispering?"

In his smooth baritone voice, he said, "I have no idea. Seemed appropriate, I guess. Looks like Freesia had a hand in this."

Hannah jumped, brought a fist up to eye level as she whirled around when someone put an arm around her shoulder. Angie took a couple steps backward nearly colliding with Willow who stood behind her.

"Didn't mean to scare you." She stepped closer to Hannah. "Isn't it beautiful? Matiah and Freesia created the paradise this afternoon. Then decided the dinner would have to be held elsewhere. They didn't want anyone messing up the wedding venue."

The closer they got to the waterfalls, the quieter the sounds, though the water continued to crash down the cliffs creating a fine mist. Rainbows sparkled on the spray from the waterfall and bounced across the umbrellas and tables. "Someone cast a muting spell over the waterfalls. Probably so everyone can hear the ceremony," Tristian observed.

"That was my handiwork," Megan said proudly, a witch-angel and Bruce's long time housekeeper. She surprised Angie from behind with a hug.

"What are you doing here?" Angie squealed wrapping her arms around the woman.

"I wouldn't miss this wedding for anything. Besides, it gives me a chance to check on my brother, Tane, and his wife."

"Does Bruce know you're here?" Angie asked.

"Not yet, but that's about to change." She chuckled as Bruce's gaze shifted to Angie and then to her while talking to his mother.

A wide smile spread across his face. He bounded down the steps of the veranda, through the tables to the edge of the garden where they were standing. He picked her up off her feet in a strong hug. "What a wonderful surprise. Mother said you couldn't..." He laughed and touched his hand to his forehead. "Oh, it was all a ploy to surprise me." He glanced at Angie. "Us. Good job."

The rehearsal went off without a hitch. Tristian was released from the rehearsal after walking Angie down the aisle and handing her off to Bruce. The task was easier than he ever thought possible several weeks ago. He grudgingly admitted to himself, that their parents would be proud of her choice and less than pleased with his behavior. However, he was none too happy with them for going and getting themselves killed, leaving all this to him. He grinned; they'd like Hannah too.

"Penny for your thoughts," Hannah said quietly, caressing sinewy muscles across his back.

"They're worth at least a quarter." He snickered, kissing her before leaving to search out two of Terra's team members to accompany him to the yacht. "Finish up here and meet me at the yacht." On the path to the beach, Terra hurried toward the house; Tristian intercepted her. "Hey, I need a couple of your guys for yacht detail."

"Okay, Jason and Trevor are securing the beach, take them. I'll send replacements shortly." She touched her headset, said something, and with a quick wave continued to the house.

All business, she was a great hire. When Tristian arrived with Jason and Trevor in tow, the yacht was a hive of activity. A tantalizing aroma wafted from the galley where the food was being prepared. An oval formal dining table of polished teak with crystal inlay in the center had eleven place settings ready for those attending the rehearsal dinner.

He carefully picked up a white china cup rimmed in gold with tiny rosebud accents while mentally counting the number of expected guests for dinner. The only surprise was Megan, and she made eleven. The china was Matiah's touch, he guessed as he set the cup back in place.

A large couch arranged in a semi-circle facing floor to ceiling windows took up the center of the living area. The furnishings matched the warm cream and dark blue accented decor, plush cream carpeting spread across the room, a golden-hued wood formed a circular staircase to the upper levels.

"Nice place," Tristian said to no one in particular. The cove was relatively calm, the slap of waves against the Seraphim was the only thing that reminded him he was on a yacht.

Mouthwatering aromas of prime rib, homemade dinner rolls, and a variety of other foods wafted through the room, mixed with the light brine brought in on a slight ocean breeze.

Standing between the dining room and living area, he brushed his fingertips over the small stainless steel wine cooler being stocked with bottles of excellent wine. He checked the labels on a couple bottles, then handed them back to the man filling the fridge and walked out onto the deck that opened off the living room. The polished brass railing gleamed in the warm sunlight.

His two security men reported everything was in order. He sent Trevor to the top observation deck, Jason to the second floor where the staterooms were located, and he chose to stay in the main living area. All the faces matched the roster Bruce had given him of Andre's employees working the event.

Tristian tugged on the sliding glass doors that closed the deck off during inclement weather. *Wouldn't need those tonight.* Tristian glanced at the clear blue sky. *It would be a beautiful night to get Hannah alone on the top observation deck.* The lilt of her voice caught his attention as she talked with one of the caterers in the dining room. He ambled toward the sound of her voice.

She'd changed into a silky green off the shoulder dress that ended a few inches above her knee and light green strappy sandals. The dress hugged her curves and flattered her creamy complexion and red hair that now hung below her shoulders. He liked her hair longer. Reaching over he twisted a curl in his finger and kissed her cheek. "You're beautiful." He touched the green emerald drop earrings he'd given her. They looked exquisite dangling from her delicate earlobes. She also wore the matching teardrop emerald necklace at her throat. Touching his headset, he asked Jason to come down and cover the main area while he showed Hannah around. The quick tour took only a few minutes, though they lingered on the top observation deck.

Before long, laughter and voices announced the arrival of the dinner guests. Tristian escorted Hannah down the spiral staircase, as the guests wandered around the living area until Andre and Matiah called everyone into the formal dining area.

Candles adorned the dining table, casting amber shadows over the crystal inlay, as everyone gathered around settling into their seats. The staff brought silver serving dishes to the table, food offered to each guest. Talk of the wedding, recent events, and the garden decor dominated the dinner conversation. Andre and Birch made toasts for long life and wedded bliss. Tristian added his own twist on a toast.

After dinner, the guests retired to the living area or the deck with glasses of wine to enjoy the beautiful star-strewn sky. Dessert, a decadent dark chocolate mousse, was served on the deck in tall tapered crystal glasses with long-handled silver spoons.

Hannah took one bite and closed her eyes. "Mmmm. This is fantastic." She scooped up another bite and slipped it into her mouth.

"My favorite," Angie declared, licking the back of her spoon. "How'd you know?" She looked from Andre to Matiah.

"A not so little demon told us," Matiah said with a laugh. "Glad you like it. Maeva fussed over it most of the morning."

Andre chuckled. "She actually had a trial run last week for us to taste. It too was perfect. Too bad you missed it," he said, scraping his spoon in the bottom of the glass for the last bite.

After midnight, as the guests were boarding the boat to deliver them back to the main house, Andre pulled Tristian aside. "Your security team is doing a great job. You wouldn't know we have security they blend in so well. If you want to stay behind on the yacht for a while, it's fine with us. Normally we don't have security on the Seraphim, but with the wedding tomorrow, you may want to leave one on the boat overnight."

"I planned on it, sir."

"Knock off the sir stuff. It's Andre." He smiled and took Matiah's hand to join his guests on the ride to the main house.

Angie and Bruce were the last to leave. "Are you two staying on the yacht?" Bruce asked.

"I think Hannah and I will spend a little more time out here, if that's all right?" Tristian said. "Make sure everyone is gone, including the wait staff. We'll leave Trevor here for the night."

"We figured as much and would like to join you, but wedding activities start early in the morning. So, we'll leave you on your own." Angie winked at the couple and tugged Bruce toward the awaiting boat.

"Oh, you can bet he planned it this way," Bruce said. "As I would, if we had the opportunity." He pulled Angie in for a kiss. "Good night," he said over his shoulder as he took another step toward the boat then they both disappeared.

"Bruce doesn't like small water crafts," Tristian said nonchalantly.

"Oh, that explained why they arrived earlier than the others." Hannah giggled. "Magic rules don't apply to him?"

"They do, but combined with his parents and Angie, the toll will be minimal." Tristian touched his headset. "Jason, you can head back to the house. Terra will have your assignments for tomorrow."

"Come on, I'll show you the rest of the yacht." He took her hand and led her across the living area to the spiral staircase.

She touched the polished wooden banister with a mermaid carved in the newel post. "This is beautiful. I'd love to have one like it in a home someday." She paused for a beat. "Maybe not a mermaid, but a bear, wolf or something…"

As they climbed the stairs to the second floor, Tristian filed that information away in his mind with a smile. Stepping onto the top landing, he shifted Hannah to the side and nearly collided with Trevor who was just coming around the corner. "Hey, Trev, I'd like you to take the night shift here tonight. There shouldn't be any action, but don't want any surprises. You'll have the day off tomorrow."

"No problem. What a place," Trevor said turning slowly in a three-hundred-sixty-degree circle. "The view at the end of the hallway—"he pointed to the other end of the boat"—is spectacular. The staterooms have a huge porthole, in addition to regular windows, plus a small deck access." He shook his head. "Never seen anything like it."

Tristian nodded and raised an eyebrow glancing toward the stairs. "Hannah and I are going to star gaze from the top deck. Keep an eye on the living area and second floor. We'll be going back to the cottage later. I'll let you know when we leave."

"Sure. I'll just make my way downstairs." He

turned on his heel and sprinted down the curving stairs.

Hannah went ahead of Tristian climbing slowly to the top deck. She sucked in a breath as her eyes went wide. "Wow, look at all the stars" She pointed to the sky. "There's the Southern Cross. Is that the Big Dipper? And that's the Milky Way."

"I'm not an expert on the stars in the southern hemisphere, but The Big Dipper is only visible occasionally here." He paused. "When the Southern Cross sails highest up in the Southern Hemisphere sky, the "upside-down" Big Dipper is seen just above the northern horizon."

Coming up behind her, he wrapped his arms around her. She tipped her head back and rested it on his chest staring at the stars.

"That's more than I knew," she said quietly.

He leaned over and brushed his lips along her neck, then covered her mouth with a searing kiss. Sweeping her off her feet, he carried her over to the double chaise and eased her down.

He smothered her lips with demanding mastery, her lips parted, his tongue slipped inside, teasing, tasting, exploring, and enjoying. She stirred his blood like no other. When he raised his mouth from hers, he stared into her smoldering green eyes for a beat. Then let his gaze wander from her eyes to her shoulders, to her breasts, then slowly, seductively, his gaze slid downward. Running his hand along her side, he reached under her blouse and cupped her breast over the lacy bra. He flipped open the front clasp, brushed the fabric away allowing her firm breasts to spill into his hand. Lifting the shirt, he buried his face between the firm mounds, licking first one nipple then the other and groaned. "So beautiful."

"Tristian," she breathed, "What are you doing?"

He chuckled. "If you don't know, I'm doing something wrong." He slid his hand inside the waistband of her pants, tugged her panties aside, felt her warm moist center, and sighed. The crotch of his pants grew tight, extremely tight. He needed her now, but he'd wait.

"That's not what I meant." She tried to push him away, but her thundering heart, racing pulse and the scent of her arousal told him, she wanted this as much as he did.

"I meant not here. What if we get caught? Trevor is right downstairs."

Reluctantly, he lifted his face from her breasts and met her eyes. "Oh, I doubt he'll bother us. Besides it adds to the excitement, don't you think?"

He felt the heat rise on her face as he rested his cheek against hers.. He loved the way she blushed. Pulling his shirt over his head, he pressed his bare chest against her warm breasts.

"Nooo. we can't." Yet her hips arched against him. She licked her lips, flicked the button open on his pants, and tugged at the zipper. Her eyes flew open wide as he gave her a devilish grin.

He'd gone commando this morning anticipating this tryst. *Hell, I'd spend every waking moment in bed with her, if I could. I'll never let her go. Never.* That realization sent shivers through him.

Contrary to her words, she relaxed her legs, allowing his fingers more access. He caressed, and teased finding her sweet spot. She moaned. "Please— not here." She bit her lip, tried to smother a long-muffled cry of ecstasy as she writhed against his hand. Panting she relaxed, and his fingers started ministrations again. "Please, let me... I want you inside...but not..."

He eased back and met her gaze. Wrapped his arms around her, enjoying her bare breasts pressed against his hard chest, and in a swirl of motion they disappeared.

Landing in a soft bed, with wispy curtains drawn around the bed and the sound of waves lapping the shore outside, he stripped her, kicked off his pants, and buried himself inside her.

She welcomed him; hypnotized by his touch, she tingled under his fingertips, reveling in the full feeling of him inside her. Flames of passion devoured her, clouding her brain, scattering her thoughts as his hands and lips continued teasing, taunting her body.

The turbulence of his desire swirled around her until the hot flow of passion raged through them in a raw act of possession. As the waves of ecstasy calmed, she savored the satisfaction snuggled against him, their legs intertwined.

About to doze off, she squealed and bolted upright. "What time is it?"

She stared over into the laughing eyes of her lover. Tristian snickered. "Relax, we'll be well rested for the wedding. The benefits of being with a time spinner."

"A what... Are we back in the cottage?" Panicked, she shoved at his arm wound around her waist, which tightened every time she moved.

"Time spinner. And no, we are not exactly in the cottage. It's been years since I've used that talent but felt the situation warranted it. Don't you think?"

"I think we better get dressed and back to the Seraphim before Trevor comes looking for us."

"He won't." Tristian released her and sat up, stretched his arms and legs. "But better make sure everything is secure before we return to the cottage."

She sat cross-legged on the bed as the curtains rippled. The entire bed began to swirl, and she fisted her fingers in the covers. He slipped his arms around her. "It'll be over in a minute, close your eyes."

When she opened them again, she was sitting on the double chaise on the observation deck of the yacht fully dressed. She gingerly slipped off the side of the chaise and stood glancing around. "Where were we?"

"The better question is when were we? Accommodations were in a faraway land where time stands still. A place I go to get away from job and life in general. Sort of one of my own creation." He offered his hand to assist her from the chaise.

Dreamily, she took his hand and got to her feet. On tiptoe, her arms encircled his neck. She pressed against him, brushed her moist lips over his, lingering, savoring every moment.

"If you don't stop, we're not going to make it to the cottage at all," Tristian murmured against her lips, his voice husky.

"Okay, okay. We could go back to that place where time ceased to exist," she whispered against his ear.

"We could—but I'm too drained by the first trip to enjoy a second."

"We need to build up your sexual stamina; I can tell." She snickered and quickly moved out of reach. His gaze followed her. "Nothing wrong with my stamina; it's the use of magic that did me in." He winked at her. "But well worth it. I'll check in with Trevor, then we'll leave."

Chapter Twenty-Five
Wedding Guests Arrive, Sacred Vows Exchanged, a Reception to Remember

In the cottage, a stream of warm sunlight fell across Hannah's face as she stirred next to a naked Tristian snoring softly in the bed. Outside, people scurried around, dishes clattered against the glass tables, bits of conversation wafted in through the open window. Tristian and she were apparently the last ones to get up. Stealthily, she crept out of bed, swung a silk robe around her shoulders, and padded over to the window. Pulling the draperies aside, she watched the flurry of activity.

Flower arrangements sat on all the tables, and the waterfall was muted again. When they'd arrived at the cottage a few hours before dawn, she'd fallen asleep to the sounds of the water crashing over the rocks, a soothing sound in her opinion. Among the early arrivals, Hannah recognized a few stylists from The Wycked Hair Salon standing at the far end of the waterfall.

She turned and pounced on the bed. Tristian was already awake watching her with an amused expression.

"Are you supposed to be helping escort the wedding guests through the portal?"

"Not anymore. Terra has it handled." He yawned wide and scrubbed his hands over his face. "But we better get up and out there before someone pounds on the door." He swung his feet to the floor and stood. "Share the shower?"

"Sure, if you'll keep your hands to yourself." She sent him a saucy smile, bounced off the bed, and the robe dropped to the floor.

"Not a chance." He chased her into the bathroom and closed the door.

As Hannah wiped the steam from the bathroom mirror, there was a light knock on the door. Tristian raised a brow in an "I told you so manner" snapped a bath sheet from the towel rack, wrapped it around his hips, and crossed the room.

"You're not going to—" Hannah said in horror.

He sent her a wink, opened the door, and lazily leaned a shoulder on the doorframe. "What can I do for you?"

The girl dressed in island attire gulped, eying him up and down. "Hannah is wanted at the main house. Something about helping the brides." Cheeks flushed, she turned and hurried away.

"Why did you do that?" Hannah asked, standing in the bathroom doorway.

He shrugged. "Someone had to answer the door." Gazing at her naked body with pure male appreciation, he chuckled. "It sure wasn't going to be you." In a whisper of movement, he was beside her and patted her ass. "Better get a move on." He crushed her against him and covered her mouth with his.

After a couple beats, she shoved him away. "Not helping."

"Sorry," he said, then under his breath added. "Not."

Quickly she pulled on the turquoise bridesmaid dress, picked up her makeup kit and shoes, then rushed barefoot out of the cottage. A quick glance back, she saw Tristian still dressed in only a towel. With a wave, he closed the door.

When Hannah crossed the veranda, the girl who'd been at the door glanced in her direction. She stood in a knot with other girls holding serving trays and whispering. They slid glances in her direction. *I'm going to kill him.*

A smiling Matiah appeared beside Hannah and touched her shoulder. "Men will be men. Willow and Angie are in the bedroom at the top of the stairs to the right."

"Thanks. Guests are arriving already?"

"Only hair stylists from the Salon. They're here to fix the bridal party's hair. So scoot."

She sprinted up the stairs, opened the door to the bedroom. Angie and Willow said in unison. "It's about time."

"Late night or should I say early morning, huh? Heard Tristian created quite a stir this morning." Angie giggled.

"Yes to all three," Hannah said, heat rising in her cheeks. One of the stylists, brush in hand, motioned her into a chair.

"I don't know what you've done to my brother. But whatever it is. Keep it up." Angie glanced in the mirror at Hannah's reflection.

Willow nodded her head vigorously as the stylist frowned, pushing her curls back in place.

"I've never seen him so relaxed, almost fun to be around." Angie snickered.

Hannah tilted her head and gave Angie a puzzled look. "I'm not sure what you mean. He's not so different from the man I met in the diner."

"You met in a diner? Really?"

"Yes, he was distressed at your leaving."

"He told you that? A complete stranger?"

"Well, I'd had a bit of bad luck and was venting to the waitress I know there. I suspect he overheard. He came over, and we kinda compared notes on life's little zingers. One thing led to the other." She smiled. "Then I was whisked away, you were snatched, and you know the rest."

"A whirlwind romance," Willow said with a sigh.

"Not exactly." Hannah shifted in her seat, uncomfortable with the conversation, peered from Angie to Willow. "All ready for the weddings?"

****

Tristian towel dried his hair and dressed in a light-colored suit, turquoise shirt with matching tie, a cream stripe running through it, casual shoes. He glanced in the mirror. *Not bad.* He stepped onto the porch to survey the area, inhaled the sweet floral scents along with a slight mist from the waterfall wafting on the breeze. Andre was nowhere in sight. He wanted to get a look at the operation center before the wedding, if possible. The unfamiliar people, caterers, employees of Andre and Matiah, made him a little edgy. Too many dignitaries in one place for his liking.

"Looking for me?" Andre appeared on the porch beside him. Tristian jumped at the deep resounding voice.

"Didn't mean to startle you." Andre chuckled. "Heard you were interested in the control center. Good as time as any to do a quick tour, before the guests arrive." He touched Tristian on the shoulder. "Follow me."

Andre led the way up the path that wound around behind the waterfall. He sidled between the falls and steep rock wall, a portion of which disappeared giving way to a narrow tunnel lit with flaming torches set in polished brass hangers. Several yards inside, Andre ran his hand along what appeared to be a solid rock ledge, it fell away to reveal a room banked by state of the art computers and monitors that beeped and hummed quietly. At the center of the room stood a six-foot wide, flat screen monitor.

"Good morning Alish. I've brought someone I'd like you to meet," Andre said as a pair of large luminous sapphire eyes appeared and blinked at them from the screen.

"Hello, Andre."

"This is Tristian; he works security for my son. I thought you could put his mind at ease regarding the security around here."

"Of course." The almond shaped eyes faded in a swirl of sapphire as the tropical paradise that Andre and Matiah called home swam into view.

"Give us a close up of the cove and Seraphim," Andre instructed.

The screen enlarged the cove area around the yacht.

"Show us the waterfall and the wedding venue."

The falls swirled into view. Matiah wandered through the tables, Owen walked around the arbor, and Tobi touched the flowers climbing the structure.

"Wow, this—I mean she is unbelievable. Hannah

has got to see this." Tristian gasped. "She's a computer guru and security specialist," he said proudly.

"Perhaps another time," Andre said absently.

"This is how you keep a finger on the pulse of the outside worlds."

Andre nodded. "At first I thought Bruce would need assistance when he won the Overlord position. But it wasn't necessary. He always had a firm grasp on what was needed. And chose your father, then you to assist him. A wise decision. Alish keeps me informed."

"Nice. Little goes on around here that you don't know about."

"There are privacy settings, which is why you were sent to the Seraphim during and after the party. Didn't really want to spy on our guests. Bedrooms are off limits for obvious reasons as well."

"Magic?" Tristian nodded in Alish's direction.

"Some. The rest is a lot of computer savvy and connection to worldwide security cameras. They exist in the most intriguing places." Andre's lips curved in a mysterious smile. He glanced up at Alish as it showed Matiah glaring at the falls, hands on hips. "Time to go."

Tristian followed his gaze and snickered. "Looks like you've been missed."

"Yes, and the guests are beginning to arrive." He jerked his chin toward the screen again as Lady Rose and Stefan entered the veranda, along with a small group of people escorted by Terra. Andre touched Tristian's shoulder, and they reappeared inside the cottage. Andre shoved open the glass French doors. "Showtime."

Andre nodded to a few, stopped and visited with others, introducing Tristian as Bruce's right-hand man.

It felt strange to be out in the open rather than lurking in the shadows, keeping a low profile. Tristian wasn't sure he liked this new spotlight.

Waiving Andre on, he stopped beside Stefan Talltree just as Lady Rose glided over to talk with a tall man accompanied by a beautiful redhead on his arm.

"Stefan, how's the world treating you?"

"Not bad. And you?"

"Good. I heard a rumor that you are leaving the employ of the Vampire Council. Striking out on your own. Any truth to it?" Tristian raised a brow in question.

"It's a possibility."

"It's more than a possibility." Lady Rose's melodic voice intoned. "He's paid his debt to the Council. I've released him with the Council's blessing. And that's what I want repeated in answer to any rumors."

"Yes, my Lady." Tristian gave a deep bow.

"Oh, stop that nonsense. I dropped my title at the door of a friend's wedding. I understand congratulations are in order on your new position as well." Lady Rose smiled. "I guess we'll be seeing more of you."

"Apparently. News does travel fast." He glanced in Stefan's direction and switched his gaze back to Lady Rose who looked in the direction of new arrivals on the veranda.

"Nice to meet you face-to-face, Tristian, under happier circumstances. Now if you don't mind, I need to mingle. Nathanial Cross and his wife have arrived from the Angel Legion. Looks like the ceremony will be starting soon." She glided off toward a group being escorted to their seats.

Tristian glanced toward the house, where Owen was gesturing for him to join them. "Gotta go. Giving my sister away today. Oh, congrats on your freedom."

"Thanks," Stefan said in a deep, smooth baritone and sauntered over to where Lady Rose sat. He shook hands with Nathanial and nodded to his wife, then settled in the seat next to Lady Rose.

Tristian sprinted up the path and steps to the veranda where Angie stood just inside the glass doors. Hannah at her side in a turquoise off the shoulder dress that hugged her curves, slit almost to the thigh. Her hair held up by a pair of combs with diamonds and emeralds sparkling across them. He let out a low whistle as his gaze lingered on her.

Owen cleared his throat, and Tristian adverted his gaze to Angie and took his place beside her. He took her hand through the crook of his arm and let out a slow breath. *This was it. She would be officially someone else's responsibility from this day forward.* Soothing chords floated on the air played by a petite woman seated behind a large harp as the small crowd quieted. *The traditional Wedding March played on a harp seems so ethereal.*

Tristian looked over at his sister, dressed in a long strapless silk gown, embroidered pastel flowers scattered over the pale pink material. *She looks so much like Mom.* He straightened at her touch to move forward behind Hannah and Freesia, walking down the rose petal covered path to the archway where Bruce and his best man, Owen, waited on the right side. Willow and Birch walked beside Angie and Tristian. Caleb smiled, his brother standing next to him on the other side of the archway.

It was like a dream, then he gave Angie over to Bruce, said something, and slipped into a chair in the front row beside Matiah. Birch handed Willow off to Caleb and eased into the chair next to Tristian. He slumped back against the chair. A vision of his mother and father swam into focus.

His father's words floated through is mind. "You've done well, son. We are proud of you. Angie's married a good man. He'll take good care of her. Now, live your life without fear. Hannah is a wonderful woman. You'll be happy together." His mother smiled, and they faded away.

Tristian swallowed hard. The raw grief of losing his parents renewed. He turned his attention to Hannah standing with Angie. Did he want to take her down the aisle and forever?

Matiah touched his arm an understanding sparkle in her eyes. "You all right?"

He nodded, words failing him.

Halfway through the ceremony, Tristian noticed out of the corner of his eye, Terra slip away from the end of the waterfall and disappear behind the cottage. He started to push up from the chair, and Matiah put a hand on his thigh, gave a nearly imperceptible shake of her head.

He glanced behind him to the empty chair beside Nathanial's wife. *Something was wrong.*

Bruce and Angie exchanged rings, Willow and Caleb followed suit, and nothing seemed amiss. Andre pronounced them husband and wife, giving Tristian a reassuring smile. He stood and rushed toward the cottage, rounded the corner, and disappeared. He reappeared at the edge of the mist concealing the portal to find, Terra, her team, Nathanial and his angels standing over several piles of ash, some still floating in the air.

Stepping out from the mist, Tristian said, "What the hell happened here. And why wasn't I informed?"

Terra turned calmly around to face her boss. "Had a bad feeling, brought the team out to check, and found these guys"—she motioned to the warrior angels—"in a battle with four demonic creatures." She directed her gaze to the piles of cinders. "A couple of additional concussive blasts from our team, and the battle was over. Didn't see any reason to interrupt the wedding. It was handled. I'll send a full written report to you by the time you return home, sir."

"Tristian, you need to get back to the wedding," Nathanial commanded.

"I don't take…" Bruce's words echoed through his mind. "You've trained your teams well; it's time you trusted them to do the job." He nodded and disappeared to reappear behind the cottage. When he slipped into the greeting line beside Hannah, she frowned at him.

"Where have you been? Is everything all right?"

"Just fine. Minor security breach, Terra took care of it." He smiled and focused his attention on the receiving line, offering his hand to the guests as they passed by.

While staff cleared the chairs away, a platform appeared for the band to set up on. The end of the line finally passed by, and Tristian relaxed, wrapping his arm around Hannah's waist. They proceeded to the table where a seven-layer cake sat among plates, napkins, and silverware.

"I'm going to skirt around tradition and toss my

bouquet now so we can get to the cake. It's devil's food you know." Angie dissolved into gales of laughter. "My favorite. Yum." She eyed Bruce who was standing beside her grinning. She turned her back to the guests and tossed the tropical flower bouquet over her head, far into the crowd. It nearly hit an unsuspecting Hannah in the face as she conversed with Birch and Tristian.

At the cries from the crowd and the look of surprise on Birch's face, she raised her hands up to shield herself and snagged the flowers in the process. Her eyes rounded and her lips formed an O as she glanced at the flowers and back to Tristian. She snickered.

Not to be outdone, Willow turned and tossed her bouquet over her shoulder into the crowd. One of the stylists caught the flowers and danced from one foot to the other. "Guess I'm going to have to find a man. Any volunteers?" she called out waving the bouquet above her head.

Freesia rushed over all smiles. "You know what this means." She laughed. "You're next to be a bride."

Birch stared at a stricken Tristian and slapped him on the back. "Well, looks like fate gave you a little shove." Guffawing, he watched as a laughing Angie put her hand over Bruce's at one side of the cake. Willow and Caleb stood on the other side, and simultaneously they sliced the cake and offered pieces to each other. Angie was quick enough to shove Bruce's piece in his mouth, smearing the frosting across his cheek. She ducked to avoid the same fate. He licked the frosting from his lips and picked up a napkin brushing the crumbs and frosting from his face, a smirk playing on the corners of his mouth. Willow gently took a bite of the cake Caleb offered and returned the favor.

Bruce spun Angie out onto the dance area for the first dance, while a caterer sliced the rest of the cake and put pieces on plates.

Birch and Freesia watched the newlyweds dance in the courtyard cleared for dancing. Freesia wiped a tear from her cheek as Birch slid a hand around her waist. As tradition dictated, Birch cut in on Caleb and swept his daughter into a dance.

"Oh, don't look so horror struck. It's only an old wives' tale." Hannah took Tristian by the hand and led him to the edge of the courtyard. "You need to cut in and dance with your sister." She kissed him on the cheek then gave him a little shove.

The earlier vision flashed through his mind, and he tapped Bruce on the shoulder. "My turn."

Bruce gave a slight bow and backed away. "Of course."

Bruce walked to Hannah, bowed, and offered his hand. "May I have this dance?"

She smiled and gave a nervous curtsy. "I'd be delighted, my lord."

"Oh, don't even start that crap." He grimaced. "It's Bruce, and you know it."

At the end of the dance, Andre stepped onto the stage and swiped the microphone. "The buffet is set up in the garden. If you're hungry, hurry over there before it's all gone."

Tristian found Hannah and enjoyed a slow dance before getting in line at the buffet. Prime rib, salmon, and tuna steaks were offered along with several styles of potatoes, wide variety of veggies, coconut bread, and assorted rolls in the warmer along with several bottles of fine wine available. Pieces of cake were arranged on a table next to a chocolate fountain. A crystal bowl of huge strawberries rested in a silver tray of ice near the fountain.

Hannah plopped four strawberries on her plate, stabbed them with a skewer and rolled them in the chocolate until they were well covered. She took a bite then put the berry to Tristian's lips. "It's yummy." She licked her lips and wiped a napkin over her mouth, catching the juice.

He steadied her hand and nibbled on the fruit. "Wonderful." He took a drink from his wine glass. "Goes well with wine." Next, he nibbled on her neck breathing a kiss at the hollow of her throat. In a husky voice, he suggested, "How about a moonlight walk on the beach?"

Chapter Twenty-Six
A Time for Us

I'm not sure we're dressed for a walk on the beach," she whispered against his ear, teasing kisses along his jawline.

"Oh, I think we can manage. Kick our shoes off beside the path, pick them up on our way back."

"Okay. Shouldn't we say goodbye to Angie and Bruce and some of the guests?"

"Oh, probably." He took her hand, entwined their fingers. They meandered through the guests saying their goodbyes and waved to the newly wedded couples. On their way to the path, they passed Andre and Matiah standing at the far end of the waterfall.

"We're going to take a moonlit stroll on the beach. Care to join us?" Tristian asked cordially.

Andre raised a brow, his eyes sparked with mischief. "I doubt you are looking for company. But I will see that the torches are lit for your stroll." He chuckled deep in his throat, giving a wave of his hand toward the path. One at a time flames flickered on each torch down both sides of the trail. A golden glow lit the way to the beach, shadows bounced on the sand as the wind teased the fire atop the torches.

Once out of sight of the reception, the path veered to the left and turned to sand. Tristian paused to remove his shoes, offered a hand to Hannah as she kicked off her sandals. He caught the hem of her dress in his hand and touched her waist, the dress gathered at that point allowing her freedom to walk without fear of ruining her dress.

"Now that's frivolous use of magic," she huffed.

He shrugged and leaned over rolling up his pant legs. "A minor infraction at best, given the fact that it's your safety that concerns me. What if you trip and face plant into the sand? Nope, not taking a chance."

She giggled. "My knight shimmering in magic." Winding her arms around his neck, she teased his lips with the tip of her tongue, then sprinted down the path to the beach.

With a laugh, he gave chase. The ocean breeze caught strands of her hair and blew them across her face. When he caught up with her at the water's edge, she pointed behind them.

"That wasn't there last time we were here."

Tristian glanced in the direction she pointed. A yellow and white striped, three-sided cloth cabana resided where there had been nothing before.

"Andre must have put it up for wedding guests that wandered to the beach before or after the ceremony," Tristian said brushing the hair from Hannah's face, letting the soft curls slide through his fingers. He leaned over and inhaled deeply.

"Are you sniffing me?" she asked in an amused voice.

"Yes. I love the lemony and sometimes raspberry fragrance of your hair." He wound several strands around his finger, then released them to bounce around her face. "Your many fragrances intrigue me."

"They do?" she asked, shyly unbuttoning several

buttons at the neck of his shirt, slipping fingers inside to caress his bare chest.

He caught her hands in his and held them in front. "Before you derail my train of thought, I'd like to talk about us."

She tilted her head up at him with a puzzled expression. "Can it wait? This is such a beautiful moment, don't spoil it with words."

He sucked in a breath and blew it out slowly. "I'm sorry, but I've been thinking a lot about us recently and it's time for a decision. Let's make use of the cabana."

Reluctantly, she followed behind him as he tugged her toward the structure. Inside two chairs covered with matching yellow striped material sat side by side. He motioned for her to sit down and pulled the other chair around to face her, eased into it. Taking both her hands in his, he stared into her sparkling but uncertain blue eyes.

"You have become a very important part of my life, a part that I am unwilling to give up. Your upcoming move to Colorado will complicate our relationship."

"But you can't ask—"

"No. I would never ask you to give up a job you love and worked hard to get. But I don't want us to end up in a long-distance relationship. I couldn't bear it." He stood, paced around the area inside.

"Tristian, we can make it work, I know—"

He paused in front of her, hands behind his back. "Just let me finish. I've thought long and hard about this. I've decided to accept Bruce's offer to manage my security teams rather than participate physically in the assignments, unless absolutely necessary."

"I'm so glad."

He raised an eyebrow and frowned at her.

"Okay, I'm listening." She picked at the hem of her dress where Tristian had attached it to her hip by magic.

"Geographically, I'd be tied to D.C. only when Bruce was absent. The rest of the time, I can handle my teams' day-to-day operations from any location I want. We've plenty of time to find a house in or around Colorado Springs that will accommodate both our needs. We can upgrade the security systems, add high-speed internet if necessary, whatever will allow you and me to work from that location." He settled into the chair again.

"I can't ask you to leave your family home," she protested.

"You're not. It's my decision. We can use my home in Maine as a vacation getaway or a base of operations when necessary."

"It sounds like we are moving from one day at a time"—she paused a beat, nibbled on her lower lip—"to planning a future together? Am I understanding you correctly?" she asked, peering at him with her irresistible blue eyes coyly from under her long reddish lashes. The edge of the cabana walls flapped in the ocean breeze catching her attention momentarily.

He waited for her full attention. "You'd be correct. "When I wake up, I want to see your beautiful face and sleep tousled hair on the pillow beside me. At night, I crave your soft, sexy body entwined with mine. I want to spend the rest of my life committed to loving you." Tristian slipped out of the chair and knelt on one knee, pulling out a red velvet box from his pocket, and flipped open the top. Inside the box, a marque diamond ring sparkled surrounded by deep blue sapphires. He took her hand in his and placed the box in her hand. "Would you do me the honor of agreeing to be my wife?"

Hannah's hand flew to her mouth, as her eyes rounded. "Oh Tristian—"

"Now before you answer, there are a few things I want to make clear. If you agree to be my wife, I want to get married as soon as possible. Our wedding will be attended by only those privy to what I do for a living."

"Tristian—my family."

"Now before you go off—listen to my reasoning and future plans." He tried to put a finger to her lips, but she backed away.

"I can't get married without my family's blessing. What kind of a wedding would that be?" Tears welled up in her eyes, though she attempted to blink them back, a single teardrop rolled down her cheek.

"It's for their own safety, right now. When things settle down and I'm out of the field for a while, then we can have a big reception in Ireland with your friends and family."

He reached out wiped the tear from her cheek with the pad of his thumb. "This is the way it has to be. I couldn't live with myself if something happened to your family because of me or my enemies looking for revenge."

"What about me?"

"I know this is going to sound bad. But you know what I do, you know first-hand what can happen. And still, you've chosen to be with me. Your family members are innocents, unaware of the danger being related to me poses."

"So we tell them. Your…our secret is safe with them."

"Maybe, but I am unwilling to take on that responsibility right now. It's a big step for me taking you into my life, given what happened to my parents, then Angie due to being mated to Bruce. But I can't help myself. I'm in love with you."

Hannah stood, handed the ring back to Tristian and walked stiffly out of the cabana without a word. The ocean breeze caught her hair, flung it around her head creating a red halo in the sun, still she walked on down the beach into the waves. He rose to follow her and thought better of it. She needed time to think. *Am I being selfish not putting her family at risk? Maybe… I can't let her go. But what if?* Pacing usually helped him sort out things, but this time. Not so much. So he waited, watching her walk along the shoreline, waiting for the waves to crash over her feet.

It seemed like an eternity until she changed direction and walked toward him. His pulse quickened, his heart thundered. *Was this it? Will she leave me? Can I compromise and tell her family regardless of the danger? How could I keep them all safe? Would they accept me, knowing what I am?* He stared at the little red box in his hand and cursed, finding no answers.

A light touch on his shoulder and her soft, soothing voice gave him a start. He looked hesitantly into her eyes, fearing what he might see. The compassion, love, and understanding he found there was unbelievable.

"Yes, Tristian, I will be your wife. I love you more than you can ever imagine. But promise me you will find a way to include my family in our celebration as soon as possible after the wedding."

"Of course, I told you I would. We'll go to Ireland, have a celebration."

"Also you need to be aware, that my sister, Brandy, and I have a deep connection. It is possible that we can't keep this from her. She'll feel my distress at having to keep our marriage secret. Or she'll feel my happiness at our wedding. I can't help it. My family—we're close—and keeping our marriage a secret is going to hurt them terribly. Also, there is a chance she could appear without warning, even at the wedding."

"If that happens, we'll tell her as much as necessary to keep her safe."

Hannah took the box from his hand and slipped the sparkling ring on her finger. She held it out, wiggling her fingers, watching it wink in the sunlight. "We have a wedding to plan. Do you have a date and place in mind?"

"As a matter of fact, I do."

"Of course you do." She wrapped her arms around his neck and brought his lips to hers. "Now how about we finish what I started earlier—" Her lips curved in a seductive smile as her sculptured brow arched.

He took her mouth hungrily, lifted her off the ground, and she wound her legs around his waist.

"Right here?" She nuzzled into his neck and kissed a trail along his jawline.

He waved an arm toward the one side of the cabana that was open facing the ocean, a flap of matching material swung across the opening. "Yep, right here."

If you enjoyed *A Warlock's Secrets*, you'll want to watch for Tena Stetler's next book from The Wild Rose Press, Inc. Here's a sample:

A Vampire's Unlikely Alliance

by

Tena Stetler

Demon's Witch Series

Chapter One
Don't Loiter On Trails After Dark

Perched on a boulder, hidden behind scraggly branches of scrub oak, Stefan sniffed the air appreciatively. In Glacier National Park, a few yards off the popular Avalanche Lake hiking trail, he watched and waited as the last stragglers made their way down the trail.

The dusky purple sky faded, his favorite time of day when the deserted trails were his alone, except for an occasional wolf, bear, or other nocturnal wildlife. The nightly routine of running the trails around Going to the Sun Road at top speed exhausted his body and reduced his bloodlust. This enhanced his ability to work among humans with little discomfort to him or danger to them.

The blood he'd appropriated from St. Peter's Hospital in Helena sated his thirst for now. But the supply was dwindling and finding a new source was at the top of his to-do list. *Was leaving the Vampire Council his best option? The blood supply was always fresh but his duties sucked.* Playing politics wasn't his strong suit, but orders to terminate the loser went against his moral compass.

Jumping down from the boulder, he landed silently on the balls of his feet and took off at a dead run, too fast for the human eye to detect. Tonight, his run covered several trails as the full moon rose over the mountain tops.

Croaking frogs settled at the edge of a pristine mountain lake, while an owl screeched overhead winging its way through the night sky. This tranquil existence was very different from his previous life.

Nevertheless, the premonitions that kept him alive as an assassin, made him feel things were about to change, almost ominous in nature.

It was nearly midnight when he cut across the Sun Road to another trailhead, so intent on his goal that he nearly collided with an attractive young woman. He skidded to a stop, spraying gravel, rocks and small twigs down the road in front of him.

A pinecone dislodged and bounced along the road past her. Tall and slender, she had miles of fiery red hair that hung down her back in a cascade of curls.

Intense emerald eyes stared back at him, as he attempted to regain his composure, not to mention balance. *What the hell was she doing here at this time of night?*

"Whoa." She stepped lightly to the side to avoid the flying debris. "You really should watch where you're going, especially at that speed." Her voice scolded, but the smile on her lips teased. "Someone could get hurt."

Pretending to pant, he shrugged, holding his palms up in surrender. "Just trying to get my run in before work. Stefan Talltree, at your service."

He stepped closer leaned over in an exaggerated bow and caught her hand, brushing his lips over the palm and wrist, inhaling her sweet scent. *AB negative with a pulse of adrenaline, perfect.* Her pulse beat a tattoo against his lips. He backed away.

Her heart thundered as she drew her hand from his grasp. "The name's Brandy. Pleased to meet you, Stefan." He liked the way her smile reached up into her bright eyes as they swept over him with an appreciative glance. Her voice had a hint of Irish lilt to it. He liked that too.

"Where do you work that requires you to report in at "—she glanced at her watch—"midnight?"

Nostrils flaring, he paused. *Blood? Not hers.* The sound of Brandy's voice brought his attention back to her and the situation at hand. "Oh, shit, I've gotta go!" He sprinted off, leaving her standing alone.

As he started down the trail, the tree branches swayed in the silvery moonlight, casting eerie shadows across the trails edge. The breeze brought with it the coppery scent of fresh blood mixed with sulfur. He turned for one last look at her as she wrinkled her nose and crept silently into the wind, tracking the source of the stench.

****

Gravel crunched beneath Stefan's feet when he crossed the parking lot. Cody had driven his old, beater of a pickup rather than his sleek, black Corvette convertible. *No hot date tonight, huh, old man?*

Stefan slid the key into the lock and yanked open the radio station door. As he walked by the empty receptionist desk, a faint scent of flowery perfume wafted past him. Turning, he rushed down the dimly lit hallway to the second door on the left. The "On Air" light glowed red above the door. Stefan waved through the glass window of the control room.

Cody flipped the mic off and motioned Stefan in.

"Well, well, look what finally dragged himself to work." Cody ran his hand over the stubble on his chin. "Come to think of it, I don't remember you ever cutting it this close. Russ's golden boy ain't perfect," Cody crowed shaking his head in mock amazement.

"Shut up. I've ten minutes before you're off shift." Stefan said, glaring as he closed the door. He took off his leather jacket, tossing it on the back of a chair located under the tiny window to the outside. Glancing around the small room, he finally located the play and traffic lists hanging on a hook above the computer monitor suspended from the ceiling.

He yanked the lists off the hook and reviewed all the commercials set to run during his shift. Stefan noted Cody had checked them all off and made sure they were in the correct time slots. Stefan's expression softened, the corner of his mouth lifting in a half grin as he looked down at the older DJ. "Thanks, man. I owe you."

"Gee, now there's something new. Hey, you get lost on the trails again?" Cody tugged his hand through his brown hair, which was graying at the temples. Then turning back to the board, he checked the minutes left on the song and made sure another was in cue. Though everything was computerized now. But old habits die hard and dead air, whether from computer error or human mistake was something to be avoided at all costs.

"Maybe." Stefan's grin faded. He snatched the playlist off the counter and quirked a dark brow, staring down at Cody. "Does it matter?"

Cody snorted and gave Stefan a sideways glance. "Or was it one of those groupies who's always hanging around at your remote appearances hoping for an intimate rendezvous."

Stefan narrowed his eyes. "You know I don't mess with that kind. Not my type."

"Hell, then send them my way. That petite brunette last week at the Flathead County Fairgrounds was HOT!" Cody wiggled his bushy salt and pepper eyebrows then grinned.

"She probably has a boyfriend. You'll be hiding out like last month after you met up with…who was it?" Stefan dropped the list of songs onto the counter. An eyebrow arched, he looked at Cody.

"Sophie. How was I supposed to know she was married?" Cody's hazel eyes twinkled with feigned innocence.

"Uh, the gold band on her left hand is usually a dead giveaway." He slapped Cody on the back and gave him a shove. "Now get out of here. I'm sure you have better things to do than shoot the shit with me."

Cody raised his hand in a sloppy salute, turned and sauntered out the control room door. The latch clicked softly behind him. Stefan checked the playlist and commercials against the computer, one final time then grabbed his headphones. It was ten minutes before his first stop set, so he swung his leg over the chair and settled in.

Leaning back in the chair, his thoughts drifted to the woman on the trail and the foreboding feeling that crept through him before meeting her.

Normally, the solitude of the radio station's midnight shift soothed him. But tonight he was edgy. Pacing back and forth across the control room floor like a caged animal, desire stirred inside him, and the unwelcome craving for naked female flesh under him. Tired of one-night stands, he wanted someone who mattered. He swore under his breath and muttered, "Never again."

Yet the need to find that red head seemed all-consuming. Even though he knew instinctively it wasn't safe for either of them...unless. Ruthlessly, he shut down the emotions swirling in his gut and turned back to the control panel. *I have a job to do.* He shoved her out of his mind, adjusted his headphones and turned on the mic.

"Cody has left the building," Stefan said in an amused voice. "I've quite a lineup for you tonight. So kick off your boots, sit back, and relax. Need to hear something? Give me a call. I'll be here all night at Big Fish radio." His deep smooth voice flowed out over the airwaves to his listening audience of night owls. With a flick of his finger, the "On Air" light went off, and his mind flipped back to the mystery woman.

Avoiding the trails for a while seemed the best course of action. She'd be an unwanted complication in his world. He couldn't be trusted and certainly not with a human female. *If she was human, why didn't she shy away tonight? Normally, warm-blood's subconscious knows I'm a danger to their very existence.*

Although he had to admit, since settling down in Whitefish, not many shied away from him anymore. *The more interesting question was...what if she wasn't human? She'd make an intriguing diversion.*

Knowing he shouldn't didn't keep him from wanting to return to the trails and look for her.

The blue flashing light on the wall signaled a phone call and yanked him out of his thoughts as he snatched the receiver. "The Big Fish, what's your pleasure?"

After a slight pause, a sultry female voice whispered through the phone. "Is this the tall, muscular hunk that prowls the trails of Glacier National Park after dark?"

Waves of lust crashed through him without warning. He stood to relieve the hard-aching ridge forming under the zipper of his jeans. Staring out the tiny window into the darkness, he said, "Well, it depends on who's asking."

"I guess you'll have to come back to the trails to find out," she purred and hung up.

Standing at the counter, he stared at the receiver. "What the hell?" he said to the empty control room, slamming the receiver down onto its cradle. Rubbing the back of his neck, he rolled his shoulders to release the tension.

A word from the author…

With the majestic Rocky Mountains just outside my window, I sit at my computer with vampires, demons, witches, faeries, and a variety of paranormal creatures gathered around telling me their stories! I am an author of paranormal romance novels. Remember the magic for happily ever after!

Colorado is home. I share my life with a wonderful husband of many moons, our brilliant Chow Chow, a terribly spoiled companion parrot, and a forty-year-old box turtle. We enjoy hiking, biking, and camping, also love water sports including kayaking and whitewater rafting, especially on the Arkansas River through the Royal Gorge.

You can find me any winter evening curled up in front of a crackling fire with a good book, a mug of hot chocolate, and a big bowl of popcorn. While growing up, if I didn't like the ending of a book, I'd rewrite it, which led to writing my own books.

http://www.tenastetler.com

Thank you for purchasing
this publication of The Wild Rose Press, Inc.

If you enjoyed the story, we would appreciate your
letting others know by leaving a review.

For other wonderful stories,
please visit our on-line bookstore at
www.thewildrosepress.com.

For questions or more information
contact us at
info@thewildrosepress.com.

The Wild Rose Press, Inc.
www.thewildrosepress.com

Stay current with The Wild Rose Press, Inc.

Like us on Facebook

https://www.facebook.com/TheWildRosePress

And Follow us on Twitter
https://twitter.com/WildRosePress